KELTIC FLIGHT

DOUBLE KELTIC TRIAD 3

LIZZIE STARR

Dokopot Books

Cover and interior design by Cat & Doxie Author Services

Photo Credit:

Zhevelev/Deposit Photos

Lakov/Deposit Photos

prometeus/Deposit Photos

BabesKovacs/Deposit Photos

okiepony/Deposit Photos

What if...?
How many times have I asked you this? How many times have you given me the answers, names, ideas for which I was so desperately searching?
How often have I not thanked you?
John, Morgan, Jason... you guys are the best.

And I love you all.

CHAPTER ONE

The fey don't dream. At least, that's what they said. Whoever they were.

Just another example of how she didn't fit in. Nanceen stared through the open portal connecting the Otherworld of Faerie to her brother's backyard in the mortal, human world. Jaye had successfully blended the two halves of his heritage, while her twin sister, Kaelea, embraced Faerie almost to the exclusion of her human half.

But neither world seemed quite right to Nanceen, and she could not find a balance similar to her brother's within herself. Nanceen scrubbed her hands through hair, cut short to defy Faerie custom, and sighed. Why couldn't she find a place to be happy? Be settled, instead of so restless all the time.

A bush to one side of the clearing rustled, and the sound drew her attention. She crinkled her brow. There was no breeze, and no one else was near the portal. Nanceen closed her eyes and reached out with her senses as she had been taught by her Uncle Derrik.

A faint, hazy patch hovered within the mass of bright green leaves and sparkled with disguised magic.

Suddenly, the haze rose from the foliage and was gone.

Nanceen shook her head and rubbed one temple. She'd swear she heard faint laughter as the haze disappeared.

Curious, she took a quick step to follow the haze, but stopped with a jolt and frowned. So that was it. Someone was playing with her, trying to lead her into a game of chase for which she wasn't in the mood. With a deep, frustrated breath, she turned her back on the unusual haze.

A quiet, deep chuckle of distant laughter trembled through her. Nanceen made a quick decision to visit Lara. More friend than niece, Lara might be able to help her work through her current dreams and unsettled emotions.

A leisurely pace took her through the brightly lit woods of her clan's homeland to the small clearing where Lara had built her home. The flat, open area in front of the small cabin was filled with toys, made of both human plastics and intricate Faerie carving. A tiny grin tugged the frown from her lips when the twins noticed her standing at the edge of the glade.

"Ceen!" Two pairs of chubby, toddler legs pumped, carrying Antin and Belle toward her. Arms outstretched, she knelt and held her breath. The collision with the children knocked her breath away and she fell onto her bottom. The twins, eager for kisses, squirmed in her embrace.

"Ceen's here!" Antin shouted. "Auntie Ceen." He planted a sloppy kiss on her cheek.

Not to be outdone, Belle touched rosebud lips to the other cheek, then wiped away the sticky kiss with her small fingers. Both children chattered happily, their high voices and four-year-old lisps filling the clearing.

Gentle as a sigh, a short, soft breeze blew past Nanceen's ear. She shivered and, expecting someone to be there, glanced over her shoulder. But the woods were empty. Except...

Nanceen blinked twice trying to bring the wispy haze into focus. It couldn't be the same as the blur by the portal, could it? What was it?

Belle pointed at the haze. "Bu-fly. Pretty."

The haze snapped out of existence. Nanceen fought to ignore

the strange emptiness left within her chest. She shook her head and struggled to set the twins away so she could stand. The force of her imagination was getting the best of her.

"Bye-bye, bu-fly." Belle pressed her lower lip to a pout and waved at the empty air, then reached for Nanceen's hand. With Antin tugging her other arm, Nanceen let the children lead her toward the cabin.

A tall, golden haired woman exited the red door as they reached the wide porch. She smiled at Nanceen and held out one hand in welcome. "Nanceen. What brings you here?"

"I needed to talk, Lara."

Lara tilted her head to one side and cast an appraising look at Nanceen. Uncomfortable under the scrutiny, she glanced away, but resisted the urge to shuffle her feet. Her niece chuckled before speaking to her children.

"Your Da is looking for you. Best go find him before he gets lost. Check behind the shed."

Shrieking with delight, the twins took off and rushed headlong around the corner of the cabin. Lara chuckled again and brushed unruly curls back from her face. "We'll have some quiet now. Come on in."

"Iain won't mind?"

The golden nimbus of curls fell back in her face when Lara shook her head. "No. He was looking out the window when you entered our clearing. He suggested we spend some time without the kids. They'll be helping him in the garden. They love it. So much, they bring half the dirt home with them." She led the way to a cozy nook and indicated Nanceen should sit at the wooden table. "So, tell me what's up."

Nanceen reached toward the ever-present bowl of chocolate, fished out a piece, and unwrapped the tiny drop. How was she supposed to describe her feelings to another when she had no idea about them herself? She stared at the light brown sweet. Where to begin?

When she looked up, Lara grinned at her. "I think I know exactly how you feel. You're restless, like you're looking for something, but you don't have any idea what that something is."

Nanceen's mouth dropped open in surprise. "How... how did you know?"

Lara sighed and snagged her own piece of chocolate. "When I looked in the mirror before I traveled to Iain's time and found him..." She popped the candy into her mouth and continued around it. "... I looked just about like you do now. It's your eyes, Nance."

::Yes. Eyes.::

A gasp passed Nanceen's lips. "Did you hear that?"

Lara's light brows drew together, and a thick line of concern formed over the bridge of her nose. She leaned forward. "Is it the kids?"

"No, no. It was another voice. It was..." The drop of chocolate fell to the smooth tabletop, and Nanceen rested her head in her hands. "I think I'm going crazy."

Lara grasped both of her aunt's hands, pulled them away, and waited for Nanceen to lift her gaze. "No, you're not. Though, I do remember it feeling that way. You'll be fine. Be patient and you, and the one you wait for, will find each other."

::Find me.::

"You're a romantic, Lara. I've been in both worlds and found no one who even begins to interest me. Perhaps I'm not meant for love."

Lara eased from her chair, circled the table, and crouched before Nanceen. She rested her hands lightly on her aunt's shoulders. "Oh, but you are. I know it."

::Love.::

Nanceen returned the kind embrace and leaned back. "Are you sure you don't hear the voice?"

"Could it be one of the kids? Belle loves to play tricks."

"No. Oh, never mind. It must be my imagination. I should go."

Concern still hovered in Lara's eyes. "Come back whenever you need to, Nance. I mean it, now. Whenever."

"Thank you, Lara. That means much to me."

Lara's gaze burned into her back as she left the clearing and passed under the thick overhang of tree branches. She wandered aimlessly, following patches of sunlight that appeared on the dimmer forest floor. With her thoughts on the memory of the voice, and the few unsettling words she'd heard, she paid no attention to her path.

A faint haze separated a strange, brightly lit glade from the surrounding trees. When she stepped into the clearing, Nanceen's skin tingled. Gazing in wonder at the tiny, grassy area, she was surprised she'd never discovered this place. Then, she shrugged and sank to the ground with her feet tucked under her. Her clan's part of Faerie was no small land, there were bound to be places left for her to discover.

She plucked a tiny purple flower from a plant with yellow-green leaves. The rise of scent from the bloom made her close her eyes and inhale deeply. It was a mix of Otherworldly scents such as she'd never encountered. Her lips stretched into a dreamy smile.

"I'm gratified you like my flowers."

It was the same voice--only not inside her head. Afraid to open her eyes, Nanceen paused before answering. What if it was just a figment of her imagination, her unknown desires becoming manifest?

"Don't be afraid."

"I'm not," she whispered.

"Open your eyes."

The voice was a clear tenor that rang with the power of magic. Had one of Faerie found her? Someone from another clan? Was this for whom she waited? Tremors chased each other down her spine. Slowly, she opened her eyes and looked around cautiously. There was no one in the glade.

"What foolishness is this? Where are you?"

"I'm here."

"Where?"

"Find me."

She rose and followed the soft echoes of the voice to the far side of the glade. A blurry haze hovered a few inches above the grass and flowers. She lifted one of her hands toward the pale golden glow, reaching to touch, to discover what magic created such a small disruption in the clear air.

"What will I find?"

"Love."

She dropped her hand to her side. "Don't say such things. I'm no fool to believe such words."

"Then, I must prove myself to you." The edges of the haze faded and it shrank in upon itself until only a tiny, winged man remained.

Nanceen stared. Words failed to pass the dry tightness in her throat. The wings fluttered briefly to lift the figure higher and closer. When he was at eye level, a slow, sensuous smile spread across his face. Turning the deep velvety blue and silver of the wings toward her, he pirouetted in the air. When he faced her again, he bowed, nearly touching his knees with his head.

"I am Korin."

"It's not possible."

He grinned. "I assure you it is, for I have always been Korin. Korin of the family Goodfellow."

"Are... are you a... a fairy?"

He bowed once again. "Aye. One of the wee folk." A hint of sadness colored his words.

"You don't exist. You're just a myth, a children's tale."

Korin crossed his arms. "I assure you, Nanceen of the Gentry, I am as real as you. As real as the humans who believe in neither of our races. Ah, my Nanceen. There is much you do not know of the Otherworld. It would seem the Faerie clans, as the mortals, are fools."

Nanceen closed her eyes. "I don't believe this. I must be dreaming." Afraid of what she would see next, her eyelids lifted slowly. She was having delusions, seeing things. This wasn't happening to her. It wasn't.

Still hovering before her face, his arms still crossed, Korin's head shook back and forth. "What shall I do so you will believe?"

"I..."

"Return tomorrow, so we may talk again." His dark wings fluttered rapidly as he turned, hovered only a moment, then sped away, rising and falling over the rolling landscape.

"Wait." The whispered word fell on the silent, empty clearing. Nanceen drew back her hand and stared at the palm. She'd just seen a man no bigger than her hand. With wings. A fairy.

She shook her head and wiped her palm against her thigh. Fairies were creatures of imagination. She gave an unladylike snort. Of course, to most human minds, so were her people.

Tiny as he had been, Nanceen had no trouble bringing his form into sharp focus. Backed by the deep blue of his wings, his hair shone with a strange combination of gold and silver. Underlain with pale blue, the silver reflected in startling, almond-shaped eyes. And his eyelashes--pale as his hair, but long and softly spiked. Nanceen smiled and admitted to herself the weakness she'd always had for lush male eyelashes. She brushed a fingertip over her own dark lashes. Why was it males were blessed with wonderful lashes when she had only a short, stubby fringe?

A shrug lifted her shoulders and a sigh filled her chest as she tried to visualize the rest of his face. She was sure he had a nose and a mouth, but she never got that far in the short moment after he appeared. The tiny man was a wonderful fantasy.

And that's all he was. She shook herself, anger at her notions made the movement stiff and jerking. Perhaps Lara was right, and the lack of a man in her life caused her strange, restless moods. But it was no excuse to create a being from a hazy spot in the normally clear air. And, if she was going to create an imaginary lover, she should at least make him the same size she was. Nanceen chuckled. It was time to return to the real world. She chuckled again. Her real world was fantasy to others, so why couldn't she have a fantasy man?

Emptiness throbbed deep in her chest. Although her mind denied the fairy's existence, her heart wished he were real. The vision of glinting sliver-blue eyes haunted her as she rose and wandered from the glade.

"Show me her."

Korin bit back a sharp retort. It was bad enough he was forced to petition his king for permission to court, to find his mate. But to expose her to the wily Fir Dhaerrig made his stomach churn. When the rat man discovered...

"Korin." The warning was explicit. The red cloaked, barrel-chested, filthy king reclined on his dirt-smudged throne, one leg thrown negligently over the ornately carved arm.

"Sire." Korin bowed his head, chewed on his lower lip, and lifted his hands. A clear bubble formed between his palms, lifted, and expanded until it was twice as tall as its maker. A gentle, whispered word swirled a smoky mist through the bubble to form a female figure. Korin could not hold back a smile when the vision of Nanceen, bent low over a thick book, solidified.

The smile died at the king's startled cry. "One of the gentry? No, man. You will not. If you must mate, take a willing fairy maid."

"I desire none but this woman."

The Fir Dhaerrig leaned forward and licked his fleshy lips. His long, beaked nose twitched, making him appear even more as the rat man so many before had called those of his blood. How one of the treacherous Fir Dhaerrig became leader of his tribe was far beyond Korin's understanding.

The obvious sexual interest his king held for the vision of Nanceen made Korin clench his teeth. His fists soon followed and hovered, quivering at his sides. The king ran one hand down the front of his loose, torn trousers to cup himself. He leaned back and laughed, drew his hand away, and flicked his fingers to make the bubble float closer.

"She is a comely thing. Perhaps when you fail, I shall pursue her."

"No!" Clapping his hands once to make the bubble disappear,

Korin leapt forward. He skid to a stop, folded back the wings that had flared with his anger, and lowered his head. "No. I will not fail."

"It is a deed never done--to mix races."

A bark of sarcastic laughter jumped from Korin's lips. "Our history tells of the time long before the separation of fairy and gentry. A time when fairy was ruled by--"

"Speak not of it, Goodfellow. If you value your meager existence, you shall not speak those names. Fairy rules fairy. There is no mixing of fairy and gentry."

"What of the tribes across the sea? What of Queen Lina?"

The Fir Dhaerrig laughed, his great belly shaking with his effort. "That whore? She weaseled her way into the Prince's heart. Imagine, born in a flower and raised by humans. Loved by a toad. She didn't even have wings, had to be carried away by a bird. Pah."

Holding back a sigh for the beautiful, much-maligned queen, Korin went to one knee. "I ask no more than the prince himself found with one from outside our race. As he gave to her, I shall give to my chosen."

"Think you to find pleasure then, Korin?" The king's laugh became a wicked, taunting sound. "I doubt you could pleasure one of her... size."

Korin looked his king square in the eye. "I have the magic to grow to the gentry's size. If she would desire it, I would find the magic to bring her to this size, to know our people as well. We shall make the final choices together."

"Such a choice is irreversible after the passing of three moons." The king's mouth dropped in astonishment then he shook his head. "No, I will not allow it."

"If I don't receive your sanction, I shall pursue my desire without it."

"You challenge my decision?" The king tensed and clutched at the arms of his throne.

"Aye."

The king's laughter rolled through his empty hall. Disgusted,

Korin turned away, already planning for the agony of losing his place in the fairy lands forever. Korin took a deep breath. His place in fairy was worthless. His family had retreated to the far reaches of the land so long ago; none remembered why they chose near banishment. Now his family was gone, and he was alone.

Nanceen was worth both the mental and the physical pain of a separation from his people. Even if she didn't choose him, he would be able to remain near her. He took a determined step toward the wide, double doors that led from the throne room.

"Wait, Korin." The king could barely make the words intelligible through his laughter. "I believe I shall change my mind."

Korin refused to let joy and hope show on his face when he turned back to the Fir Dhaerrig. If the fairy knew the effect of those words, Korin's life would be made even more miserable than it already was whenever the king took notice of him.

"Yes, I have changed my mind." The king lifted one hand and studied the chipped, dirty nails. "However, there are conditions."

"Conditions, sire?"

"Oh yes. You must succeed in a series of challenges I set for you. Succeed and the maid shall be yours. Fail, and wingless banishment awaits. Do you accept my challenges?"

"For the love of the maid, Nanceen, I do."

The king clapped his hands twice. A long, feathered quill and a curl of parchment appeared before him. He tapped the side of his face with the end of the feather as he concentrated. After turning a twisted, self-satisfied smile to Korin, he wrote.

Korin held his breath for three heartbeats, then let it out slowly. What kinds of challenges would the sneak who was their king assign him? Would they be physical? Korin tensed and relaxed his well-toned muscles. A physical challenge should be no problem. Mental? Perhaps he was not so well accustomed to such things, but there would be a way to succeed, and he would find it. Would the rat king assign him a task of bringing more treasure to the already overflowing coffers, hidden where even the leprechauns couldn't find it? Korin gave up speculating and, while he waited, the image of Nanceen filled his inner vision.

"Eh, Korin. Are you ready to hear your challenges?"

He took another deep breath. "Aye, sire."

"Should you succeed, which I doubt, you shall hear the sound of a bell. A mark shall be made upon one side of this page. Should you fail, a mark shall be made under the name of your king. Me." The Fir Dhaerrig laughed. "The length of time for the completion of the challenges is one changing of the moon. From dark to dark again is all the time you have to tally more marks upon your side of the page. This challenge is sealed by fairy law, and shall be witnessed by a hand's number of my people. I shall even give you the honor of choosing those witnesses. There will be no question of the legality of this challenge."

Korin nodded. "I understand, sire."

"Then, call your witnesses. Get on with it. The dark moon falls upon the human world this night. I want to make sure you have all the time you need." He laughed and spread his hands to make the parchment lie flat in the air as if supported by a table. The king leaned back, tossed his leg over the arm of his chair, and looked expectantly at Korin.

T he witnesses had come, studied the parchment, nodded approval and scurried from the hall. After reading the conditions and uncaring what consequences might come from the rash action, Korin shook the parchment in his king's face. "These are your challenges?"

The red-cloaked Fir Dhaerrig steepled his fingers under his sharp chin, tapped the tips together in a light, dancing rhythm, and grinned. The crooked cant of his lips twisted his face to a malicious leer. "Until the marks are made and witnessed, you can always back away, Korin Goodfellow."

"Once a bargain is made, no Goodfellow has ever turned his back on the challenge."

"Then what are your concerns?" The king's face softened to a confused expression, but his beady eyes continued to glitter with wicked intent.

A shudder passed through Korin and he brought his wings tight against his back. He took a deep breath, cleared his mind, and dropped the parchment back to the invisible table.

"I do not understand the challenges you set before me, sire."

"Eh? Have I made them too difficult? Will you be forced to concede to my will and forget the gentry maid?"

Knowing that even the destruction of his body would not drive the essence of Nanceen from his spirit, Korin shook his head. "No, sire, I will not concede."

"Then perhaps part of the challenge is to understand the tasks placed before you."

"As you decree, sire."

The Fir Dhaerrig rose ponderously to his feet and took a step toward the parchment. "As you decree, sire," he whined. "As you decree." His voice settled to harsh tones and he slapped his hand on the parchment. "Korin Goodfellow, I so decree. And, since you continue to challenge me, I decree one further condition.

"Think again if you plan to seduce the maid to win her to you. You shall not join with her until..." The king let a serious, contemplative look fill his features, then tapped his finger against his chair. "Until four of the other challenges are met."

Korin returned a cool smile to the king's expectant expression. He had not thought to use seduction, but the thought of lying with Nanceen, of touching the soft warmth of her skin, made him weak.

Eyes narrowed, the Fir Dhaerrig's mouth twisted to a frown. "Should you lay with her, should you mate with the gentry woman before my conditions are met, the agreement is forfeit. As is your life. Do you understand me, Goodfellow?"

Korin gave a sharp nod.

"The witnesses have acknowledged the document. If you desire to continue with this useless farce, make your mark, Korin of the family Goodfellow."

Korin's wings unfurled and quivered with the force of holding his anger in check. He snatched the quill from the air, drew the distinctive design of his mark, and shoved the page toward the king.

Suppressed laughter turned the king's face the bright color of his cloak. He turned his hand so the back of his fingers pressed against the parchment. A faint glow surrounded his middle finger. An acrid smell drifted past Korin, and he turned his face from the wafting odor.

"Done." The king snapped his fingers. "The document is marked and witnessed."

A duplicate parchment appeared before Korin. He glanced quickly at the page, rolled it into a tight cylinder, and stalked from the chamber. When he reached the clear air he leapt high and let the light breeze carry him far from the rancid stench of the king's chamber. How had a Fir Dhaerrig, a creature who cared for nothing but his own amusement, become king?

Korin sat on a low branch and spread the parchment over his knees. His heart sank as he read, reread, and tried to understand the challenges. One cycle of the moon. It was not much time.

CHAPTER TWO

Awakening with the vestiges of a highly erotic dream still tingling across her damp skin, Nanceen stretched and smiled at the timbered ceiling. The movements pulled her silky nightgown across her sensitive breasts and tightly peaked nipples. She wiggled her shoulders to increase the wonderful feeling, rolled to her side, and snuggled into the feather bed.

Her window framed a bright sun rising over the Faerie world, highlighting the tops of the lush trees. The rays warming her face were cool compared to the heat burning through her. If the fey truly didn't dream, they were certainly missing a wonderful way to spend the dark hours of the night. How could images from her mind be so complex--she burrowed further under her light blanket--so stimulating?

Every puff of breeze through the window was soft as a lover's kiss. Every brush of material against her skin--the touch of a lover's hand. But nothing compared, nothing even came close, to the soft, electric caress of his wings.

Wings? Nanceen jerked to sitting and rubbed her hands over her face. It was true. Her dream lover had wings. Deep blue and silver wings. Butterfly wings. Strong, sensuous wings that had wrapped her in a cocoon of...

She slammed her palms against the feather bed, making two muffled thumps in the quiet morning. "No," she whispered, but wondered what she was denying. The dream? Heat flowed to the tips of her breasts. No, a dream was a dream. That her dream lover had wings? The heat crawled up her neck and into her face and she chuckled softly. Dreams were purported to be filled with strange, disjointed images. Why should her dreams be any different simply because she was half Faerie?

Did she deny that she met a creature of myth the day before? Nanceen crawled from the bed and stood at the window. The breeze lifted her damp hair from her scalp, cooling her. Yesterday's experience must have been some sort of a waking dream. What would cause such a delusion? Such a handsome, compelling delusion.

A tickle at the back of her mind hinted at the real reason for her restless dreams and her early morning denial. She shook her head fiercely, turned from the window and stared at the jumbled mess of her bed. The echo of a clear, male voice-- made tiny by the size of the man--curled itself around the thoughts she sought to deny. Deny as she would, the fact remained and stared back at her from her dream memories.

She was attracted to--okay, more than attracted to--a figment of her own imagination. Nanceen sank to the bed and cradled her head in her hands. She was going crazy, becoming demented, losing her hold on reality. Laughing, she flopped onto her back and laced her fingers behind her head.

Reality? How did one define reality? And whose reality? With a snort for the philosophical turn of her mind, and determined to start the day normally, Nanceen rolled from the bed. One final glance out the window wouldn't hurt, so she angled her face toward the light.

The morning dawned to glorious brightness. She took a deep breath of clean air and began to turn away. A faint haze blurred a section of the distant forest. Pulling her lower lip between her teeth, she paused uncertainly. The haze reminded her of him, of the imaginary one of her dreams. And that was the direction of the clearing she'd found, where she imagined the fairy.

The hazy shimmer called to her. It beckoned to her heart, tugging like a physical chain, drawing her to the window ledge. Curious, but unwilling to succumb to the strange, intense lure, Nanceen hovered a few steps from the window. Finally, she closed her eyes, drew a long, shaking breath, and turned her back on the window. There was no way she'd wander around Faerie looking for an imaginary clearing and an even more fantastic fairy man.

A deep sadness, so intense it caused a pain centered in her chest, nearly returned her to the window. What could it hurt? Maybe the glen was real and filled with butterflies. Only her loneliness made the tiny winged creatures into a man. The pain lessened. Her resolve grew. She would not look for something that wasn't there.

She told herself so, over and over, as she dressed and entered the common room of the cottage she shared with her sister. Kae was already gone. Nanceen snatched a shiny green apple from a bowl on the table and rushed from the cottage. The sooner she was away, the better for her sanity.

At first she thought to visit Lara, but her home was in the same direction as the glen. So Nanceen turned the opposite direction and strode with wavering purpose toward a portal to the mortal, human world and visit with her brother.

After reading the document through a fifth time, Korin folded the parchment tightly and, with a snap of his fingers, stored it safely away in a small bag hanging from his belt. Looking at the page again wouldn't help him decipher the king's warped conditions. Korin had memorized each nuance, every word, in hopes of finding some meaning to help him in his quest.

He sighed dramatically and leaned back against the crook in a small tree branch. Hidden by the thick, green leaves, he watched Nanceen's small cottage unobserved. A rueful grin touched his lips when Nanceen rushed from the building, hesitated, glanced toward the distant glen, and turned away.

It was as he suspected. She would go to the mortal world, looking for answers.

Answers. How was he to answer the challenges put forth by his king? Although Korin found the Fir Dhaerrig and his ideas difficult to comprehend, the rat man was still king. And, as such, still to be obeyed.

But what if he couldn't solve the riddles? Would he be willing to risk all, give up all, for the love of a woman? Korin shook his head--he honestly didn't know. His heart screamed yes, but some feeling lodged even deeper within him created a long list of reasons why such a decision would be unwise.

A slight change in the air had him fluttering inches above the branch. Even though Nanceen had passed through the portal into the non-magical, human world, Korin still sensed her. And the threatening aura nearby.

The fluttering of his wings became a dark blur as Korin sped toward the portal. He skirted the faintly shimmering oval and using his own magic, entered the human world. He surrounded himself with the faint haze and followed the essence of Nanceen's passage through a yard reminiscent of Faerie, across the hot, gray stone of a street, and into the broad, grassy expanse of a park.

There she sat cross-legged on a small rise, her elbows resting on her knees, her chin braced against her interlaced fingers. Korin frowned. He sensed danger, but the scene was peaceful and calm. One other human--a man, hands clasped behind his back--stood watching her. Was this the danger?

Korin hovered uncertainly, but when the man moved closer and sat beside Nanceen, the decision was made. Tightening the disguising haze around him, Korin moved closer.

"Excuse me?"

Nanceen jumped at the modulated tones of a man's voice. She shaded her eyes against the sun and looked up at the silhouetted figure. His arm swung out to indicate the ground next to her. "May I join you?"

Nanceen shrugged. "It's a public park." She wasn't sure if she was irritated that her contemplations were interrupted, or glad of the respite from her tumbled thoughts. The man's face remained in shadow until he collapsed gracefully onto the grass beside her and flashed a grin full of even, white teeth.

"I am Titus."

Nanceen looked away, but found her gaze drawn back to him. Coal black hair framed a face more suited to a blond. His eyes were a muddy brown, the pupils circled by a lighter colored ring. She lowered her head and grinned. Why did humans find it necessary to change their appearance through hair dyes and colored contacts?

But who was she to judge--she hid much of herself from the human world. Why should she consider herself different? So, she turned her grin toward him. "Nanceen."

"Pleased to meet you. Not many will talk to a stranger these days." Titus leaned back on his elbows and stretched his long legs. "I'm new in town and haven't taken the time to go through the proper channels to meet people."

"Welcome to the area, Titus." Not feeling up to chitchat, Nanceen sighed and searched her mind for a way to make a reasonably quick, yet graceful, escape. Something about the man disturbed her. Shivers crawled across her skin like a parade of ants.

"Thank you, Nanceen." The speculative undertones of his voice made the ants crawl in a wild, disruptive pattern. Suddenly the feeling was gone. Warmth surrounded her as if a security blanket had been draped over her.

Titus frowned and glanced around the park. His eyes narrowed as he searched the open landscape. The frown faded and his brilliant smile returned.

Nanceen guessed his expression was calculated to win friends and influence people. And it might have worked, if not for the itching under her skin. Titus seemed to come to a decision and cleared his throat with a soft rasping sound. "Ah, this is a pleasant city. I have been considering setting up a business venture here."

Not really interested, Nanceen asked politely, "Oh? What kind of business are you in?" Her mind wandered, and she didn't listen to his answer. The sense of security became a caress so like the winged caress of her dream that Nanceen gasped.

"Is everything all right, my dear?" After Nanceen's nod, Titus continued. "I've been many things; in many parts of the world. I've picked up a few tricks and trades and thought I might try a catering business this time around."

Nanceen chuckled and let her eyes grow wide as she glanced at him. She laughed again, but held out her hand to prevent the flare of anger she recognized in Titus' eyes. "No, I'm sorry. It's just funny you should mention catering."

"Why is that? Oh, perhaps you are a caterer yourself. You would make lovely competition."

Waving away the compliment, Nanceen explained. "No, not me. Although I do help out sometimes. It's my brother, Jaye, who does the party planning. He's been in business for a long time and is very successful. It may not be easy to compete against Zeroun's."

A speculative light flared in Titus' eyes and he leaned toward her to rest his warm palm against her bare arm. "But I do so relish a challenge."

The angry buzz of a bee flew past his nose and Titus jerked from Nanceen. She silently thanked the insect as she rubbed her arm. Unable to chase away the uncomfortable tingles, she scooted back a few inches and glanced at Titus from the corner of her eyes.

He glared at the space between two low-lying bushes and blew out an angry breath. However, his expression was calm and pleasant when he returned his gaze to her. "One of the problems with the outdoors." He glared again toward the bushes. "Pesky insects. However, I must leave you, now. It has been a pleasure. Perhaps we shall meet again, Nanceen."

Before she could say a word, he rose to his feet in one fluid motion and strode away. Nanceen watched his lithe movements until he disappeared around a curve the shook her head. What had just happened? A bee saved her from an uncomfortable situation? She turned to look at the bushes and blinked twice and tried to focus on a patch of haze. So like the haze that greeted her in the small clearing, she nearly called out to it.

No, she told herself fiercely. It was just her imagination--a daydream brought about by her nighttime visions. And there was only one way to prove the folly. She had to return to the glen and show her heart there was no tiny, winged man waiting for her.

P anting heavily, Korin sank onto a woodchip and ran his fingers through his hair. Nanceen was leaving, but he was unable to follow. Completely changing form in the Otherworld was difficult enough, but to do so in the mortal world where magic was limited had exhausted him. Even his wings ached. The rapid beats needed to lift the fat, rounded bee's body were far from the gentle flight that normally carried him easily through the air.

Across the park, Nanceen crossed the road and returned to the portal's location. He smiled. Hopefully, she would be at the glen when he was able to cross back to the Otherworld.

From the other side of the grassy expanse, the man also watched her. Korin's hard breaths filled with anger. There was no magical aura about the man, but there was danger. The prickly hairs on the back of Korin's neck stood erect. If the human dared to trifle with his Nanceen...

Korin rolled his eyes to the bright, blue sky and drew in enough breath to chuckle. The happy sound lifted his spirits and filled him with renewed strength. He would deal with the human if necessary, as he would deal with the puzzles set forth by his king. And win the love of Nanceen.

With a single flutter of his wings, Korin rose from the wood-chip. Finding a weakness in the fabric between the two worlds took a few moments, but he was soon at his glen, sitting on a broad leaf, waiting.

CHAPTER THREE

Once she returned to Faerie, Nanceen's determined footsteps slowed. Her feet grew heavy and dragged her down into her doubts. Her logical mind, a strange inheritance from her Faerie mother, repeated a monotonous litany. *There were no such things as fairies. No such being as a tiny winged man. No. No. No.*

But to each negative thought, her heart whispered yes.

The path took her close enough to Lara's cabin to hear the twins' high, joyous calls. Unable to face the young exuberance, or her niece's knowing looks and questions, she skirted the area. She even tiptoed past the turning of the path and chuckled at the folly of the actions. As if trying to find a new glen in a well-known forest, hoping a tiny man was waiting for her, wasn't folly.

She needed to prove it to herself that it *was* folly. And so, ignoring the fresh blossoms on the low hanging branches and the melodious calls of the small birds, she moved quickly through the Faerie woods. One thought, one need drew her forward. Her feet shuffled a path through the littered undergrowth. Her eyes searched for the golden glow of sunlight piercing the dimmer forest.

And finally, there it was. There were many glens, any number of small glades throughout her clan's part of the Otherworld, yet she knew this was the one. Hesitating while still under the over-hang of branches, she rested one hand against a rough tree trunk. The dusty prickle of the bark kept her focused. A deep breath caught in her throat. Now, she had to face the empty glade.

One slow step brought her out from under the trees. A second step disturbed a small animal hiding within a low, bushy plant. Nanceen took another deep breath and rushed to the center of the open area. She stared into the cloudless blue sky and chewed on her lower lip. Afraid of what she would see--or what she wouldn't see--she lowered her gaze slowly.

A soft breeze caressed her cheeks and the lingering scent of unfamiliar blossoms surrounded her. When she scanned the glen, only the bowing grasses greeted her. Feeling a fool once again, she whispered, "Are you there?"

::Find me.::

Nanceen shook her head to clear the reverberating echoes of the soft voice. "I'm not playing games with a figment of my imag-ination." Tempted to stomp her foot, the niggling doubt held her still. "If you're here, show yourself."

::As you wish.::

A slight fluttering sounded to one side. Keeping her lower lip caught between her teeth and reminding herself to continue to breathe, Nanceen turned slowly toward the sound.

"I'm glad you came back."

The mellow voice, even more melodious than when only in her head, sent tingles of awareness through her. Rubbing her arms, she tried to press the goosebumps back into her skin. Her dry mouth formed words, but no sound rose from her throat.

"Bide with me a short while?" The fairy rose slowly until he hovered at eye level. A cautious smile stretched his lips, but he said no more.

Nanceen remained silent as she studied the fine angles of the tiny face, the small, masculine figure accented by a gauzy tunic, a long, dark vest, and tight, form-fitting breeches. Dark, cobalt wings moved slowly, effortlessly, keeping him aloft. A deep longing filled Nanceen and she sighed a soft "Oh."

The fairy's smile grew wider. He gestured to a soft, grassy knoll at one side of the clearing. "Will you join me?"

She gave no thought, and nodded. The fairy flitted away, and Nanceen took cautious, even steps to follow. Suddenly, she stopped and covered her face with her hands.

"What am I doing?" she asked with a desperate exhalation of breath. Fear for her sanity displaced the odd longing. She couldn't sit in a clearing, talking to a being who didn't exist. She didn't want to give in to fantasy. A bitter laugh burst from her lips. She was fantasy. Why shouldn't she have her own?

Because the logic she and her sister had cultivated within the bounds of the Otherworld and the fun-loving Faerie would not allow her to succumb to a fantasy. No matter how attractive. Thoughts of her sister kept her from taking the steps forward that her heart begged her to make. The logic of disbelief turned her away from the grassy knoll and the winged figure waiting for her.

But fear made her run from the glen.

CHAPTER FOUR

T he leaf dipped with Korin's movement as he reached to one side and snatched at the length of a nearby blade of grass. He tugged until a bit broke off, stuck the end in his mouth, lay back and chewed thoughtfully. Floating high above him, clouds filled the clear sky. Their flat, gray color matched his mood. He sighed and turned to his side, propped his head on one hand and stretched his wings.

As much as he hated to admit, the first of his king's conditions would perhaps be the hardest to meet. It was the only clear requirement listed on the parchment. She must believe in him.

Korin tossed the shredded stem away. There had been a time long ago, even to the fairy, when both humans and the gentry readily believed in the smallest of the sidhe. Even after the human's religious beliefs forced the gentry underground, then to the Otherworld, the diminutive fairy were honored, or at least remembered, with sweet honey cakes and fresh milk. Korin smacked his lips. It had been a long time since he'd tasted the creamy white ambrosia of milk.

Until humans began to blame the wee folk for their troubles. When aided by the priests, their beliefs in fairies disappeared.

But how had the breach with the gentry occurred? Even the

legends skirted the issue. There was no history to help him, and Korin was unsure how to proceed. Without Nanceen's belief in him, fulfilling any of the other conditions would be useless.

Useless. That's what he was. The niggling doubt became a surety. Somehow, the Fir Dhaerrig had manipulated him. But at what cost?

Korin flopped to his back, folding an edge of one wing under him. Wincing, he adjusted his position and covered his eyes with one forearm. There had to be a way to make Nanceen--no, he could not make her do anything. He would find a way to convince her of his reality. And the existence of his people. One word flashed through his mind. Over and over until the rapid flashes burned behind his closed eyelids. *How?*

A shadow covered him, cooling his skin. Cautious, he lifted his arm from his eyes and opened them. A face loomed over him. Startled, he scrambled to a sitting position and scooted back until he pressed against the plant stem.

"Hi, bu'fly man."

The child's whisper sent waves of relief over him. Occasionally there were children who saw fairies, until adults taught the belief out of them. Sadness followed the relief. If children could only retain their beliefs, perhaps the breach between races would be healed. And he wouldn't be fighting to claim love from one of the gentry.

A chubby finger moved closer and he held still. Gently, the child touched the tip of one wing and giggled. "Pretty."

"I thank you, child. How are you called?" At the confusion in her dark brown eyes, Korin asked, "What is your name?"

The rosebud mouth formed a silent 'oh'. "I'm not supposed to talk to strangers." She giggled again. The clear sound filled Korin with a strange hope. "Who're you?"

"I am Korin, young mistress." He rose, bowed deeply, then spread his wings to their fullest.

"Bu'fly man. Kor'n."

Korin winced at the childish lisping of his name, but cast a brilliant smile to the engaging girl. "Kor-in, young mistress. Are you able to say Kor-in?"

"Kor'n." Dark brows drew together as she concentrated in forming her mouth around the syllables of his name. "Kor-in."

A deep chuckle rose from Korin. "You may call me bu'fly man if you wish."

The enthusiastic nod bounced the dark waves of her hair around her face. She reached toward Korin again. Then she lifted her head and her smile grew wider. "Daddy."

Korin glanced in the direction of her gaze to the tall, dark haired man who gestured at the tiny girl. He was the man who lived in the nearby clearing. A grin tugged at one side of Korin's lips, it was the place he'd first seen Nanceen.

The child bent close and the warmth of her sweet breath flowed over him as she whispered. "Bye, Bu'fly man." She ran and flung herself into the man's arms.

Korin remained still. Unaccustomed jealousy rose at the tender way the man and daughter greeted each other. When the child pointed back toward him, he knew he should shrink into the shadows, but stood firm. The man's gaze landed on him and the dark eyes held his for a long moment. With a brief nod, the man gathered the girl into his arms and disappeared under the trees.

The breath escaped Korin's lungs with a whoosh. The man had seen him. Acknowledged him. The man was not merely indulging the child's fantasies. He recognized Korin as a sentient being. This was a strange occurrence, one that brightened the dim hopes Korin sheltered in his heart. If one man could see him as he was, why couldn't the woman he loved see him so as well?

Renewed determination strengthened the beat of his wings when he lifted from his leafy refuge. The low rumble of thunder echoed overhead and thrummed through him. The Otherworld would soon be under the power of a rare storm. Thinking this change in the weather suited his mood well, Korin flew swiftly toward his home. Once the sun shone again over Faerie, he would search out Nanceen. Perhaps the combined darkness of the storm and the moonless night would bring him inspiration.

. . .

The cottage was still and dark. Nanceen chewed on her lip and opened the door then reached for a match to light the lamp centered on a round table. A folded sheet of thick paper propped against the lamp made her sigh. Nanceen picked up the page and held it so she could see her sister's spidery script.

Nance,
I've gone south to the edge of the African continent. There are rumors one of the desert clans has discovered scrolls that survived the fires that destroyed the fey library at Alexandria. 'Tis also rumored these scrolls contain a history of the Otherworld and early relations between Faerie and the human world. If so, this is a remarkable discovery, one I must experience firsthand.
I'm not sure when I will return, but if you need me, send a message the usual way.
Enjoy your time without me.
Kae

She had drawn a crude smiling face next to her final state-ment. Normally, Nanceen would relish the time alone, but not now. Not when she needed desperately to talk with someone about her delusions.

Kaelea, with her love of history and knowledge of many races, both human and Otherworldly, would surely have words of wisdom for her confused twin. Nanceen crumpled the note and tossed it across the room. How dare she run off when she was needed?

But if you need me...

Nanceen was sure her sister would return at a moment's notice. Yet, in all honesty, what could Kae do except listen? And, no matter how Kae tried to listen, her mind would be obsessed with the possible find of ancient knowledge. Nanceen could find no blame in that. Kae had few interests, and spent little time away from their clan's lands. This time away would be good for her as well.

"I hope you find what you're looking for, Kae."

Wandering around the cottage's common room, Nanceen picked up one item after another and set each down just as quickly. Unable to focus on a task, or even a simple thought, she sat, stretched her legs out before her, and stared at the ceiling. She wasn't ready to face her parents with her strange tale. Too often during her years of growth she had given them cause to fret and worry over her. As an adult, she was loath to do so again.

There must be someone she could talk to about all this. Someone who would try to understand--and not condemn her for foolish notions.

Lara. Her niece always had a willing ear. No doubt she had some concern after Nanceen's last visit. Nanceen shook her head. She was getting very good at not casting herself in a positive light. Much too good.

Thunder shook the tiny glass bottles lining a shelf high on the wall. A brief smile touched her lips. It had been a long time since rain fell in Faerie. Thunder rumbled again, closer, and the whistle of rising wind whipped around the corner of the cottage. She needed to hurry so grabbed a plaid shawl from a hook near the door and stepped from the building.

Wind tore at the shawl, nearly ripping the soft weave from her fingers. A bright streak of multi-forked lightning creased the sky. A dead silence filled the Faerie glade before thunder followed another bolt of lightning. Nanceen took a deep breath and rushed from the minimal shelter of her porch. With an anxious glance at the dark sky, she ran beneath the overhang of branches and through the woods.

The thunder chased her. Each horrendous clash threatened to stop her in her tracks. Soon she had gone too far to return home, and only the imagined warmth and safety of Lara's cottage drew her forward. Electricity filled the air and with each lightning flash her hair rose slightly from her scalp. Large, cold drops of rain splattered through the leaves and fell around her.

What had she been thinking? A storm in Faerie loosed the wrath of the elements. Rare though storms were, few ventured from their homes when the darkened skies roiled with thunder and stark flashes of light illuminated the driving rain. Just another example of her foolishness.

The huge, cold raindrops blinded her until she pulled the shawl over her head and held the edges far out before her. It would be easy to become lost in the storm's confusion--confusion that paled when compared to her reasons for entering the storm in the first place. Pausing under the doubtful safety of a huge tree, she focused her thoughts. Lara's cottage. She had to get to Lara's cottage.

A sense of warm comfort surrounded her for a brief moment and the rain seemed to lessen to one side. She leaned into the warmth, squinting through the rain to find Iain's worried gaze staring down at her. He grinned and rain ran from the tip of his nose.

"Seems to be a bit of a blow in Faerie this night." He wrapped one of his arms around her shoulders and angled Nanceen toward another path. "Come, Lara is waitin' fer ye."

Snuggled into the protection Iain offered, Nanceen glanced at him. "A bit of a blow?"

"Aye. The storms along the coast when I was young were much worse. Wi' nae trees to block the wind from the sea." He chuckled. "'Tis much more pleasant in these fair lands."

Moments later the cabin, with its bright red door, came into view. Lara opened the door and the light surrounding her welcomed Nanceen and Iain into the dry, cozy building. After thanking Iain with a kiss, Lara fussed over Nanceen, made her change into dry clothing, and sat her before the fire wrapped in a fluffy blanket. Lara allowed her children to greet Nanceen, then sent them back to their father. When they were settled in a far corner, playing games with bits of string, Lara turned her attention to her aunt.

"So, what's up?"

It would do no good, but still, Nanceen tried to evade the question. "Why should anything be up?"

"There are few Faerie crazy enough to brave a storm of this magnitude--unless something is up." To prove her point, a crash of thunder and a blast of wind shook the small cabin. Lara glanced quickly toward her children before she focused on Nanceen. She said nothing more, only waited.

Nanceen remained silent a long time. Now that she was here, she had no idea how to broach the subject of tiny men with wings. She stared at her folded hands until a thick, pottery mug appeared in her vision. Taking the offered hot chocolate, she gave Iain a timid smile of thanks. He nodded and returned to the kitchen area.

The twins sat at the table, a small bowl placed between them. Iain reached into the cooler, removed a pitcher, and poured a small amount of milk into the bowl.

Lara asked the question that hovered on Nanceen's lips. "What are you doing?"

"Nae but teachin' the bairns the ways of the good folk." Nanceen stiffened and held her breath. Lara chuckled and shook her head. "What tales are you telling them now?"

"No momma." Belle shook her finger at Lara. "It's for the bu'fly man."

With a sharp, painful jolt, Nanceen's heart skipped a beat. The child had mentioned a butterfly man once before, just before she first met--him.

"Aye, fer the butterfly man, sweetling." Iain ruffled his daughter's hair, then offered his son the same treatment. Antin twisted away, took Iain's hand and twined his small fingers through his father's larger ones. Iain turned his gaze to Lara. "I only do as yer great grandmathair taught me. In order to receive the blessin' of the wee folk, ye must offer somethin' in return. 'Tis said the good people will do much blessin' fer milk and honey cakes."

"Good people?" Lara raised her eyebrows.

"Aye. Fairies. Nae as our clans, but the tiny winged folk." Nanceen choked on her cooling hot chocolate. The heat of embarrassment at drawing attention to herself rose to cover her face and she waved away Lara's concern. She set the mug on a side table, clasped her hands tightly, and waited for Iain to say more.

"Legends. If you'll pardon the expression--fairy tales." Laughter hovered just below Lara's words.

Iain crossed the room and knelt beside Lara. "Nae tales, sweet. In my homeland sightin's were few, but the old folk believed, so the wee ones blessed them. Beatris often left milk and honey cakes on the windowsill in times of stress, an' in times of happiness. The offerin's always disappeared, though I ne're saw one o' the good people." He paused. "Until this day."

Nanceen gasped and grabbed the arms of her chair. She leaned forward. Someone else had seen a fairy? Had Iain seen *her* fairy? She closed her eyes. *Her fairy*. When did the winged man become hers? A deep, pent up breath escaped through her slightly parted lips. When she admitted she believed in him.

She opened her eyes to Lara's confusion and Iain's enigmatic grin. He touched his wife's arm to gain her attention. "But, we have nae honey cake. Dinna ye think chocolate cake would do as well? 'Tis nothin' so fine as chocolate."

Deep red covered Lara's neck and cheeks. Nanceen grinned and glanced away. Iain's legendary love of chocolate was minute compared to his love of wife and children. She held back a chuckle. At least his love for Lara didn't give him a bellyache.

"Da," Antin demanded, "gotta finish."

Iain leaned forward and let his lips linger against Lara's flushed cheek. Then he rose and turned to the children. "Aye, my brave bairn. Come, you put the cake on the plate and we will set the feast just outside the door." He glanced back at Lara and Nanceen and winked. "I dinna ken yer mathair wishes fairies in her house just yet."

While he busied the youngsters and readied them for bed, Lara and Nanceen sat in uncomfortable silence. Nanceen was unable to read Lara's expression, nor was she able to further broach the subject. Even though the idea of the wee folk seemed to be on everyone's mind, how could she admit that she'd seen one? Perhaps that would be easy, but would they think her crazy if she admitted to the attraction she felt for the tiny man? And where could such an attraction lead? Nowhere.

Iain returned and sprawled into a chair. Lara turned to him. "And just when did you see a fairy?"

"This verra day."

Lara jammed her hands against her hips. "And where was this fairy?"

As if trying to contain a laugh, Iain chewed on the corner of his bottom lip. His eyebrows lifted innocently and he began. "I was lookin' fer yer daughter."

"Since when is she my daughter?"

"When the sweetling is nae doin' what she should, then she is yer daughter. I have only well behaved bairns." His laughter encouraged the women to laugh with him. A measure of Nanceen's confusion and doubt lifted and disappeared. But the answers she needed were no clearer.

"So, what did my daughter do?"

"Och, only wandered off--again. I found her in a glade I'd nae seen before." Confusion clouded his features for a moment before he continued. "'Tis nae far from here. She was bent over a flow-erin' plant, chatterin' to somethin'. She left the flowers when she spied me. Told me the butterfly man was there. When I looked, I saw a large, blue-winged butterfly." Iain paused and rubbed his eyes.

Nanceen scooted forward in her chair, eager to hear Iain's next words. Yet, she feared those words as well.

"Just before I turned away, 'twas as if my vision cleared. 'Twas nae butterfly. 'Twas a winged man. From his expression, he knew the moment I recognized him as fairy. I dinna ken why one o' the good folk is near."

"I... I do." Nanceen's voice cracked. "He's here because of me."

CHAPTER FIVE

The storm grew into one of the worst to ever hit the Otherworld. Wind rattled Korin's home, shaking it to the foundation. He paced across the large room and stared out a triangular window into the darkness. Lightning illuminated the wildly thrashing branches and the driving rain. Firm footsteps carried him to the other side of the room. The view from that window offered no hope for abatement of the fierce weather.

Was Nanceen safe? His imagination placed her wandering the forests of the Otherworld, drenched and frightened, the storm tearing at her until she collapsed. Korin shook his head to clear the vision. She had to be safe. She wasn't foolish enough to step into the storm. Was she?

Worried because his presence had distressed her and made her run from the glade, Korin feared she would not use the logical mind he so admired. Thunder sounded further away and he turned back to the window. Was the storm finally moving off?

His own logic slipped away and he rushed to the door, threw it open, and stepped into the storm. Wind pulsed around him, driving him back inside. How could he face the storm? What form could he take? He straddled a bench and leaned his elbows on the table. If only his ability to move between the human world and the Otherworld would also allow him to move between one place and another in Faerie.

Slapping the table with flat palms, Korin pushed to his feet. There was only one way to reach Nanceen. Before he could succumb to reason and stay in the safety of his home, he rushed out the door and planted his feet firmly on the soggy ground. His eyes closed, he spread his arms wide and lifted his face to the roiling sky. He furrowed his brow in deep concentration. Even as the wind threatened to tatter his wings, the soft membranes folded close to his back. Hot pain seared through him, and he choked back a cry. Spasms of agony shook his body until the wings absorbed, leaving twin dark discolorations centered between his shoulder blades. Korin moaned and slumped to his knees.

Blasts of wind drove rain through the slits in the back of his clothing. The cold drops careened down his spine. Korin shivered once, spoke a harsh, guttural word of command, and began to grow. Stumbling to his feet, he ran before he reached full human height.

Rain plastered Korin's clothing to the planes of his body, but he ignored the chill of soggy material and increased the speed of his passage under the waterlogged leaves. He ran blindly and stumbled when his stretched muscles tightened into agonized knots. With his increased size, the forest looked different and he lost his way in the darkness.

Frustration filled him and he turned in a tight circle to search the depths of the forest for a recognizable clue. Water, snaking down the short strands of his hair, blinded him, and he dashed the drops away with the back of his hand. He wanted to howl his frustration, growl out his anger at the weather, but the cold blasts of wind stole his breath. His frustration turned to despair. What good would he be to Nanceen when he couldn't even find his way through the forest?

What good was he at all? His head hung forward, and his shoulders slumped under the weight of his dejection. He would have stood there through night and welcomed the discomfort except some call, deep in his mind, made him turn his head to one side.

Through the curtain of rain came a flicker of light. Korin drew his brows together and squinted against the weather. Shelter. He would warm himself, rest a few moments. Then he would be able to make sense of the forest and find his way.

He kept his gaze focused on the light, fearing that if he looked away the golden glow would disappear. The muddy ground sucked at his feet, finally pulling one of his soft, low- cut leather boots from his foot. Korin ignored the wet grass and mud squishing between his toes and, leaving the crumpled, soggy leather behind, trudged forward.

The light grew larger. He would have thought it a cheery sight had he not been so miserable. Barely able to set one foot before another, he lurched into a clearing and faced a sturdy cabin. The red door beckoned him, and he forced his screaming muscles to take another step. A wide, covered porch offered him shelter from the renewed fierceness of the storm. Knocked forward by a blast of wind, he fell to his knees at the bottom step.

He lifted his gaze and spotted a small bowl protected by a wooden box turned on one side. Beside the bowl was a tiny plate with a square of a dark brown cake. He crawled up the steps, struggled to his feet using a post for support, and inhaled deeply. Mixed aromas assailed his nostrils. The wet forest nearly blocked the sweet, rising scent of fresh milk. Korin blinked twice and rubbed the water from his face. An offering to the fairies? Who still followed the almost forgotten, long ago traditions? He turned back to the clearing, and finally recognized where he was. The home of the child, and the man who had acknowledged him earlier.

He'd heard rumors the man was from a time far in the human's past. Could it be he came from a time when there was still a connection between humans and fairies? Korin eyed the dish of milk. His mouth watered for a taste of the white, creamy ambrosia. One taste--one taste would give him strength to continue.

Korin took one step toward the door. Accustomed to the weight of his wings, he overbalanced and fell forward. His head hit the solid, red door with a resounding thunk and he slid to a crumpled heap on the woven doormat.

"What was that?" Lara lurched from her chair, skirted the edge of a low table, and made for the door. Iain was there before her, one hand raised to hold her in place. Nanceen sat frozen, staring at the door.

Iain listened with his ear close to the wood for a few moments. Then, he shrugged and pulled open the door. A pile of dripping material rolled onto his feet and moaned. He dropped to his knees next to the inert mass. Carefully, he turned the figure over until he lay on his back. The man moaned, opened his eyes a mere slit and lifted one hand to his temple. Iain pushed the wavering hand away.

"He'll be needin' ice fer the bump."

Lara leapt into action and crossed the room in a few strides. By the time she turned back with ice cubes wrapped in a cotton towel, Iain had pulled the man completely into the cabin and shut out the storm.

Breath hovered at the base of Nanceen's throat. She knew who the drenched stranger was, but shook her head to deny that knowledge. This was a man--a long legged, full-sized man. And he had no glorious butterfly wings.

Of course there were no wings. Nanceen bit back a strangled laugh and rose from her chair. "Who is it?"

Iain hesitated, then took the ice from Lara and placed it carefully against the stranger's temple. "I dinna... ken."

The man moaned again and drawn by the sound, Nanceen moved closer. She couldn't see the man's face. What wasn't covered by the towel was blocked by Iain's wide shoulders. Angling to one side, she could almost see the man's features, but Iain reached out to hold the ice in place as the man moved.

"Dinna squirm so much. If ye dinna keep the ice in place yer lump will be large as yer head." He chuckled when the man froze.

"May I sit?"

Another chuckle rumbled from Iain. "Of course. Just hold the ice so it does nae slip."

Facing away from Nanceen, he sat with awkward, jerky movements, as though he was accustomed to carrying weight upon his shoulders. His muscular back showed through two long slits in the back of his tunic when he moved. Droplets of rainwater fell from short hairs curling against his neck and ran beneath his collar. He shivered.

Nanceen reached behind her for the quilt tossed over the back of her chair and moved forward to drape it over his shoulders. She studied how the rain had darkened both the gold and silver of his hair and plastered the soft curls against his scalp. Using his free hand to pull the material tight at his chest, he snuggled under the quilt.

"I thank you. The warmth is welcomed."

The voice--tenor and clear even though his teeth chattered with cold--filled her with relief and longing. The sound echoed through her, tingled her nerve endings until she crossed her arms protectively over her breasts. It was the voice of her dreams, the voice of the tiny winged man from the glade. But how?

She hesitated before touching a damp curl with one finger,then took a long, slow breath and spoke. "Is it you?"

A shimmering bubble protected the fairy king from the wild wind and driving rain. He frowned at the cabin and rubbed the back of one hand beneath his long, pointed nose. The storm brought Goodfellow and the gentry maid together. Not at all what he'd planned. Shading his eyes with his hand, he peered into the dark storm.

"Show yourself, Howlie."

Raucous laughter sounded over the gusts of wind pummeling

the impenetrable bubble. The Fir Dhaerrig tugged on his ragged cloak and shouted again. "Before me now, Howlie. Appear."

Wind swirled around the king, made him roll his gaze to the sky and shake his head. A small creature, barely more than a mere light space in the darkness, dropped from the wind, turned in a joyous circle, and bowed to the king. It doffed a bright red cap and bowed again. "Sire."

The Fir Dhaerrig stared into the distance over the creature's narrow shoulders.

Howlie turned another circle, as if trying to get his body to face the same direction as his backward pointing toes. "'Tis great havoc, is it not, sire? A delightful mess for the gentry forest."

"Aye," the king was forced to concede. "But not with the effect I had anticipated."

"But, me did as you commanded, sire."

The creature's stricken expression brought a mirthless laugh to the king's lips. "Aye. Perhaps too well, Howlie. Instead of keeping 'em apart..."

"Who, sire? Keep who apart? Me help more." Howlie bent his crooked knees, pulled his cap tightly over long ears, and prepared to leap into the passing wind.

"No. No more, Howlie. Let the storm go."

"Aww, sire. 'Tis fun. An' the mountain gnomes will be angry if you disrupt their game."

The king blew out a huff of air. It was terrifically difficult to meet his own desires while keeping his subjects happy. He cast a wicked grin at the cabin, shrugged and clasped Howlie on one shoulder. Not all his subjects. "Tell the bowlers to take their game to the mortal world. That should please them. In fact, Howlie, why don't you ride your storm over the humans? Frighten a few children. As a reward for the work you've done here this night."

Howlie jumped up and down, clapping his hands in glee. Wild laughter called a gust of wind to him. He paused before catching hold of the wind and turned his face to his king. "Thankee, sire." He swung onto the wind and with another gleeful shout, rode over the trees.

In the sudden silence the Fir Dhaerrig let his protective bubble dissipate and he turned from the cabin. His thoughts were already filled with new tricks and stumbling blocks for the spawn of Puck.

T he whisper-soft touch on his hair froze Korin mid-breath. When he heard the quiet, wondering voice, the towel dropped from his suddenly lifeless fingers. Ice scattered across the polished floor. Afraid the knock on his head had made him delusional, he closed his eyes and spoke without turning. "Nanceen?"

He sensed her moving in front of him, felt the slight vibration of the wooden planks beneath him when she crouched. Tentative, warm fingers touched his face. Leaning his cheek into the gentle pressure, he let a sigh of contentment brush past his lips. He opened his eyes to the most beautiful sight he ever thought to imagine. "Nanceen."

"It is you. How..."

A small, dark-haired blur launched itself into Korin's lap. Small, chubby arms wrapped tightly around his neck and soft lips planted a wet kiss on his cheek. "Bu'fly man."

Korin tore his gaze from Nanceen's confused expression and gently unwrapped Belle's arms from their stranglehold. "Yes, child. It's me."

Belle turned to where a young boy half hid behind the man's leg and stuck out her tongue. "See. He comed. Daddy was right."

The boy looked at his father. "Da?"

The man ruffled the child's golden curls and grinned. "Aye, Antin. 'Tis yer sister's butterfly man." He took a step forward. "But, I dinna think I should call ye butterfly man."

"Daddy, his name's Kor'n."

A blonde woman moved beside the man. "Corn?"

Belle laughed. "No, momma." She moved her mouth soundlessly as if trying to remember how it felt to say his name correctly. "Kor-in. His name's Korin."

Korin patted the small shoulder. "That's right, child."

"I'm not child. I'm Belle." She pointed to the family group. "That's my momma an' daddy. An' my brother, Antin."

Twisting in Korin's lap, she jabbed her pointing finger. "An' auntie 'Ceen."

Korin couldn't resist saying her name again. "Nanceen." Caught in the act of reaching for an errant ice cube, she slowly turned her gaze back to him. "Korin."

Their eyes caught and held. Time stood still. The dawning of true belief rose in her dark eyes. Was he close to fulfilling the first condition? She held the rewrapped ice cubes to his temple.

"Eww." Belle squirmed off Korin's lap. "You're all wet."

The woman took her daughter's hand. "And it's time for you two to go back to bed." She cast Korin a quick glance. "Will you be here in the morning?"

"I shall." Korin nodded carefully. "If I may rest here until then." *If Nanceen will stay as well.*

"No problem. Belle, you'll see Korin in the morning." She smiled at Korin. "I'm Lara. My husband's Iain. Welcome to our home."

"Aye, welcome." Iain cocked his head, listening. "The storm wanes. But 'twould be best if Nanceen remains here as well." He bent to kiss his children. "Off wi' ye."

Nanceen still held the ice to his forehead. The heat of her body warmed him and she scooted closer, then burned him; igniting the desire he fought to keep under control. The heat of her body drew him closer still.

Iain cleared his throat. Nanceen blinked and leaned back. Her hand fell away from him. The loss of both her heat and the comfort of the ice confused Korin. He looked up at Iain.

A sheepish grin brightened the man's face. "Uh, Korin... 'tis best ye get dry. Or ye may be addin' a cold to yer discomfort. Come. I dinna think we have clothing to fit ye here, but yer quilt should be enough for now."

A shiver reminded Korin of his damp clothes. He touched Nanceen's hand. "I shall return."

"I know. Korin? You are real, aren't you?"

::Yes. As real and solid as the walls surrounding us. As real as the storm that brought us together this night. As real as my love for you.::

Nanceen's gaze jerked to his. Two tiny lines formed between her brows, and he longed to smooth the worry away with his fingertips. She granted him a slow shy smile. "I understand."

Rising to his feet, Korin grasped his pounding head in both hands. Nanceen stood beside him and steadied him when he stumbled under the pain. She leaned close and he gratefully took the strength she offered. She stood on tiptoe and whispered, "I believe in you, Korin. You are real."

From the far reaches of the cabin came the squeal of a child's laughter.

CHAPTER SIX

N anceen stared at the closed bedroom door. How did it happen? How did she suddenly come to believe in fairies? One fairy anyway. How did he become a size she could touch, hold, experience?

Alone in the cabin's great room, she paced from one side to the other, her intense gaze seldom leaving the door. Her thoughts tumbled over each other, swirling in confused waves, much like the wind that had blasted her to Lara's cabin.

Inordinately pleased that Iain had insisted she stay the night, she hoped to learn more about the fairy who claimed to love her. How could he love her when he didn't know her? Yet, the tangle of emotions fighting against her logical mind hinted at more than just her concern for his well-being. Sensual tingles, a remnant of her dreams, made her feel as if she knew him--intimately. Perhaps the night would give them time to truly begin to know each other.

The slight squeak of a floorboard signaled the men's return. She rushed to a chair and leaned back, trying for a nonchalance her trembling muscles wouldn't allow. So she scooted forward to perch on the edge of the chair, clasped her hands tightly and watched the door.

Iain entered the room first, his wide shoulders blocking Korin's lankier frame. As they passed the round dining table, Korin paused, leaned on the back of a chair, and took a long, shaky breath. When Iain turned, Korin waved away his concern. "The storm drained me of energy. I shall recover with rest, and perhaps food."

Lara entered the room. "You haven't offered anything to our guests? Iain, what were you thinking?"

"Och, sweet. There has been nae time." He planted a quick kiss on Lara's cheek as he strode past her and into the kitchen area. "Mayhaps a bit o' ale will strengthen ye."

Korin tugged at the quilt wrapped around him. A faint flush covered his face. "I would prefer..." His voice lowered to a whisper. "... milk. If you have some."

At Iain's nod, Korin left the table, kicking the bottom of the quilt away from his feet as he walked. He sat on a couch facing the fire and wrapped the quilt securely over his lap and shoulders. One side of his lips quirked and pulled at the fullness until he smiled.

The pounding of her heart beat against Nanceen's chest. His was a dazzling smile, inviting and sweetly sensuous at the same time. She licked her suddenly dry lips. Smoky darkness filled the silvery blue of his eyes. There had been other men, both human and Faerie, who had turned lust-filled eyes toward her. She recognized the signs. But none had affected her so deeply, so immediately.

She was being drawn into those eyes, pulled into the depths of his emotions. The Faerie had often been accused of using a glamour to seduce hapless humans. Although Lara had disagreed with them, she and Kaelea had often scoffed at those tales and legends. Until now. Now she understood. She didn't know if fairies used magic to ensnare humans...

A body blocked Korin from sight, and Lara handed her a fresh, steamy cup of cocoa. Cold from the sudden loss of Korin's heated gaze, Nanceen sank into the depths of her chair, pulled her own quilt around her shoulders, and stared into the swirling chocolate drink.

"My thanks."

Korin's voice drew her attention back to the room, and the man. It was difficult to consider him a fairy, grown now to such a pleasing height. But, to her surprise, she did miss his wings. Somehow, the soft, cobalt and silver shapes complimented him, made him complete. Made him a fairy. Fairy and Faerie. She was going to confuse herself. Better just to call him Korin.

He accepted a tall glass of milk from Lara. Joined by Iain, the four sat silently with their drinks and their thoughts. Lara curled next to Iain. He wrapped his arm about her shoulder and she rested her head against his chest.

A flare of jealousy burned through Nanceen. From the soft, knowing smile on Korin's face she suspected he knew her thoughts. When one eyelid lowered in a slow wink, she was sure he did. Hiding her humiliation behind her large mug, she took a careful sip, continuing to watch Korin over the rim of her cup.

He turned his simmering gaze to the tall, clear tumbler in his hand. Holding it at eye level, he turned the glass first one way, then another. Firelight flickered and caught tiny prisms of colored light in the glass. He smiled in delight and caressed the outside of the glass with the tip of one finger. A shiver trembled over Nanceen's skin.

Bringing the glass close under his nose, Korin's eyelids drifted closed and he inhaled deeply. An expression close to ecstasy softened his face. He lowered the glass and opened his eyes to stare into the milk. Slowly, he traced the rim of the tumbler with his fingertip. Three times around the finger traveled, each time slower. Nanceen tried to control the shallowness of her breaths, to ignore the image of his sensuous caress touching her, the slowly tightening circle of pleasure his hands would create upon her.

Suddenly, he dipped his finger into the glass, swirled it once through the milk, and brought the milk-covered digit to his lips.

He lapped at a suspended droplet then, with a sigh, sucked the entire finger into his mouth. Twice more he dipped his finger, twice more the finger slipped into the moist depths of his mouth.

Nanceen bit back a tiny moan and squirmed in her chair. He only played with a glass of milk. Her nipples tightened, tingled with want, and a spiral of desire stole her breath. Her hands shook and she grasped her mug more tightly, belatedly noticing how her fingers curled around the handle and softly stroked the length. But Lara noticed and threw her a wicked grin.

Korin brought the glass to his lips. Instead of drinking, he only tipped it far enough to lap at the edge of milk. The tip of his tongue slid back and forth against the glass, drawing minute bits of milk into his mouth. And eliciting a gasp from Nanceen.

A rumble sounded from low in his throat. With both hands wrapped around the tumbler, he angled his head back and drank deeply. Sounds of pleasure, soft moans, and sighs accompanied his drinking.

Nanceen bit her bottom lip. The pleasured sounds caressed her as a lover would. Was this how he might sound when wrapped in her arms and deep in the throes of physical passion? Needing to direct her thoughts elsewhere, she glanced toward Lara and Iain. Both had leaned forward, watching Korin in amazement. She followed the line of their gazes.

He emptied the glass and pulled it a fraction of an inch from his lips. Eyes nearly crossed, he watched a last drop slide down the smooth surface and hover on the rim. Patient, he waited until the droplet fell to his outstretched tongue. As he savored the last drop, he closed his eyes, sighed, and lowered the glass to his lap.

As if sensing them watching him, Korin opened one eye. The other eye popped open and his light brows rose. Straightening his back, he set the glass on the floor and spread his hands in apology. Highlighted by the dim light from the fireplace, a ruddy flush crept up his neck and filled his cheeks. He cast a quick glance around the room. When his eyes met Nanceen's, he held her gaze, the silver-blue growing deep and smoky.

"I barely remember the last time... I tasted milk."

. . .

T he soft movements and stretching of Nanceen's sleep had pushed Korin into a small corner of the large couch. One of her slim hands rested over his thigh, the fingers curled lightly and pressed against his skin. For one brief flash of a moment he wished her hand lay on the outside of the quilt, rather than innocently caressing his leg. Then the flash was gone. He angled further into the couch arm and captured her restless hand under his.

The first rays of dawn filled the eastern windows and shone in to highlight her face. Korin longed to kiss the places where sunlight glistened upon her skin. He ached to taste her sun-warmed skin. Growing increasingly uncomfortable, he shifted, shoved Nanceen's hand away, and closed his eyes wearily.

"Didn't you sleep?"

The soft question made him smile. He turned his face toward Nanceen and opened his eyes. Her heavy lidded eyes and flushed cheeks stole his breath and he could not speak.

So, he shook his head.

Nanceen's brows drew together and concern swirled in her dark eyes as she struggled to free herself from the tangle of her covering. "I should have...stayed...awake, too. Uh." Finally putting her feet on the floor, she took a deep breath and glanced sideways at him.

He shrugged. "There was no reason. You were tired--so you slept." Rearranging the quilt covering him, Korin sat cross-legged facing her. "I didn't need to sleep."

Her frown crinkled her forehead in a decidedly cute manner. "You look exhausted."

"I'll recover."

"But I really wanted to talk to you last night. Find out everything..."

"Everything?" Korin cocked one eyebrow.

Pink infused her cheeks, and Nanceen turned her face from

him. It was cool without the warmth of her gaze, so he touched her arm. "I have nowhere to go. I am yours."

The pink blazed bright red and she stared at him, but her eyes offered nearly as much as his simple, innocent statement. Oh, the things they could discover about one another. He leaned forward, but the quilt held him in place, reminding him there was more he wanted from Nanceen than just a bedding. He wadded the patterned material in his lap. Even without the strictures of his bargain with the king, he would wait until the time for the physical act was perfect.

As if sensing his decision, a faint disappointment flickered in Nanceen's eyes before a shy smile eased her lips. "Maybe we could spend the day--"

"Many days."

Nanceen chewed on her bottom lip. The skin grew red under the abuse and Korin touched her arm again. "Today we shall talk only and learn about each other."

"I'd like that."

Noise from the hallway broke the spell of intimacy. They were forced further apart when Belle leapt to the couch and wrapped her arms around Korin's neck. "Bu-fly man." She placed a noisy kiss on his cheek and leaned back to look at him. "Sorry. I'm supposed to call you Kor...Korin now."

The young face looked so hopeful and sweet, Korin had to laugh. He returned the hug and kissed her forehead. Glancing over the girl's sleep mussed hair, he caught a wistful expression on Nanceen's face. All else faded. Belle slipped from his lap and skipped away. When he learned more of his Nanceen, he would understand the strange expression.

K orin took Nanceen's hand as they stepped from the wide porch. When Korin bent to pull his shoe from a mud puddle, Nanceen turned halfway back and waved at the couple standing arm in arm in the doorway.

"Those clothes will be great for the weekend," Lara called

after them. "But I think Korin needs something different for this evening."

Nanceen turned completely to face her niece. "The weekend?"

Laughter preceded Lara's next statement. "Remember? We're going to the Renaissance Faire. We've been planning for months. Remember?"

"Oh." Confused, Nanceen rubbed her tired eyes. "That's right. Tonight?"

"We promised Bryce we'd go to the N B Tween with him."

Not wanting to share her time with Korin, Nanceen glanced sideways at him. A brilliant smile greeted her and he nodded. "It will be fun." He leaned close to her ear. "There shall be time enough for us... alone." The tiny kiss he placed on her earlobe made Nanceen shudder with delight.

Lara chuckled again. "We'll meet you there at eight. Don't make me come looking for you."

Korin sketched a slight bow. "We shall arrive on time. Again, my thanks for your hospitality."

"And the milk?" Iain joined in Lara's laughter.

A bronze-red infused Korin's face, but he laughed as well. Then he gathered Nanceen's hand in his and his smile was only for her.

She basked in the glory of his happiness. His eyes sparkled merrily and the picture of him cavorting through a flower-filled glade, the leader of a troop of dancing fairies filled her thoughts. His eyes darkened slightly, and a new vision filled her imagination. Instead of the trooping fairies, there was only the two of them, surrounded by flowers, dancing the dance of lovers. Burning filled her face, and she turned back toward their path.

Walking in silence, they passed through the forest until they reached a clearing before a small stone building. Two Faerie women sat before the structure, leafing through slick-paged magazines. At Korin's frown of confusion, Nanceen giggled.

"Since my lady aunt, the Queen, permanently opened portals to the human world, the Faerie discovered the need for appropriate clothing. It caused a bit of a stir the first few times we tried to obtain clothing in the human world. Besides, many Faerie don't understand the concept of money."

"I have enough coin."

"I don't doubt, for your people. However, human currency is varied by locale, in denominations that are difficult to remember. We'll get you clothes here, and you'll let someone else take care of the money part." Afraid she may have offended Korin, she stammered to silence.

But he merely gave her an understanding grin and nodded. "That would be best. And, perhaps, I shall avoid milk as well, except when we are alone."

The twinkle in his eyes and the way his lips twitched told Nanceen he was teasing her. She slapped him playfully on the arm, then caressed the muscle with the palm of her hand. Just touching him...

Korin lay his palm over her hand and stilled the movement. He squeezed her fingers lightly before lifting her hand to his lips and pressing a kiss to her fingertips. How could he take her to such delight with so simple an action? What would happen-- when he kissed her? Nanceen's lips were dry, and she flicked her tongue out to moisten them. When... when would he kiss her? She rose to her tiptoes and leaned toward him.

Korin smile turned reluctant and he released her hand. Nanceen ached to cry out to him, to beg him to ease the tingling of her lips. She reached toward him, but he shook his head and canted it toward the stone building. Tearing her gaze from his, Nanceen discovered the Faerie women, magazines forgotten in their laps, watching them with undisguised interest.

"Clothing first. Then we shall... talk."

The up and down movement of her head brought Nanceen from a hazy world containing only the two of them and back to the clearing. She gave him a rueful grin and turned toward the building.

The Faerie women oohed and ahhed over Korin. Nanceen bit her lip to keep from telling the clothiers exactly what they could do with their magical measurements. Ignoring her, they scurried to bring magazines and opened the well-worn pages to show Korin items he could choose. When they brought out the bridal magazines to show him tuxedos, Nanceen cleared her throat loudly and stepped closer to the group.

"We're going to a bar--not a night club. He needs..." She paused for a moment and eyed Korin. She would hate to hide his muscular legs beneath some sort of baggy pants, or the breadth of his chest with a crisp, button-down collar. "Jeans," she continued. "And, a polo shirt." She glanced at his soft boots. "Your shoes should do fine."

One of the women giggled while the other nodded in agreement. "How worn would you like the jeans?" she asked.

"Comfortable, but nice enough for an evening out." While Nanceen had plenty of appropriate clothing for both Faerie and the human world, she had to allow herself to have confidence in the women and their ability to dress Korin.

Raising their arms, they paced around Korin. He twisted and turned trying to watch them. Nanceen wondered, a bit guiltily, if she should have warned him about the procedure. He didn't seem stressed over the women's muttered words, but grinned as if he were enjoying himself.

A glow of dull, washed-out blue light rose from the floor while a similar emerald green dropped over Korin's shoulders. The glows met just below his waist then swirled away.

Nanceen nodded in satisfaction, but had to remind herself to breathe as Korin turned in a circle and showed her his back. Jeans were definitely made for him--fitting looser in the leg, but tight across his buttocks. If she were the drooling type, she would be. The denim material was lightly worn and faded in just the right places. The polo shirt accented Korin's chest, without being tight and binding.

The three Faerie women sighed together.

"Where are my other clothes?" Korin faced the clothiers with his fists planted against his slim hips.

"Do not fear, sir. Your belongings are right here." The woman pointed to a stool. Korin's clothes were neatly folded, a small bag and a creased parchment topped the pile.

Korin rushed to the stool, picked up the parchment and opened one corner. After peering closely at the page, his deep breath stretched the shirt across his chest.

Weak kneed, Nanceen moved closer and tried to peek at the parchment. Korin folded the page tightly and, after looking down at himself, slipped it back into the small bag. He held one hand out to her. "Is there anything else we must do?"

Nanceen shook her head. After fastening the pouch to a belt loop on his jeans, Korin gathered the rest of his clothing and tucked it into a paper bag Nanceen held open for him. He held out his hand to her. Silently, she let him weave his fingers through hers. She spoke a quick thank you to the Faerie clothiers before he led her from the building.

By unspoken agreement, they turned toward Nanceen's small house. But, as they neared the cozy structure, Korin found himself dreading the confines. He halted at the door, suddenly wary of entering the place that was hers. Unable to vocalize his discom-fort, Korin took the bag containing his fairy clothing from her and asked simply, "Could we just walk awhile?"

A long breath, colored with relief, whispered through her slightly parted lips. Offering her a tiny smile, Korin acknowledged the uncomfortable newness of their relationship. And although he knew much of her from his observations, she knew little about him, and was wise to be wary. He appreciated her logical mind, and he would give her time to know him.

He waited while she went inside alone. Long minutes passed as he stared into the woods and tried to discern the source of his discomfort. He thought he would leap at the chance for a time of seclusion with Nanceen. During the night, as he watched her sleep, he'd realized she needed time. Time to know him. Time to completely believe in him. Time to let that logical mind relax and loosen the love in her heart.

Finally, he heard her behind him and turned. She had changed into jeans of her own. The blue material hugged the shape of her legs. A loose, gauzy top hung to her hips. She held a yellow apple out to him.

Korin bowed slightly as he accepted the fruit and closed his eyes as he took a bite. He chewed slowly, letting the juice fill his mouth before swallowing and opening his eyes. "Ah, daughter of Eve...to tempt me so."

Her apple stopped half way to Nanceen's mouth. "Daughter? Of Eve?"

Korin chuckled at the confusion in her eyes. "Merely a name some of my folk call humans."

"I'm only half human."

"Yes. You are daughter of Eve and child of the gentry. A tantalizing and irresistible combination." He cast her a wicked glance, took another bite, and spoke around the chunk of apple. "You have tempted me and I did not resist."

Nanceen rolled her eyes to the sky and bit into her apple. The crisp sound hovered between them and she giggled. "You're teasing me. Aren't you?"

When he didn't answer, she rested her hand on his arm. The press of her palm against his skin strengthened his awareness of her and he kept his expression serious. The heat of her touch took the breath from his lungs, and he couldn't maintain his ruse. He chuckled. "Human females are named daughters of Eve, and we know the tale of the temptation of her lover. Beyond that..."

She lowered her gaze. "Where, then, shall we walk?"

"I have long wished to visit the human world with a knowledgeable guide. And since we have promised to meet Lara there, could we go now?"

"Can you go to the mortal world?"

Korin nearly recounted his adventure of the previous day, but bit back the tale. He didn't wish to frighten her by admitting how long he had watched her. "Fairies have the ability to use weakened areas in the veil to move between worlds. Much like your portals, except none but a fairy may pass. There are often fairies in the human world. Often we are seen as butterflies...or bees."

"Can you go through a portal?"

"I've never tried. As I am, I am too large for my normal transport. Will you take me through your portal?

Nanceen took his hand. "Of course. We'll have plenty of time for you to explore before we have to meet everyone at the N B Tween."

CHAPTER SEVEN

"I isn't gonna tell 'im."

"Nor me. I values me skin. 'Im's sure ta take a switch to us." Two, tiny, dirty brown men peered around the corner of Nanceen's cabin and watched the couple walk away. One turned to the other and shook his head. "Ne're did go inside. How we 'sposed to do what 'im's say?

The second fairy shrugged. "Dunno. I isn't gonna tell."

"Tell what, fool?" The harsh voice of the fairy king made the two hunch together like frightened rabbits. Shaking, they turned as one to face the Fir Dhaerrig.

The king stood with his bandy legs spread wide, thick arms crossed over his protruding belly. A frown lowered his eyebrows until they met over the bridge of his nose. "Well?"

The taller of the two brown creatures nudged his companion in the ribs with the point of his elbow. A second poke provoked a lifted fist, but the king cleared his throat and the action froze. The taller fell to his knees.

"Pardon, 'ighness. Them's din't go inside. Only the gentry. Now, they's gone."

The Fir Dhaerrig tapped one foot. Irritation hovered around

him like waves of heat in a summer sun. Waiting for a pronouncement of punishment, the fairies quivered in dire anticipation.

"Where did they go?" The king spoke slowly, an unspoken threat underlying his words.

"Ta gentry portal."

"To the human world?"

"Ya. Ta there. 'Ighness? Wha' cha gonna do wi' we?"

"Get out of my sight and I won't do anything. Send the boggart to me, and I will forgive your lack of action."

"As 'is 'ighness wishes." One of the tiny brown men crawled forward to fawn at the king's knees and kiss the hem of his filthy tunic.

"Off with you. Do not fail me again." The king disappeared with the slight popping sound of disturbed air.

"I's don' wanna find the boggart. 'Tis scared I is."

"We's gonna do it. We's has to. Don' wan' no punishment. Don' cross 'im. Sooner done, sooner back ta drinkin'."

fter the short walk to the portal, Korin felt Nanceen's gaze on him when he paused before the faint shimmer. Despite the frequency with which the gentry and humans moved from world to world, he wasn't sure how this magic would affect him.

He didn't want to show weakness before Nanceen, so he gave her a wide smile and tugged her quickly into the shimmer.

Gentry magic against his skin was akin to the touch of a lover's hand. Stimulated, his skin tingled, and he longed to rub his arms to capture the feeling. Was this what it was like for Nanceen and the gentry? If so, it was no wonder they passed often between worlds.

A glance at Nanceen's calm and curious expression let him know the transfer did not affect her in a similar manner. Then the sensuous tingles were gone, replaced by shards of pain. He stumbled.

Although Korin had stepped confidently into the portal, his

steps faltered when he entered the human world. His entire body trembled. The shivers transferred themselves to Nanceen through their clasped hands. She'd never been with anyone who had such a violent reaction to a portal. Nanceen turned to face Korin. But then, she'd never known a fairy before. Trying to mask her confusion, she took his other hand. The trembling was electrifying and the fine, short hairs on her arms lifted.

Korin's eyes widened and he jerked his hands from her grasp. He stumbled back a few steps before sinking to his knees. His shoulders sagged and he took a shallow, ragged breath.

Concern flooded Nanceen and she knelt beside him. Hesitant to touch him again, her hand hovered inches from him for a moment before she rested her palm against his forearm. "Are you... what happened, Korin?"

He lifted his head as though his neck barely supported the weight. A weary half-smile only partially eased her concern. He took another breath, deeper this time, and his lips settled into a somber line. "Mayhaps, my race is not meant to pass through a gentry portal."

"What happened? Tell me."

"Ah." His voice cracked. "Ah, an interesting experience, endearment." A flush crept over his pale face and his gaze slid past her.

Nanceen barely noticed his words as she focused on twisting the hem of her shirt in her hands. "Are you okay?"

Korin touched her wrist and her nervous hands stilled. "I'm fine. But it is not an experience I wish to often repeat. There is a strange force within the portal, Nanceen. Mayhaps it is there to prevent the loss of magic from the Otherworld. And, alas, I am a magical creature."

The words and his wistful expression startled her until she looked more closely at him and noticed the mischievous twinkle in his eyes. His gaze turned liquid silver and his hand tightened imperceptibly on her wrist.

How could he tease her so shortly after--after experiencing such pain? If the tingle of electricity still at her fingertips were any indication, the passage must have been painful for him. In fact, tight lines of pain still crinkled at the corners of his eyes. She wanted to smooth those lines, and lessen the deep furrow in his forehead. She didn't know what to do.

Korin rested the tips of his fingers against her arm. The sharp electricity was gone, yet a stinging heat remained. Nanceen let a soft sigh pass her lips at the amazing feeling and covered Korin's hand with her own. They remained kneeling on the short grass lawn, gazes locked. Nanceen searched for answers in the silver depths. A hint of--something--nearly broke the surface of his gaze, but was deeply hidden away.

"We..." She leaned toward Korin. Adjusting the angle of his body, Korin matched her lean, tilted his head to one side, and softly kissed her lips.

"Yes, we should go. You must show me this human world." Excitement lit his eyes. "I'm looking forward to the new experiences."

Freed from the sensual intensity, Nanceen gave a relieved chuckle and rose to her feet. Holding out her hand to Korin, she nodded. "We won't go far right now, just across the street to one of my favorite places."

"Good. I have only been to this world a few times, and only as a fairy. It will be wonderful to travel freely." He took her hand, but there was no pull upon it when he stood.

"Have you recovered from..." Nanceen swung her hand in the general direction of the portal.

Korin grinned and danced a spritely jig before her. He grabbed her hands and twirled her in a high stepped dance. Laughter bubbled from her lips, stole her breath, and forced her to pull Korin to a halt.

Taking deep draughts of air, Nanceen grimaced at Korin. When she released his hands, he continued to dance. Nanceen planted one fist against her hip and lifted her other hand. "Okay, you've recovered. But you're wearing me out. Stop, please."

Immediately he halted, hung his head, and peered at her through the thick fringe of his light lashes. "I'm sorry. My people take the greatest of joys in the dance. We dance for happiness, we dance in misery, and dance only for dancing sake."

"Don't be sorry. The Faerie often dance as well." Nanceen let her hand drop to her side.

"Ah, the celebrations of the gentry. I've only watched from afar and longed to join your stately folk. So similar to the dances of my kind, yet so different. I don't know how to explain it."

"Perhaps, someday, we could dance together."

Korin closed his eyes, smiled softly, and sighed. "A wish I've held since the time I first saw you. 'Twas at such a gathering. You and your sister danced together, filling the moment with indescribable beauty."

His eyes opened, his grin faded, and he swallowed heavily. After turning his face away, Korin took a shuddering breath. "What is this favorite place?"

Nanceen's skin burned, both from the color she knew filled her face and from deep within her. One glance from the strange man and her bones melted. She had no doubt her blood boiled as well. Many men had tried to garner her attention. Why now did a creature she'd once thought mythical hold her in thrall? Stranger still, she didn't care.

"The park across the street."

"What?"

"There's a slight hill in the park across the street. I like to sit there, watch the people, the birds. It's almost a bit of Faerie in this human world."

"Then, shall we watch the world go by as we learn of one another?"

"I'd really like that." She took Korin's hand and led him from her brother's backyard, across the cracked gray of the paved street, onto the lush grass of the small park. At the top of a slight rise, she stepped away from the cobbled path before sinking to the ground with a sigh.

Korin's warmth caressed her as he sat cross-legged beside her. She watched from the corner of her eyes as he stared in wonder at the world around him. He'd said he had been in this world before, yet his face showed a rare mixture of awe and delight. One side of her mouth pulled into a lopsided grin. Of course, it would look different if this were the first time he'd seen this world from a human-sized perspective.

A sudden case of prickles crawled across her shoulders, stealing the joy of the moment. Nanceen glanced around the wide open expanse of the park. Someone was watching them.

T itus stepped from the shadows of a stone and wood picnic shelter, but kept himself hidden behind the branches of a thick pine tree. Parting the prickly needles, he glanced at the backs of the pair seated closed together on the hillside.

Taking an immediate dislike to the man, he tried to ignore the figure and concentrated on the woman. He stared until she glanced around and rubbed the back of her neck. Then, he smiled and moved from behind the tree.

Although she was a lovely woman, he didn't want her, felt no physical reaction within him to signal desire. But he did consider her to be a possible key to his plans. Yet unformulated plans. He knew... somehow...

Nodding to himself, he turned away. Jaye Zeroun and his entire clan were doomed.

S itting in silence, Nanceen watched Korin. Sunlight glinted off his silvery, golden hair, sparkling, dazzling her. She easily sensed the magic within him and was amazed the humans who passed by on the jogging trail noticed nothing. But those unfortunates would not have the benefit of Faerie blood or a magical upbringing.

Still... she sighed. Maybe it was the way he made her feel that created the magic. A shake of her head did nothing to chase away the fanciful notion. So in order to put Korin and her feelings into a more logical perspective, she needed to know him better. Hopefully, he would give her straight answers to her questions. The tales often told of how fairies spoke in riddles, how they hid the true meaning of their words behind poetry and song.

"Tell me about your family."

Korin slowly turned his face toward her. "I beg pardon?" He blinked and gave her an impish grin. "I'm sorry. I'm so amazed by this world. It's so different than either of our homes. And yet... yet, I feel a sense of belonging here. Mayhaps it is a lingering memory of the time when all races shared this world." His grin faded. "When the humans still believed."

Needing to comfort his sudden sadness, Nanceen rested her hand on Korin's knee.

He caught her fingers and entwined his own through them. "You asked about my family?"

Nanceen nodded. It was all she could do under the intensity of his gaze.

Resting one palm over his chest, Korin bent forward in a graceful, seated bow. "I am Korin, of the clan Goodfellow. My family rises from ages past, from the loins of Robin Goodfellow."

He paused at the confusion narrowing Nanceen's eyes. Long and convoluted, the history of his race, and the connection with the gentry, was difficult to explain. His family traced back to long before fairies and gentry turned to separate worlds. For now, he would only tell her what he knew of Robin. A rush of sadness filled his chest, and he struggled to keep the emotion hidden. No need for her to know now he was the last of his family.

"Long after the sire of my sires passed into the netherworlds, a great bard of the humans learned part of his tale. To this day, humans know of Robin Goodfellow."

"The name is familiar, but I don't know where I've heard it."

Ah, he is known by the name given him by his master, the king of the fairies. This was the name the bard used." Korin lowered his eyes and peered at Nanceen through his lashes. Would she believe him?

Leaning toward him, Nanceen gave him a look of pure exasperation. "Okay, so who was this ancestor of yours?"

"The Puck."

"You're joking." Nanceen angled back in surprise.

"I do not jest when I speak of my family."

"I didn't mean to doubt you, Korin. If he was Puck, then the bard must be--"

"Shakespeare."

"You're kidding."

"I do not--"

Her shoulders sagged and she held up one hand to stop his denial. "It was just a phrase of amazement, Korin. I'm not doubting you at all. I know Shakespeare's tale well. It's my brother's favorite play." She cast him a shy smile. "I don't know why it should surprise me, anyway."

"Then, you no longer doubt me?" Hope filled Korin's chest. He took a deep breath and waited for her answer.

"No. I haven't doubted who, or what, you are since last night." The look of speculation and curiosity she gave him stole the breath he still held and it whooshed, whistling past his lips. Nanceen giggled.

"Shall I tell you more?"

"Were the tricks he played on the lovers true?"

Korin's hand lifted again to his heart. "You wound me, endearment."

Nanceen arched her eyebrows. "So they were. The plant is real as well?"

"Why would you wish to know?" Frowning, Korin squinted at her.

"For my sister." She shrugged. "Kaelea is always in search of the sources and beginnings of our ancient legends, and the meanings of the stories. She'll love to meet..." A stricken realization jumped to her eyes. "Is that okay? I mean, do we need to keep your identity hidden?"

Korin rushed to reassure her. "Only in this world, and only from unbelievers. Be there humans who believe--why shouldn't they know me?"

"Umm, I'm not sure that would be a good idea right now. There are far too many unscrupulous--"

A shadow fell across them, and Nanceen bit back the rest of her words. She glanced up just as Titus knelt beside them, carefully placing himself to show off an expanse of tanned leg while he tightened the laces of his jogging shoes. Korin stiffened. The tension in his muscles made the air between them quiver. Nanceen touched his arm, shook her head slightly, then gave Titus half a smile.

Ignoring Korin, Titus returned a full smile to her. "And so, we meet again, Nanceen."

"Titus."

Titus rose to his full height, stretched his arms over his head, and leaned from one side to the other. The movements pulled his cut-off shirt higher and highlighted the definition of his abdominal muscles. "A fine day to be outside, isn't it?"

Keeping her fingers lightly against Korin's arm, Nanceen shaded her eyes with her other hand and looked up at Titus. She had to bite her lip to keep from giggling. Titus had preening down to a fine art. Not that he didn't have the looks to work with--but she preferred Korin's innocent, unschooled sensuality.

One of Titus' eyebrows lifted as if he knew her thoughts. A shiver ran down her spine, and immediately Korin's muscles bunched under her hand. She glanced sideways at him and nearly gasped at the intensity of the anger infusing his expression.

Titus turned his gaze briefly to Korin, gave a slight nod, and lifted one long, fingered hand in a wave. "Gotta run. I'm sure we'll see each other again, Nanceen." With that, he turned and rejoined the joggers on the path.

The vibrating tension under her hand lessened, but Korin's eyes remained focused on Titus' back. Nanceen had the strange feeling that her fingers were the only thing that kept Korin from flying at Titus and--and what? True, Titus was confident and self-important, but she'd shown no interest in him.

"He's not important, Korin." Slowly, he turned his gaze to her. His face was unreadable, but still she tried to decipher the expression in the silver smoke of his eyes. Reluctant to glance away, but unable to bear the intensity, she looked down at her watch.

"Oh my, it's getting late. We need to leave if we're going to meet the others."

"Must we?"

It was tempting to leave Lara and the others to their own devices, but weeks ago she had promised to join them this weekend. Slowly, she nodded.

The smile on Korin's lips was tight and forced, but she chose to ignore his strange mood. "Then we shall go." He rose fluidly to his feet and lifted her along with him. There was a moment's hesitation as he stared in the direction Titus had gone before he turned back with a true smile gracing his lips. "Come, I'm ready for a new adventure."

CHAPTER EIGHT

After a bland, greasy meal Nanceen called fast food, Korin walked hand in hand with her toward the center of town. He supposed by human standards it would be considered a lengthy walk, but the moments with Nanceen made the time pass quickly. The sky darkened and the first dim stars twinkled despite the competition of the city lights.

Staring at the tall, heavy buildings, Korin tried to keep his amazement under control. In his small size, he had seen such buildings from a distance and barely imagined the grandeur of the gray and brown structures. Now, standing at the base of such a building, he couldn't fathom the true size, or understand how humans could build such grand edifices. He laughed as lights flashed, highlighting the highest rooflines and rivaling the stars in color and design.

Korin returned his gaze to the woman next to him and the laughter faded from his lips. Unable to decipher the strange emotion hovering in her dark eyes, he held her gaze a moment longer, then turned his face again to the sky. "I find it hard to know the words to describe this sight."

Nanceen's gaze followed his to the top of the building, and a grin pulled at her lips as she spoke. "It is pretty amazing."

Unable to look away from the movement of her stretched neck as she spoke, Korin angled to face her. Nanceen shrugged one shoulder. "I've spent so much time in this world. I guess I take these buildings for granted."

A dry lump grew heavy in his throat. Korin stared at Nanceen until she lowered her face and turned toward him. Heat filled his face and he looked away. Compelled by the feel of her eyes on him, he looked fully at her.

A tiny furrow formed in Nanceen's brow, bringing her eyebrows close together. "What is it?"

The concern in her voice and the light touch of her hand on his arm lightened his heart, and brought a smile back to his lips. How could he not help but smile at her? How could he not do anything to keep a smile upon her lips and a twinkle in her eyes? His breath caught for a moment. More than the happy glint, he wished for another emotion to fill her expression. If only he could find desire within those depths, it would be a mirror to her soul and to his own feelings.

Time. It would take time. And time was not in his favor. His hand slipped to his side and he fingered the pouch containing the agreement he'd made with the Fir Dhaerrig. Wrapping his hand around the small bag, he pressed it against his leg to reassure himself he had not made a foolish contract. There would be ways to fulfill the terms. If only he would be able to find those ways.

The pressure of Nanceen's fingers drew his thoughts back to the city streets. With a quick glance at the waxing moon, he smiled at Nanceen. "Amazement at this world and wonder at the fact you are beside me. They overwhelm me."

A nervous giggle erupted from Nanceen's lips. "You are a charmer, aren't you? Come on, we'd better hurry so Lara doesn't wonder where we are."

A few blocks later, Nanceen directed them around a corner and stopped before a plain, black door. A small sign gave the only indication this doorway was any different from others lining the buildings along the street. A deep throbbing rose from the pavement beneath his feet, a primal beat that called his heart to dance. Two young men rushed past them and opened the door. Loud music flowed over them and drew Korin eagerly toward the dark doorway. Nanceen chuckled and followed.

After the evening light of the streets, the interior of the building was an amazing contrast. The shine from bright, colored lights bounced rhythmically off dark, satiny walls. A haze of smoke hovered high near the ceiling before disappearing through slatted metal vents. A mass of humans crowded a small raised platform, gyrating to music pouring from tall, boxy speakers. Dancers had even climbed to the tops of the speakers and moved blindly to the beats.

A wistful smile touched Korin's lips. Dancing he understood. This music was louder, harder, more raucous than most fairy music. Only the dwarves and other earthy creatures had music that seemed to throb from the depths of the earth. Secretly, he'd always loved the dark, overpowering, pervasive beat. Fully intending to join the dancers, he took a step forward. Nanceen held firmly to his hand and tugged him instead to the tables crowded to one side of the large room.

Reluctant, he turned from the music. But his steps lightened when he spied the fair, blonde curls covering Lara's head. She sat between two men. Korin's eyes narrowed, neither man was Iain.

Catching sight of their progress through the crowd, Lara waved and gestured broadly at them. Nanceen plopped into a chair next to the dark-haired man. It left a space for Korin between her and the other man.

Nanceen leaned close to his ear, but still had to shout over the music. "This is Lara's brother, Jaysson." She patted the dark-haired man on the arm, then nodded in the other man's direction. "And that's their cousin, Bryce."

Lara's brother held out his hand. Korin grasped it and was rewarded with a firm handshake and a wide smile. The man across the table gave him a jaunty salute before scanning the crowd over Korin's shoulder.

"Don't mind him." Jaysson leaned over the table. "He's always looking for someone, and never finds 'em. What can I get you guys from the bar?"

Korin turned a hopeful glance to Nanceen and she chuckled before shaking her head. "No milk tonight, Korin." She squinted one eye in thought. "How about a couple of those dark brews? Do they still get them from the brew pub down in the Market, Jayse?"

Bryce leaned sideways. "Sure do. The manager here and the pub's owner are lovers." The music stopped suddenly and Bryce's last word was loud in the echoing silence. A bright pink flushed his fair skin and he rolled his eyes. "Bring me one, too, will ya, Jayse?"

Nodding, Jayse pushed off from the table and moved through the crowd to the bar.

When Nanceen turned back to Korin, his face filled with dismay. "Will there be more music?"

"After they get set up for the strippers." Bryce grinned and leaned both elbows on the small table. It rocked toward him on uneven legs.

"Strippers?"

Bryce shook his finger at Nanceen. "Didn't you tell him this was amateur strip night, Nance?"

"But, what are strippers?" The whispered words tickled her ear, but she resisted the urge to brush away the soft breath. Deep inside, deep where she didn't want to examine, her body responded to Korin's closeness and the tenor of his words.

So she grinned at him. "Wait, you'll see." The thought of watching him watching college students vie for prize money by taking off their clothes appealed to her. This spicier side of human life had embarrassed her the first time Lara dragged her along to the bar. Now, she simply enjoyed watching the imaginative moves and occasional pitiful attempts at musical seduction.

Jayse returned with tall, dark brown bottles and set them around the table. Before he sat, he waved at a shadowed figure.

"Nightshade, come join us."

The muscles in Korin's forearm jerked. Nanceen followed his gaze to the slender man moving smoothly through the crowd. A shudder ran through Korin, and his leg trembled against hers. But when he turned back to her, he smiled.

"It's nothing. Just a name from my family's past." Nightshade sat in the chair Bryce snagged with his foot and snatched the bottle from his hand. After taking a long sip, he wiped the lip with his hand and passed the bottle back. Bryce glared into the half empty bottle, but grinned at Nightshade. "You owe me."

"Of course."

"Are you dancing tonight?"

Nightshade rested the tips of his fingers against his chest. "Moi? No. One of my girls is giving an exhibition before the amateurs begin. Show the pretenders how it should be done." He eyed Korin with lifted eyebrows, and sank back against his chair. "Carouselle is trying out one of my costume designs tonight."

"Nightshade manages professional exotic dancers over at The Panther's Back," Bryce explained, "and designs most of their costumes."

Nightshade dipped his head. "With help from a good friend, of course."

Nanceen took a sip of her beer and glanced at Korin. Why had the name Nightshade caused him such a start? And why did he try to cover his reaction with an inane explanation?

Before she could form a question, the lights over the dance floor began to pulse. First together, then in patterns of ever-increasing complexity, the flashes signaled the crowd to find their seats. As conversation fell to a dull murmur, the first strains of soft music rose from the gigantic speakers. A spotlight arched across the floor and came to rest at the side of the raised platform. Eyes hidden behind sunglasses, a tee shirt clad man waved broadly to the cheers of the crowd.

He bent toward a microphone. "I'm your deejay Gobe Quix. Tonight is amateur night."

Cheers rose again and the stomping of many feet vibrated the floor. The deejay made shushing motions with his hands and grinned at the silence. "You all know the routine. Wanna dance? Line up and give me your music."

The sound of chairs scraping the concrete floor made him take off his glasses and peer at the crowd. Feigned amazement lifted his eyebrows. "Woo hoo. It's gonna be a great night to show what you've got. And as an added incentive, our hosts at N B Tween have upped tonight's prize money. Top dancer takes home..." He paused dramatically and scanned the crowd. "... Five hundred dollars." A wild cheer and competing hoots made Nanceen cover her ears.

Then she leaned back and watched Korin. Fascination etched across his angular features. Even in the dimmer light over their table, his eyes shone silver. Well, he wanted an adventure. And from his reaction, he'd never seen anything like this in his world.

"... if they can find a pocket to carry it in." The deejay waited until the laughter died down before he sat, poked at a couple of levers on his console, and dimmed the dance floor lights. "Ladies and gentlemen, N B Tween is proud to present a special treat for you. While the amateurs get ready to strut their stuff, we have a real pro. Since her dancing career started here at an amateur night, she's graciously consented to dance for us. Give it up for... Carouselle."

The spotlight swirled around the dance floor as the volume of music rose. The brassy sounds of New Orleans zydeco filled the bar. Suddenly, the light flashed to blue and settled on a still figure sitting on one of the speaker platforms.

A mask of short blue feathers and sparkling rhinestones covered the top half of her face and molded to her head. Only a few spiraled strands of hair peeked from under the skullcap. Slowly, she drew a long strand of beads from around her neck, twirled it like a lasso and tossed it into the crowd.

Nanceen glanced at Nightshade. His lips were pressed tightly together, but satisfaction shone in his eyes. He leaned toward the center of the table while he kept his eyes on Carouselle. "We've wanted to do a Mardi Gras number for a long time, but could never come up with the right costume or music." He pointed at the stage. "This is it."

While watching the gyrating moves of the dancer, Nanceen

also watched the reactions of the men at her table. Jayse's expression held a tiny grin and he lifted his bottle in salute when he caught her watching him. Korin swayed with the music. Bryce stared open-mouthed as Carouselle shed parts of her costume and continued to toss beads into the crowd. His eyes were soft, dreamy. Nanceen frowned; it was a strange reaction from the young man.

When Carouselle left the stage, Bryce tugged on Nightshade's long, billowy sleeve. "Who is she?"

Nightshade shook his head. "Professional ethics, my dear boy. I can't tell you. The real names of my dancers are theirs alone to tell. And, I caution them strongly against it. There've been too many cases of men--or women--stalking them."

"You can tell me. You know me."

Shaking his head again, Nightshade touched the back of Bryce's hand. "I can't."

"Introduce us."

"I doubt we could catch her before she leaves the bar. She's off on vacation. Even I don't know her plans." He paused and gave Bryce a sympathetic look before he rose. "I'm sorry."

Silent, Bryce slumped in his chair, tipped his beer, took a long swallow, and glared at Nightshade's retreating back. As if realizing the whole table was watching him, he grinned, shrugged, and took another drink. Bottle empty, he rose and made his way to the bar.

Amateur dancers took the spotlight in rapid succession. Some were good and had obviously practiced, while an excess of alcohol was the only thing that brought others to the stage. The deejay announced each one, played the music, and had some ribald comment at the end of each dance.

A muscular man, with tight abdominal muscles and a smooth chest, had stripped down to a brief thong. Korin nudged her shoulder with his. "What is the thing he wears?"

Nanceen choked on a sip of beer. Waving away Korin's apology, she chuckled. "That's a thong. One of many forms of underwear."

"Underwear? Such a strange thing."

"Don't you..."

Korin shook his head and grinned wickedly. "It seems an unnecessary and cumbersome scrap of cloth. What purpose does it serve?"

"The clothiers didn't give you any underwear?"

"No. Mayhaps because I had none to start with?"

Heat blazed across Nanceen's cheeks as she imagined what wasn't beneath Korin's stylish denim. Korin lifted her hand to his lips and pressed a brief kiss to the back of her fingers.

"I shall return shortly. Is that acceptable?"

"Of... of course. I'll be right here." When Korin stood, she glanced at Lara and received a slow, dramatic wink.

Korin moved swiftly through the crowded tables and stood next to the deejay until the man looked at him. Korin gave him a wide smile and said, "I wish to dance."

Frowning, the man looked him up and down. Korin assumed it was his rather plain clothing that confused the man. But, after watching the many dancers, Korin realized it wasn't what was worn; it was how the clothing was removed. So, he watched a young woman gyrate as the deejay watched him. And waited.

"Well, man. You just barely made it. There's just time for one more contestant before we announce tonight's winner. What name do you wanna use when you dance?"

"Korin."

"Uh, okay, Korin. Got your music?"

"I was hoping you would choose for me." Korin let his gaze leave the dancer and he stared at the deejay.

The man smirked and chuckled. Korin was reminded of his king, the Fir Dhaerrig. "What kinda music did ya have in mind?" He picked up a long necked bottle, took a swallow, and watched Korin closely when he lowered his drink.

"Something--magical."

"Yeah, right." The deejay smirked again, then lowered his eyebrows in thought. A delighted chuckle passed his lips as he pointed toward the two shallow steps leading to the dance floor.

"You wait over there until I announce you. Then the stage will be yours."

Korin moved toward the indicated spot. The deejay shuffled through a box of thin, plastic cases and muttered under his breath. "Magical, huh? I'll give him magic. Where the hell is Lost Highway?"

Korin bit back a grin and angled his body so he could speak to the deejay without facing him. "Fourth from the back." He laughed out loud at the man's startled exclamation. Applauding politely, he stepped closer to the stage and nodded at the young woman who gathered her clothing before she brushed past him.

The dance floor darkened suddenly; only the lights over the bar at the far end of the room cast any illumination. As he'd watched the dancers before him do, Korin moved to the center of the floor and waited. Although many had struck strange and interesting poses, he simply stood still. Excitement and expectation for the dance caused tremors of delight to course through him. It had been a long time since he'd truly felt the joy of anticipation.

"And now... last, but hopefully not least..." Gobe Quix's voice echoed through the speakers over Korin's head and reverberated throughout the bar. A single bright light swirled back and forth above Korin. He wondered absently for a moment what kind of music the man chose for him. Shrugging his shoulders, he decided it didn't matter. However, the absence of his wings was another concern. He'd never danced without them.

"Watch now, friends, as Korin puts a spell on you."

The spotlight dimmed briefly before it flashed to life with a rainbow of colors. A hard, driving beat pulsed across the stage and into Korin's heart. As the lights came to rest on him, bathing him in solid brightness and heat, he tipped his head back slightly, spread his arms, and smiled.

Even through the deep intensity of the music, he heard Nanceen gasp. This dance would be his gift to her, his surprise to bring the lightness of a smile to her face.

I put a spell on you. The dark, sensuous voice sang words of longing. *Because you're mine*. And drew Korin into a wild, sinuous dance. *'Cause I'm yours, yours, yours anyhow*.

Easily adapting moves he'd witnessed earlier, Korin undulated across the stage. Better to feel the music, he closed his eyes. Slowly, within the rapid beat of the music, he shed his shirt.

Assuming Korin left her side to find the men's room, Nanceen was stunned to silence when the deejay shouted his name. She frowned at the dirty tabletop. It had to be someone else; she misunderstood the name.

Lara poked her shoulder and slid her chair closer to speak into Nanceen's ear as the music pulsed to life. "Did you know he was going to do this?"

Nanceen shook her head.

"Ooh, he's good."

Embarrassed for him, Nanceen refused to look at the stage. She clenched her hands tightly around her bottle and stared until her knuckles turned white. The normal catcalls present on amateur strip night were silent, and her shame grew. If they made a fool of him, how would she be able to explain it to him? What would that do to his spirit?

Lara poked her again. "Really, Nance. Look at him. He's got the crowd mesmerized."

Reluctance tugged at her and insisted she keep her eyes lowered. Finally, taking a deep, deep breath, she looked at the dance floor. Korin had his back to them; the movements of his arms rippled the muscles beneath the smooth skin of his shoulders. Nanceen's gaze was drawn to twin dark shadows that marred his back. Just inside his shoulder blades, the marks were about the length of her hand. She glanced down to her palm, then back to Korin. Realization struck her as he whirled to face the bar. His eyes opened slowly and the feverish intensity of his gaze captured hers.

Heat blazed through her. Each hard, insistent, musical beat corresponded to a smooth movement of his hands running over his chest and down his flat abdomen. With a gasp, she realized the button of his jeans was undone and the zipper slipped down halfway.

"Oh, my God."

Lara touched her shoulder. "What's wrong, Nance?"

She couldn't turn from Korin, so spoke into the air over the center of the table. "He told me he doesn't have any underwear." Ripping her gaze away, she turned a helpless expression to Lara. "No underwear. Nothing under his jeans. He can't do this Lara. He'll be arrested."

Lara scooted her chair toward her brother and whispered urgently to Jayse. His eyes popped open wide and he laughed heartily. Lara slapped him on the shoulder. He nodded before rising to his feet.

The spinning spotlights centered on Korin. He stood nearly motionless, only the movements of his hands flowed with the erotic music. What was he waiting for? The jolt when their eyes met again brought a gasp to Nanceen's lips and a wide smile to Korin's.

His hands slipped under his denim waistband. The soft material inched down his hips to expose more golden skin. Nanceen whispered, "No." Korin's seductive smile only grew lazier. He turned his back on the crowd, but glanced over his shoulder as the jeans slid soundlessly to the stage.

The final beats of music pounded, but Nanceen couldn't feel it over the rapid beating of her heart. The last notes faded away and Korin turned to face the audience. A tight, black pouch covered the parts best left hidden in public. One side of his mouth lifted and he winked with a slow seduction Nanceen knew to be only for her.

Complete silence met the end of his dance. Not even the deejay uttered a ribald comment. After a few seconds, wild cheers filled the bar. Beer bottles bounced as fists pounded against the rickety bar tables. Korin bent in a slight bow and stepped from the now static spotlight.

CHAPTER NINE

"I did something wrong?" Korin ran his fingers over the edges of a stack of twenty-dollar bills. Confusion marred his features and made a tiny knot of guilt rise in Nanceen's chest.

"Yes. No. Oh, I don't know. I thought you should keep a low profile while in this world. But your dance didn't do any harm."

"I enjoyed it. Do you think the people here enjoyed it?"

Nanceen chuckled. "You won first prize, didn't you? Really Korin, it was almost as if you really did put a spell on the audience. On me. Like you mesmerized us. There was no sound, no conversation while you danced. It was amazing." *Like you.*

Before Korin could comment, a pair of giggling college-aged women stopped by their table to offer continued congratulations. Nanceen squinted at them, wanting them to leave quickly. Why was her reaction to the reactions of other women to Korin's dance so strong? Was she jealous? She honestly didn't know.

The musical tones of a cell phone drew their attention to Lara's voluminous bag. Grimacing, Lara pawed through the contents until she found the small, annoying phone. She held one hand over her free ear and leaned over to try and block the noise from the bar. Her eyes opened wide, she frowned, then grinned and held the phone out to Korin.

"My daughter wants to say goodnight to her bu-fly man.' She won't go to bed until she does. Will you talk to her?"

Korin's dazzling smile made the knot in Nanceen's chest grow tighter. Perhaps she was jealous.

He held the phone to his ear and after saying hello, listened intently. "Yes, Belle. You shall see me again soon. Yes, you must do as your grandmother says and go to bed. Not tonight, dear one, but soon. I shall tell you a story that will bring the sweetest dreams."

In a moment of unusual silence in the bar, the clear, tinkling sound of Belle's laughter could be heard. Korin smiled again and handed the phone back to Lara.

Lara gave him an apologetic grin. "Sorry. Belle's even more headstrong than I was at her age. Hopefully, she won't give Mom any more trouble--tonight."

The adults around the table chuckled, and Bryce reached over the table to nudge Lara's arm. "I, for one, am glad you were so--precocious. I'd hate to have missed this night." After renewed laughter, each sat back with their own thoughts.

Korin tapped the pile of money before he folded the bills in half. It made a satisfying bundle. Although he didn't really comprehend the human's monetary system, he knew he held a sizable amount in his hand. He contemplated what to do with it as he felt at his side his small leather bag. Intending to slip his winnings inside, he opened the bag beneath the tabletop.

But as he loosened the drawstring, a wave of heat pulsed from the small opening. The crackling sound of dry, burning wood, too high for the humans around him to hear, followed the heat. Concerned, Korin drew the tiny bit of parchment from the bag.

It was hot, but cooled instantly at his touch. Carefully, Korin laid the agreement on his leg and tucked the money into the bag before staring at the folded sheet. It took a strong dose of self-will to touch the cooled parchment and slowly unfold it. Even in the dim bar lighting, he easily read the words he had committed to memory.

Korin blinked in amazement. The agreement had changed. A thin, bright purple line crossed through the words of one of the Fir Dhaerrig's conditions. Holding his breath, Korin traced the words with his fingertip. *To mesmerize without magik.* He glanced at the empty space designated for scoring the completion of the conditions. A second mark had formed below his name. The space for the king remained blank.

Korin laughed out loud and shrugged when his new friends gave him questioning looks. Nanceen leaned close. Her breast pressed against his arm. "What is it, Korin?"

The heat of the altered agreement was a mere spark compared to her body against his, and nothing compared to the burning that pressed against the tight underwear he'd magicked for his dance. Wondering why human males would subject themselves to such binding, he shifted uncomfortably. The silky material soothed along the growing firmness at his groin. He gasped, perhaps this was why...

"Korin?"

"Oh, I beg pardon, Nanceen." Korin cleared his throat, squirmed again and bit the inside of his cheek against the continued sensations. "I was merely wondering what to do with my prize."

Jayse tipped his chair back on the two hind legs and gave Korin a look so full of knowing that Korin's face heated under the scrutiny. "Are you coming to the Ren Faire with Nanceen tomorrow?"

"I believe that was the plan."

"You might find something you like there."

"A grand idea. I'm sure I shall." *With Nanceen at my side.*

Nanceen was still pressed against his arm. Had she any idea the effect she had on him? Her flushed face and the brightness of her eyes when she looked at him made him believe she did.

Her hands clutched spasmodically at his arm. "We need to get an early start, don't we, Lara?" She glanced at her niece for confirmation.

The golden nimbus of Lara's hair bounced as she nodded. "Yup. That's why Iain and I are staying at Mom and Dad's tonight. Granted, the journey back home to Faerie is short, but we'd have to lug the kids both ways."

"A terrible burden, to be sure." Jayse laughed.

Lara returned his laughter. "Hard enough to leave them behind. Hopefully, this way we can be on the road before they even wake up. Then Mom will have to deal with them." She glanced from Nanceen to Korin and back again. "Are you two going back to Faerie?"

Korin stiffened. Unwilling to face the agony of the portal again so soon, he turned a pleading glance to Nanceen. Worry reflected in her eyes as well before she shook her head. "I think you've got the right idea, Lara. I think we'll stay here. I'm just not sure where. Your folks' house sounds pretty crowded."

Jayse held up one hand to stop the flow of Bryce's low, earnest words and turned a grin toward Nanceen. "Uh, I think Bryce and I might do a little bar-hopping tonight. You guys are welcome to stay at my place. I don't have a guest room, but the couch is plenty big enough for two." He cast them another knowing glance. "If you don't mind being cozy."

He jerked and glared at Lara. "Aw, come on, sis... you didn't have to wear such pointy-toed shoes, did you?"

Nanceen stared at the table and her face filled with heat. She tried to imagine what it might be like being 'cozy' with Korin. They'd already spent one night on the opposite ends of a couch.

A gentle finger pressed upward against her chin, lifted her face, and angled it toward Korin. Deep concern, mixed with other emotions she dared not try to name, swirled in his eyes.

"I do not wish to travel the gentry portal tonight," Korin whispered. "It will be much easier if we stay."

The jangle of keys being pushed across the table tore her gaze from Korin and she focused on Jayse.

"Here." Jayse patted the keys. "The way Bryce is mooning over that dancer, I don't even know if I'll make it home tonight. You guys go on, and I'll see you in the morning."

Before Nanceen could open her mouth, he grinned. "Yes, I'm sure. Get going, Korin looks beat. Must be all that dancing."

"I've got to go, too," Lara added. "I told Iain he could drive tomorrow. But, I need to be alert while he does. He thinks he's doing a good job, but I've almost worn a hole in the floor on the passenger side of the van pressing on invisible breaks. I'm gonna take over the driving long before we get to the Faire." She pushed back her chair and rose. "Can I give you a ride to Jayse's place?"

Nodding, Nanceen stood as well. "Thanks, Jayse." She reached for the keys and turned expectantly to Korin.

The parchment still lay over his leg and he struggled with one hand to fold it and stuff it back into the bag with the wad of money. He tucked the bag into his pocket as he stood. With a brief nod of farewell, he followed the women from the bar.

Glad for a chance to relax in a neutral space, Nanceen kicked off her shoes and curled in a corner of an overstuffed couch facing the fireplace. The apartment hadn't changed much in the many years it had been used as a refuge, both from the Faerie and human worlds. Her brother had been wise to keep the apartment, even after he married Allyn, since both of their children had used the large, spacious rooms as their first adult homes.

She watched Korin pad silently around the great room. He stopped and peered from each window, stared at every piece of art gracing the walls and touched many of the ancient musical instruments lined up on a deep shelf.

When he stopped before the fireplace, she grinned. "Korin? Why don't you flip that switch on the wall? The one next to the mantle."

He turned a quizzical look to her and moved toward the side of the wide fireplace. There was no hesitation when he reached for the switch, but he leapt back in surprise when a fire flared to life in the dark firebox. A startled cry of joy accompanied the single clap of his hands.

"Magic in the mortal world?" he asked as he backed from the hearth.

Nanceen chuckled. "Oh, yes. The magic of technology. The one magic humans are able to accept--even when they don't understand it."

"Amazing. Wonderful." Still watching the fire, he sank to the floor in front of her and leaned back against the couch.

The silence surrounding them was natural and comfortable. They sat together, not touching, watching the play of the flames.

Unwilling to delve into her own thoughts, Nanceen wondered what Korin was thinking. What did he think of his brief foray into the human world? She stretched one leg and grinned. It was profitable for him at least. The longer she spent in his presence, the more she longed to know him. And, if she cared to admit it to herself, the more she simply longed for him.

He was of a race far different from hers. And yet, when he was human-sized, they seemed so similar.

"Why did the races of the Otherworld split apart? It must have been a long time ago if fairies became a part of Faerie legend." Nanceen paused and sighed. "It's confusing to say fairy and Faerie."

Korin angled his body forward and wrapped his arms around his knees. "Perhaps we should follow the custom of my people-- and name your folk gentry."

"That seems so... so formal. But, unless something better comes along..." She contemplated what to ask next.

"Yes. It was long, long ago." Korin's somber words confused her for a moment until she recalled her initial question.

"Ah. Do you know anything about what happened? Was there some event that caused the split?"

Korin sat back and nodded. "Our folks had been as one people, Many tribes ruled as one people for many ages. Perhaps even before the humans filled this world. But of that, I do not know. Our king and queen, gentry the Bard named Oberon and

Titania, grew weary of the Otherworld. And weary of the curiosity of the new humans as well. They thought to pass beyond the mists, beyond the boundaries of both worlds."

"They died?"

A deep sigh lifted Korin's shoulders and tension tightened the muscles of his neck. Nanceen gave in to part of the longing and rested her hands on his shoulders. The muscles quivered under her palms so she softly kneaded and stroked them to ease the tension.

Korin released another sigh and pressed back into her hands. Nanceen rubbed more firmly and slid her hands under his shirt collar. His skin was warm, smooth, and just touching him seduced her senses. Concentrating only on relieving his tension, her mind barely registered the fact he continued speaking.

"No, I don't believe they died, not in a sense any of the magical races would understand. But deep within every fairy being there is a place of calm, a peace of spirit whenever our king or queen are thought about." However, that calm was now missing within him, and Korin's spirit soared under Nanceen's ministrations.

Nanceen's hands moved rhythmically on his shoulders. He tightened his lips against a sigh of pleasure, for he knew it would turn instantly to a groan of need. When her thumbs circled and pressed on the knot at the base of his neck, he let his head fall forward limply, and gave into the sound of pleasure.

Nanceen's silent chuckles vibrated through her healing touch. Her hands moved lower, and pulled the front opening of his shirt tight against his neck.

"Nanceen."

"You don't need to say anything more right now. Let me... your muscles are so tense."

"Uh, Nanceen, if you continue this way, you'll choke the life from me."

The marvelous pressure of her fingers ceased. "Have I done anything wrong?"

Korin twisted his neck slightly to loosen the pressure at his throat. "Nothing wrong, never anything wrong. But you're pulling on my shirt." He gave a small chuckle. "It has become uncomfortably tight around my neck."

Nanceen's hands flew from his back and shoved at the bunched material of his shirt. The fabric slid across his shoulders. But, missing the warmth of her fingers, Korin hardly noticed.

"I'm sorry. I didn't know." Nanceen rested her hand on his shoulder and moved her fingers lightly against his neck. "Scooch forward just a bit."

Korin tried to angle his body so he could glance back at her, but she gave his shoulders a gentle shove. "Move up just a little, so I can sit on the floor behind you."

Korin followed her instructions and held his breath as she slid from the couch and settled behind him. Her thighs pressed against the sides of his hips and he shuddered. It was almost too much sensation, too much of what his body longed to experience. Fire and heat pooled in his groin and pressed his sensitized skin against the tight clothing.

Gentle hands pushed on his shoulders, leaning him forward again. Nanceen's fingers slipped under the hem of his shirt and skimmed the skin of his back. "Try and relax."

Relax? How could he, when every muscle cried out for her touch, when the only thought in the whirl of need that once was his brain was turning and burying himself, deep and hard, between those thighs? Korin chewed on the inside of his cheek. How could he relax when each stroke of soft hands over his back was as stimulating as those same hands caressing the firming bulge of his need would be?

"Korin?" Her sweet, warm breath flowed past his ear. The sound of her breathing became shallower, harsher. She inched closer; the heat of her core branded him through the material of his jeans. "This would be even easier, if you'd take off the shirt."

"Yes." His voice was a hoarse croak. As she pushed the shirt toward his shoulders, he shrugged out of the arms and let her pull the soft material over his head. Holding his breath, he waited.

Nanceen's sigh was soft as a midsummer's breeze. Her hands

flowed over his back, lightly caressing, teasing his skin with unspoken promises. Limiting the movement of her hands, she leaned even closer, shrinking the small space between them.

"What are these dark marks on your back?" The tip of one of her fingers traced a pattern near one shoulder blade, then moved to trace a similar design on the other side of his back.

She'd asked him a question. The answer floated to the top of his mind, but blew away as she retraced the pattern on his back.

"Are they scars?"

There was concern, and perhaps fear in the question, and those qualities settled into his mind until he was able to think somewhat clearly. As her finger began another tracing, he knew he must answer quickly, or he never would.

"Those are the places..." He swallowed heavily and tried to bring moisture to his dry mouth. "...where wings appear. My wings...there...in my natural form."

"Oh, I see." Warm lips pressed against one of the marks. Nanceen's slid her hands from the center of his back to his sides and around to the front of his body. Skimming the taut, quivering muscles of his abdomen, she curled her arms under his and brushed her fingertips across the tight buds of his nipples. One hand rested there, her palm covered the pectoral muscle, and her fingertips patted a light pattern on his skin. The other hand drifted down to curl over his leg and inner thigh.

If he moved a fraction of an inch, she would cup him there as well. And if she touched him there, even just the barest of caresses, he would--Korin clenched his teeth and willed his aching body to stillness. "Are you... are you trying to... seduce me?"

CHAPTER TEN

Words of denial hovered heavily on Nanceen's lips, but she could not speak them.

She'd never been able to lie, and even stretching the truth made sweat cover her forehead and the tips of her ears turn red. *Was* she trying to seduce him?

Her fingers twitched against his thigh. He gasped and the movement rubbed his back against her breasts. She tingled. Never had she wanted a man so badly. Even the erotic dreams of him-- for now she knew it was his face that hovered before her eyes and his dream body that covered hers--were pale re-creations of the intensity he aroused in her now.

"Nanceen?" Her name was another gasp upon his lips. Boldly--God, she'd never felt so bold--she ran the pad of her thumb over the tight bud of his nipple. As she pressed her lips to the arched length of his neck and whispered, "Yes," she moved her other hand to rest lightly over the bulge at the juncture of his thighs.

Korin's hips bucked once and pressed the ridged length into her palm. "No," he croaked, "you mustn't. We can't."

Again she whispered against the tight column of his neck, just below his ear. "Yes, we must. You can't deny you want this, too." She stroked him and smiled into his neck at the lifting of his hips.

"I… I cannot." Korin tried to move away, but her hand at his groin kept him close.

Nanceen slid her hand from his chest, stroked across his abdomen and leaned back slightly so she could touch his back. She placed tiny kisses upon the darker skin where he said his wings would be. When she traced the oblong discoloration with her tongue, Korin cried out and wrenched away from her caresses.

He moved only far enough to turn and face her. His chest rose and fell rapidly. A soft sheen of sweat covered his upper lip. Nanceen smiled. He could deny her no more than she could him.

"No, Nanceen. I cannot. Not…now."

One of her hands reached toward him of its own accord. "Why?"

"We…cannot."

Nanceen lowered her brows and glared at him. "Are you trying to tell me our bodies aren't compatible?" She choked back a laugh at the absurdity of the notion. "Korin, shortly before we met, I started having dreams. Some have said that since the fey have no souls--"

A sharp sound of denial and the jerking shakes of Korin's head interrupted her. Although she ached to bridge the distance he'd set between them, she waited patiently until Korin lifted his gaze to her. Her bones melted at the intensity of his silvery stare. A deep breath did nothing to calm her and only stretched the material of her shirt tightly across her sensitive breasts.

Korin's eyes moved lower as if captured by the movements of her breathing. Tight tingling swirled from the tips of her nipples to her lower belly. How could he continue to deny her?

After taking another deep breath, she continued with the thought that had nearly been lost in her haze of desire. "Since they have no souls, they do not dream. My dreams were beautiful, sensual." She paused. "Erotic. And who I thought to be a faceless, anonymous lover, I have come to realize is you. By whatever magic, you came to me at night and left me in the morning-- empty and longing. In those dreams I felt you above me, below me… inside me."

The tips of her ears burned and the heat moved quickly to cover her face and neck. Korin's eyes grew wide; his silvery pupils large and luminous in the firelight. His lips moved silently, and Nanceen couldn't help but imagine their firmness moving against her skin. She moaned and let her eyelids drift closed.

"You dreamed of me?" Stunned by her words and unable to believe he'd actually heard them, Korin repeated them in a whisper. "You dreamed--of me?"

Nanceen's eyes opened to reveal a glistening hope and palpable desire. She nodded. "Many times. How did you--?"

"I did nothing." Korin shook his head. "I don't know the magic needed to invade a sleeper's dreams. It's not one of my abilities." He paused, ducked his head and cast her a shy grin. "But, that's not to say I wouldn't visit your dreams if I could." Amazed at this turn of events, Korin fell silent. This had to mean something more than just a simple dream. The timing, the mere fact she dreamed of him. And of making love with him.

His body reacted to his renewed sensual thoughts. The physical evidence of his desire was hard, painful and aching to find freedom in the glorious confinement of Nanceen's body. A niggling presence in the depths of his consciousness and the memory of the king's prohibition held him back.

"Then, how did I dream of you before I even knew of your existence?" Her confusion did little to lessen the sultry light in her eyes or the pouty, kissable set to her lips.

Korin shrugged. "I have no answer to that, endearment." Curious, he couldn't hold back his question. "I pleased you--in the dreams?"

A deep rose blush infused her already pink face. Holding his gaze, she nodded. "Yes. Very much. Except..."

"Except?" Whatever his dream persona had failed to do, Korin vowed he would fulfill. When he was able. His heart dropped. When he was able had such a ring of never. He was ready to ignore the now urgent denials in his mind and leaned forward.

"Except, you always left me."

The air whooshed from Korin's lungs. "I will not leave you, Nanceen. For now that I know you, you are my heart."

She stared down at her hands. "Pretty words, Korin. I'm sure you spoke such words to me in my dreams as well. The tales often speak of how the fairies speak only what the listener wanted to hear."

Korin rose to his hands and knees. When Nanceen lifted her gaze, they were nose to nose. "I speak the words from my heart, Nanceen. I will not leave you--unless you request it of me. Please...believe me."

"I...I think I do." Tears shimmered in her eyes. "Then why, why won't you make love to me now?"

How could he tell her--when he couldn't explain the prohibition to himself? Then, from a hidden place in his mind came a flash of clarity. He could not join with her, find release within her, but he could offer her pleasure. Lifting one hand, he curled a finger under her chin, tipped and angled her face, and kissed her.

Light exploded behind his closed eyelids and a shock wave of feeling coursed through his body. He panted in the aftermath. If a simple kiss stole the strength from his muscles, how would he survive the loving? Another flash of understanding, a memory perhaps, helped him realize he would need to grow stronger. The transformation from his tiny fairy body to a body that could bring pleasure to a gentry maid had stolen much of his strength. He grinned. The king's prohibition worked in his favor. By waiting until additional conditions were met, he would be stronger and more able to love Nanceen as she deserved.

He crawled next to Nanceen and pulled her close to his side. She snuggled against him and moved to touch his groin. Laying his hand over hers and pressing her palm to his belly, Korin shook his head. "No, Nanceen. I cannot. But, please, endearment, let me love you as I can."

"Why do you use that word--endearment?"

"Ah, my sweet endearment." Korin cupped her cheek with his palm. She leaned into the caress and closed her eyes. "There are no words in any language that mean enough to me. No one word can express how I feel for you. So, when I say 'endearment,' you may hear any--or all--of the endearments your heart desires. Choose the words to show you how I feel. Nanceen, my endearment, do you understand?"

Confusion once again filled her face and she chewed on her lower lip. After an eternity of waiting, she nodded slowly. With a deep groan, Korin covered her lips with his, touched his tongue to the reddened fullness, and slipped into the sweet warmth of her mouth. The silky length of her tongue met his and returned each stroke, each curl and dance.

The flash of colored light burned the backs of Korin's eyes. But he would not stop the kiss. His own discomfort was nothing compared to the joy he offered and received in return from Nanceen. The light faded to a pulsing throb, similar to the lights above his dance at the bar. Nanceen moaned against his lips and her hands rested in trembling stillness against his chest.

Only the feel of Korin beneath her hands kept Nanceen grounded, kept her from spinning away into a universe of sensation and light. Although she ached to touch him, she was afraid that if she tried his kisses would stop. Then, then she would surely die. So, she kept her trembling fingers firmly against Korin's chest. He could do as he wanted, and she would not allow herself to chase him away by doing more than he would accept.

She didn't understand. He obviously wanted her; his body couldn't lie. Perhaps there was some prohibition to the mingling of fairy and gentry. If so, he risked much to be with her. If not... her thoughts faded until only the press of Korin's lips, the gentle movements of his hands, and the sounds of his harsh breathing became her only reality.

He laid her back on the thick carpeting and stretched out beside her. When he wrapped one leg over hers, she whimpered with need. His knee pressed her legs apart and the hard heat of him pulsed against her thigh. The glide of his fingers under her shirt arched her back. For once, she was inordinately glad her half-Faerie body did not require a bra. His palm closed over one breast and she cried out with surprise.

"Do you like my touch, endearment?"

Nanceen tossed her head back and forth and tried to arch her back higher to press closer to the circling motion of his hand.

"Do you? Shall I continue?"

Her eyes slid open and she stared up at Korin's grin. His breathing was as shallow and harsh as her own. His eyes filled with shining silver. He lifted his hand from her skin.

"No. Don't. Please, Korin."

He chuckled, but the sound was strained. His groin rubbed rhythmically against her thigh. "You wish me to continue?"

She swatted at his arm. "You know I do."

"Ah, then." Korin lifted the loose hem of her shirt and stuck his head beneath it. He sucked at the skin to one side of her navel, then traced the tiny depression with his tongue. Slowly, pushing the shirt before him, he worked his way up her body until he could kiss the underside of her breasts.

Laving her skin, he traveled the cleft between her breasts and pulled the shirt over her head. Lifting himself on stiff, shaking arms to gaze at her, he straddled her thigh. She had to touch him, feel his skin, taste the salty sweat on his brow. She lifted her hands, wrapped them over his shoulders, and stroked down his back.

"Nanceen."

"I won't do anything. Just let me touch you."

With a groan, he lowered his body to lie half over her. He bent his head to take the turgid tip of her breast into his mouth. He drew firmly on the peak as he traced one hand down her belly. She held him tightly as he loosened the button of her jeans and slowly lowered the zipper.

His mouth moved to the other breast, leaving the first damp tip to cool in the night air. But she didn't cool. She became hotter, as if she were burning along with the flames in the fireplace. When one of his fingers slipped beneath the elastic of her panties and into the cleft of her womanhood, she jerked and bit back a deep moan.

Korin lifted his head. "How will I know if I please you, if you don't tell me?"

He slid one finger along the cleft and over the hard nub. A sharp cry burst from her lips. "There." A smile filled his voice. "Now, I know."

The continued assault of his hands and mouth stole what was left of her thought. She clutched at Korin's shoulders and arched to his touch. When an impending scream of pleasure rumbled at the base of her throat, Korin pressed his lips there. As she cried out her release, Korin thrust his finger deep into her and continued to circle the tiny, nerve-filled nubbin with his thumb. He scraped his teeth over one distended nipple and carried her amazingly past her first peak, and into her second.

"Korin? I... can't..."

But he would not let her rest until she moaned his name a third time.

CHAPTER ELEVEN

Nanceen woke in the early morning, long before the sun even considered rising into the sky over the city. She stretched and bunched the length of the family plaid Korin had tucked over her in her hands. After drying the dampness from her palms, she reached for Korin. He wasn't beside her.

Panicked, she sat against the couch and searched the dark room. Only city lights reflecting through the windows illuminated the area. About to rise and search for him, Nanceen glanced out the wide French doors to the balcony.

Korin stood with his back was to her. Arms stretched out to the sides, he lifted his face to the sky. He remained frozen in position for a long moment. Unwilling to disturb whatever he was doing, Nanceen relaxed and sank back to rest her head on a cushion and watch silently.

Finally, Korin lowered his arms. His shoulders rose and fell as he took long, deep breaths. The ripple of muscle across his back glinted in the artificial light, and her hungry gaze followed the length of his spine to where his jeans hung low and rumpled on his hips. The material pulled tight across his buttocks when he stretched his arms over his head and bent forward slightly.

She gasped in delight.

He turned. Eyes wide, he stared at her for a moment. Then, he smiled a slow, sensuous smile, licked his lower lip as if tasting it, and stepped toward her.

The firm evidence of his arousal had to be painful, for he had not found his own release. Now, no matter what he said, she would ease him, show him it was okay, and love him as he had loved her. She sat forward and reached for him.

Korin took her hands, turned them palms up, and bent to place lingering kisses in the depressions in the centers. He knelt beside her and shook his head. "I know what you're thinking. I'm afraid it isn't possible yet, my endearment." Still holding her hands, he raised them over her head and pressed her back against the cushions. Stretching his body next to hers, he held her wrists together with one hand and pushed away the plaid to bare her body to his heated gaze.

When his liquid silver gaze lifted to hers, Nanceen sighed and arched her back. How could he make her tingle and ache just by looking at her? Still holding her wrists above her head, he lapped his tongue over the tip of her breast. With a soft cry, she lifted her shoulders from the floor.

Taking the plaid, he draped the material over her hands and tucked the ends under a pillow. Even though she could pull her hands from under the material, she understood and accepted the gentle confinement. She nodded and Korin gave her a lopsided grin.

"Thank you." He bent over her and tasted the skin on the underside of her chin. Using his tongue, he traced patterns down her neck and across her chest. He braced his hands on either side of her body and laved, nipped, and kissed his way across her skin.

She was hot, so hot, and melting by the time his mouth hovered just below her navel. Pressing her feet into the floor, she lifted her hips and encouraged him to taste her completely.

Despite her whimpered pleas, Korin shook his head and slid down her body until he could begin on her toes. He honored every inch of her skin with his mouth, until his breath huffed through the triangle of curls waiting in aching anticipation for his touch. "Please, Korin... touch me." Nanceen stretched her arms, hooked her fingers under the frame of the couch and rolled her spine. "Touch."

After another long, cool breath of air over her damp skin, Korin's mouth covered her and his tongue slipped between her folds. Her release was instantaneous, shattering, and she gasped his name over and over until the jerking of her body ceased.

A moment later, Korin pressed her legs further apart with his shoulder, and thrust his tongue deep inside her.

After her third incredible release, she realized he had never touched her with his hands.

A phone rang. Nanceen groaned and rolled away, leaving Korin curled on his side, sleeping. She crawled to the end table and slapped at the surface until her hand came in contact with the slim, cordless phone. "Yes?"

"Well, morning sunshine." Lara's cheerful voice made Nanceen frown and she squeezed the phone tightly. "Are you guys gonna be ready to leave in about half an hour?"

"Uh, I suppose. You woke me up." Nanceen grumbled under her breath. Usually she woke with the same lilt in her voice. But she didn't usually have such an intense, sleepless night. Her nipples peaked at the memories of the three times Korin took her to multiple heights of pleasure. She glanced back at him.

Awake and smiling at her, he pillowed his head on his hands, looking extremely pleased with himself. Nanceen stuck out her tongue. The leisurely roll of his tongue over his lower lip curled longing deep within her. She nearly dropped the phone.

"Are you there, Nance? We'll be by to pick you up in half an hour." Lara laughed again. "Leave Korin alone and get ready." The phone went dead.

Nanceen returned the phone to the end table. "We have to get ready to go to the Renaissance Faire. Iain and Lara will be here to pick us up soon."

"You have my clothing in your bag. You're sure it will be appropriate?"

Nanceen closed her eyes to imagine the flowing tunic and vest and the tight breeches Korin wore in the Otherworld. The outfit would be more than appropriate. She sighed and her eyes popped open. "Your clothes will be fine. But I have to return to the Otherworld for mine."

Pain dulled the silver of Korin's eyes. Nanceen rushed to his side and caressed his cheek with her palm. "I'll go change and be right back. There's a portal here in the apartment. You wait here. Why don't you take a shower and change while I'm gone?"

The smile returned to his full lips and brightened the room. Nanceen hated to leave.

"Go on. I shall be fine here. A shower may do wonders to revive me."

Nanceen glanced down the length of his body. A tight bulge still filled his jeans. Why had he given her so much and taken nothing for himself?

His curled finger lifted her chin. "There was pleasure for me, Nanceen. Don't worry. The time shall come, mayhaps soon. I don't know. Now, go dress for me in your finery. I shall be your humble servant this day."

He brushed a soft kiss across her lips. He started to rise, but returned to take her mouth possessively, urgently, tantalizing her mouth with soft scrapes of his teeth and dancing thrusts of his tongue. When she gasped for breath, he rose and stumbled toward the bathroom.

Finally able to rid himself of his underwear, Korin shimmied out of the tight scrap of cloth and tossed it on the top of the pile of his human clothing. He reached his arms over his head, stretched to stand on the tips of his toes, and sighed. Even though his body still thrummed with the need for release, he was well pleased with the past night. He had learned much of Nanceen's body and of the places that gave her the greatest pleasure. Still tasting her kisses and the flavor of her skin, Korin licked his lips. The sweetness stole strength from his legs, and he leaned against the cold porcelain of a pedestal sink.

He needed to focus, to put his lust into a proper perspective. He wanted more from Nanceen that just physical satisfaction. It would be easy to find that elsewhere if he so desired. *No.* No longer would casual fulfillment be enough. A grin pulled his lips and he stared at his reflection in the mirror centered above the sink.

A sudden frown furrowed his brow. He would love his gentry maid for all of time, even if he could never join with her. A glance down brought another fervent wish to his heart. *Let her be mine-- in all ways.*

The clear shower door wouldn't budge when Korin pushed on it. He tried again, and the panel shuddered. Frustrated, he growled at the door and gave it an angry swipe with his hand. The door slid easily on its track and Korin's frustration turned to laughter.

He was equally delighted with the large showerhead he could twist to create different pleasing patterns of warm spray over his body. He sniffed the contents of a large bottle of soap and nodded in approval of the fresh essence of wood and the outdoors.

An unbidden image of Nanceen resting on a thick carpet of soft grasses and tiny wildflowers brought his semi-aroused body to full life. Korin groaned and stood, head down, eyes closed, and willed the darkness to take the vision of Nanceen's welcoming smile. Water pounded the tense muscles of his shoulders and ran down his back to caress the sensitive skin usually hidden by his wings.

He groaned again. Mayhaps he needed to follow the ancient path of a male alone and ease his longing. One hand slid across the wet skin of his abdomen but paused when his palm covered the slight bump of his navel. He shook his head and sent water droplets streaming into his eyes. The touch, the empty feeling of release would not be enough. It would never be enough. If he had to resort to such actions, he was not deserving of his Nanceen. He would wait.

Korin turned off the shower, stepped from the steamy enclosure, and dried quickly with a large, deep blue towel. He donned his clothing and took a happy breath. So much more comfortable than human clothing, he twisted his shoulders to feel the swipe of the loose tunic over his back. The slits, where his wings would normally protrude, tickled his skin with hints of warm air.

He pulled on his breeches, tied the corded waist tightly, and danced a rapid jig. Much better without the confining underwear. The freedom was addictive, and he continued his dance as he made his way back to the living room.

Sobering with a short jerk, he ran his hands through his hair, lifting soft spikes over the top of his head. He returned to the bathroom, neatly folded the human clothing, and clutched his small bag tightly in his fist. The rustle of the fairy parchment against the money drew him further into a serious mood.

As he tied the bag to a loop on the waist of his breeches and shortened the strings so the bag was snugged tight against his body, Korin debated his next actions. Should he consciously struggle to determine what would fulfill the conditions of the agreement--or should he trust in his love for Nanceen and the will of fate?

He shrugged; he didn't know. Today was meant to be another adventure, one he would gladly take with Nanceen and his new friends at his side. One thing he did know--he could not allow a repeat of the past night. Delightful as it was, he no longer believed he could withstand the joy of being with Nanceen--of watching her eyes glow with desire--to listen to the sounds of her pleasure and the way his name passed her lips without burying his need, and himself, deep within her.

Calm. Calm was needed for the day. He glanced around the great room, cast a small magik to tidy the area, and slipped out to the balcony.

The dawn light preceding the sun barely streaked the sky over the tops of the nearby buildings. He wished for grass between his toes, but the soft breeze carried the scents of distant flowers. It would suffice. Lowering himself to a cross- legged position, he straightened his back, took three long, deep breaths, and focused on the false horizon of the roof on a low building. His vision blurred and he closed his eyes.

Nanceen's body tingled with sensuous memory and the promise of future delights. Not that she minded losing the sleep. Still, a quick shower would revive her after the short night. And, maybe calm her body's responses enough so she could make it through the day.

However, the gentle spray piped from the warm underground spring reminded her too much of Korin's kisses and the hot, damp paths left by his tongue. She cut the shower short, quickly towel dried her hair, and stood, wrapped in her towel, staring at a selection of clothing.

Originally, she had thought to wear a simple skirt and tunic with a brightly colored sash to the Faire. Now, since Korin had spoken of finery--she rethought her choices.

This weekend at the Renaissance Faire was dedicated to fantasy, so there would be many dressed in their own interpretations of fairies, elves, and other mystical creatures. Nanceen paused and fingered the material of a deep red, velvety gown. Since mortals usually attributed what they knew of the fairy world to authors such as Shakespeare or Spenser or the fairy tales they'd heard as children, light, filmy clothing and wired wings would be the norm at the Faire.

Her thoughts stopped with a jerk. Korin said he was a descendent of one of the characters in a Shakespeare play, but that the history happened long before Shakespeare lived. In the play, fairies were ruled by members of the gentry. So that meant...

She grimaced at her attempt to make sense of a convoluted logic and she had no idea where she was going with her ideas. Besides, now was not the time to debate worlds or ideologies with herself. Now was the time to transform herself into a true member of Korin's gentry.

She reached for a favorite gown, one she often wore when in attendance for her aunt, the clan's Queen. The soft, silky material caressed her like a lover's touch--like Korin's touch, and she almost pulled the dress back over her head. She lifted a multi-chained, knotted necklace and fastened it around her neck to partially cover the skin left bare by her low neckline. A string of glittering purple stones circled her neck. A matching string rested low on her hips to keep the floating layers of the dress somewhat in check.

Silver ribbons attached at her shoulders caught the breeze when she turned. The shimmer reminded her of the changeable lights in Korin's eyes as he moved from delight to passion. As a finishing touch, she attempted to calm her short curls and set an open mesh cap of silver and tiny purple stones on her head. Trailing fringes skimmed her upper back and she laughed. Made for her by Faerie smiths when her hair was still long, she hadn't worn the headpiece for many years. Today, it felt like the right thing to do.

Just like Korin felt right to her. A flash of sadness dampened her rising good mood. What prohibition was there be to prevent Korin from making love with her? She wanted more than he had been able to give her--she wanted all of him, every inch of him pressed against her, moving with and inside her. What was it that he couldn't tell her?

As she moved from her room, she glanced across the cabin to her sister's door. Nanceen brightened and felt a nearly physical weight lift from her shoulders.

Kaelea loved the study of myths and beginnings. Perhaps, since the folk of Faerie considered the small, diminutive fairy a myth, Kae might know something about them. If nothing else, perhaps Kae would take some time from whatever it was she was investigating now and help.

Sitting at a wide desk, Nanceen reached for a sheet of parchment and a pen. She paused to compose her thoughts, then wrote swiftly, covering the small sheet with flowing letters.

Kae;
I know you're probably immersed in your investigation, but I need a favor of you. If you have knowledge of what I'm asking, please let me know as soon as possible. I've met

She scratched out the last two words and watched as they faded magically from the parchment. Chewing on the end of the pen, she closed her eyes in thought. How should she phrase her need without sounding as if she'd lost her mind?

Do you know anything about fairies--like in the tales Allyn told us when we were children? Beings like those from a Shakespeare play? Could they be more than myth? Even in myth, what kind of magic do they possess?

I know these are strange questions, dear sister, but ones I must know the answers to them soon.
I hope your investigations go well and you discover whatever it is you're looking for. You know me, Kae, I don't remember why you've gone.

Nanceen grinned. Kae would smile as she read the words. Nanceen had never understood her sister's desire for arcane knowledge and usually only gave the barest attention to Kae's rambling dissertations. She might have been better off now, if she had paid more attention. She tapped the nib of the pen against the parchment. It would be better if she could talk to Kae face to face, but since she didn't even know where her sister was.

Please try and find some time for my questions. And let me know what you know, as soon as you can.
I do miss you, Kae. And I have much to tell you when you get home.

Nanceen signed her name and followed the signature with a

small design she and Kae had developed as young girls to use when sending secret messages to each other. As she left her cabin, she tucked the folded parchment into a small box set to one side of the porch. Unseen Faerie messengers would take the missive to Kaelea. Feeling she'd done all she could, Nanceen hurried toward the nearest portal, held her destination firmly in mind, and returned to the mortal world.

A silent apartment greeted her. The barely audible hum of an air purifier made a soft, white noise background to the silence. Nanceen gave the great room a cursory glance. The cushions and pillows scattered during the night had been returned to their proper places. The plaid was folded neatly and tucked over the back of the couch.

Where was Korin? A moment of panic tightened her chest. The fear he may have left the apartment--left her--choked the breath at the base of her throat. The necklace felt tight and grew tighter as she struggled to take slow breaths.

Just like the dreams. He had given her amazing pleasure and, like those dreams, had disappeared with the coming morning. Tears burned behind her eyes and found release to coat her lashes. Why had she hoped...?

A slight, bobbing motion at the edge of her vision caught her attention. She paused in open-mouthed amazement.

On the balcony, Korin sat in what was easily recognizable as a meditative posture. But he floated two feet off the decking.

Nanceen bit her lip to keep from crying out her relief and astonishment and moved quietly toward the balcony. She paused in the doorway and studied Korin's face. Relaxed, a tiny smile stretched his lips. His lashes lay golden against the ruddy glow of his cheeks. His breaths were soft, barely lifting his chest. She hated to disturb him, so she watched as he rose slightly when a fresh breeze blew across the balcony then settled back to his original position.

After a slight trembling of a muscle in one cheek, Korin's eyes opened slowly. His irises were a dull pewter--cold, nearly colorless circles in his eyes. Ever so slowly, his lids lowered. The slow motion blink hid his eyes from her. Just as slowly, the lids raised. Now, glimmering silver filled his eyes. He turned his head toward her and smiled broadly.

"You're back."

Not trusting her voice, Nanceen nodded.

Bouncing slightly in the air, Korin stretched his legs, lowered his feet to the deck, and stood. One step brought him to Nanceen's side, and he placed a soft kiss against her cheek.

"You shouldn't do that."

Startled, Korin took a short step back. "I shouldn't greet you with a kiss?" What had he done now?

"No." She stumbled over her words to reassure him. "Oh, no. That's fine. You shouldn't be, uh, floating out here where someone might see you."

Korin's lowered his brows. "How high was I?"

Nanceen lifted one hand, glanced at the low wall surrounding the balcony and adjusted her hand lower.

"I was not above the barrier?" She shook her head and he gave her a smug grin. "Then, no harm was done?"

"No, but you... oh, Korin. The people in this world wouldn't understand. Please, be careful."

"I shall, endearment." He had to touch her, so he cupped her cheek with his palm and ran the pad of his thumb over her lashes. They were damp. "What's this? Tears? If it causes you tears, I shall keep both feet firmly on the ground."

"That's not it." She smiled, but her lips quivered in betrayal of her lingering, confused emotions.

Gentle, Korin brushed his finger again over her lowered lashes, capturing a tear. "Then what, Nanceen?"

A sob gasped from her lips. "I thought you were gone."

"Gone?" He traced the back of his finger over the curve of her cheek. "Where would I go, when you were to return here?"

"In my dreams--"

"I am not a dream, endearment. I believe I have more sense than to act as the dream fairy did. I will not leave you until the moment you wish me gone."

"Is that all you are, Korin? A figment of desire I can wish away at any moment?" She pressed her hands flat against his chest. His heart beat hard, trying to pound his love for her way into her palms.

"I am real, Nanceen." His curled finger moved to disturb the fringe of beaded chain behind her ear. "And you, you are my gentry princess, a Faerie maid to delight the senses." He moved his finger lower and traced one of the chains lying low on her chest. "A delight I shall never grow tired of."

He leaned closer and ran the tip of his tongue along the pink shell of her ear. He grinned when her entire body shuddered in response. Her arms snaked around his neck and she angled her face to accept his eager kiss.

Korin would have kissed her forever, and a day longer, but a door slammed inside the apartment. Keeping his mouth against Nanceen's, Korin's lifted his heavy eyelids and watched the doorway.

Awkward, fumbling movements sounded from within the apartment, and finally a voice called out hoarsely. "Nance? Where are you?"

Jayse's haggard face and slumped body followed his voice to the balcony. "Oh, there you are. Lara and Iain are waiting downstairs. Iain's impatient to get on the road since we have a three-hour drive." He whirled around, stopped with a jerk, and grabbed his head with one hand.

Nanceen tried to wiggle from Korin's embrace. He tightened his arms around her and turned their bodies so she could see Jayse. Nuzzling her neck, Korin kissed the flush rising on her skin then whispered against her ear. "He doesn't care. Why should you?"

Jayse grabbed the doorframe and spoke without facing them again. "I need to grab my stuff. You guys go on down, and I'll be there in a couple of minutes." He mumbled to himself and moved toward his bedroom.

When he was gone, Nanceen relaxed and leaned against Korin's chest. He tightened his hold. "I know I shouldn't be embarrassed. It's just..." Her words, softly spoken, rumbled through his chest and threatened to destroy his hard- won calm.

"It doesn't matter, endearment." He pressed his lips to her cheek. "Come, we should go. You must tell me about these human Faires."

Nanceen giggled and shook her head. "No, I think I'll let you find out for yourself. You wanted adventure." She took his hand and tugged until he followed her.

It was impossible to keep a silly grin from his face. Nanceen's moods were changeable, moving swiftly from embarrassment to teasing. And now he knew how quickly passion overcame her. The more he knew of her, the more he loved her.

Walking close to him, Nanceen's hip brushed his small bag and the parchment crackled loudly to Korin's ears. His smile faded. There were still the conditions. And if he couldn't fulfill them, his Nanceen would be forbidden to him. Unless he forswore fairy. Could it be done? Would he?

The questions consumed him until they passed from the building and crossed the street. Nanceen knocked once on the side door of Lara's deep blue van, interrupting her niece's exploration of Iain's mouth.

"Seems a popular pastime this morn." Korin chuckled, delighted when another blush filled Nanceen's face.

She slapped him playfully on the arm and reached to slide open the side door. She gestured for Korin to enter the vehicle before her. Trying to climb into the van with long, flowing skirts and arranging them so she could sit comfortably took a few moments. By the time Korin and Lara got her settled, Jayse had emerged from the building and stumbled to the van. He tossed a bundle of clothing to the rear bench and crawled inside, collapsing on his back with his legs still extended in the narrow aisle.

"Tough night, bro?" Lara covered her laughter with her hand and they all turned to watch his tight, pained movements.

"Mmph."

"Is Bryce in the same condition?"

"Worse. I'm gonna sleep. Wake me up when we're pulling into the parking lot. I'll change then." Jayse covered his eyes with his forearm, mumbled something incoherent about Bryce, and fell silent.

Soft laughter filled the front of the van, and Iain maneuvered the vehicle on to the street, through the city, and to the highway.

CHAPTER TWELVE

The hours to Kansas City passed swiftly, even though there was little conversation. An occasional light snore from the back seat reminded them of Jayse's presence. Lara seemed reluctant to talk as she kept her eyes on the road. One of her hands clutched convulsively on the armrest. Nanceen admired her control and the ability to let Iain drive, even though it frightened her.

Nanceen contented herself with watching Korin. Giving up on secret glances, she watched him with open admiration. Almost bouncing in his seat like a young child, he watched the passing farms, the barns, and white houses highlighted in the rising sun. He would crane his neck to study each small town they passed. Two tiny frown lines formed above his nose each time he saw the pointed steeple of a country church and although Nanceen wondered what he was thinking, she was hesitant to ask and spoil the quiet atmosphere in the van.

Soon they reached the outskirts of the city, and Iain pulled into a gas station to let Lara take the wheel. Skirting the metropolitan area, they passed large sports complexes and huge manufacturing facilities.

Grumbling noises from the backseat of the van indicated

Jayse had risen from his comatose state. And before long, his tousled head peered over the seat. Rustling and bumping, followed by a series of grunts and whispered expletives, made Nanceen giggle.

Korin glanced at her in question.

"It's hard to change clothes inside a moving vehicle," she explained and waved her hand toward the back seat.

"Damn right it is. Ow." Jayse rested his arms on the back of Nanceen's seat and leaned forward. "Good thing I didn't come in fighting regalia today."

"Armor?" Korin squinted in confusion. "There is fighting?"

Jayse laughed, then pressed his palms against his temples. "Any fighting at this faire is for entertainment only. In fact, everything is choreographed and scripted. When I fight for re-enactments and at small faires, the fighting is real--even if the weapons are only padded sticks."

"Ye dinna bring yer sword today?" Iain rested one arm over the center console and angled to face the others.

Jayse ran a hand through his hair and shifted the messy, short, dark brown waves to some semblance of order. "Naw. Weapons are forbidden except on special days. Even then, it's required for all blades to be peace-tied." He brushed at wrinkles in his loose, cotton gauze shirt. "This day, I am but a simple man. A farmer perhaps."

Iain snorted with laughter. "Och, ye are nae farmer. A jester perhaps."

"Ah, but give me wings, and a fairy I'd be. I always wanted to be mythical."

Nanceen held her breath, chewed on the inside of her cheek, and glanced from Iain to Korin and back again. Iain's eyebrows lifted slightly, but he made no other indication of the effects the simple statement had on the other occupants of the van.

Shoulders stiff, his expression stony, Korin faced forward. Afraid he had taken offense at Jayse's words, Nanceen reached one hand to him. Holding her palm a fraction of an inch above his arm, she hesitated.

"We're here." The cheerful tone of Lara's voice was strained. "Hang on, there's a ton of ruts in the parking area."

The bounce of the van brought Nanceen's hand in contact with Korin's arm. He jerked once before his shoulders relaxed and he turned a sad smile to her. "In time."

"What do you mean?" She leaned closer.

Korin shrugged and shook his head, ending with a slight backward motion to indicate Jayse. Then his smile grew wide and curious as the massive gates of the Renaissance Faire enclosure came into view through the windshield.

K orin attempted to see everything at once. The gaiety, the colors, the bold and bawdy actions of the people intrigued him to speechlessness. From around a corner, three--were they men?--appeared, dressed in rough, dirty robes covering them from neck to toe. The men called out to the crowd, coming close then backing away. Unable to tear his gaze from the fascinating sight, he nudged Nanceen. "What are they?"

"Those? Those are lepers. They beg and are often chased away by others. It is dangerous to touch them, for people had long thought to touch them would spread the disease."

"I must help them." He took a step to the side, but halted at the firm grasp of Nanceen's hand around his wrist. Twisting, he tried to free his arm.

"Korin, it's pretend." He froze, lifted his gaze to hers and met eyes filled with compassion. "Everything here is pretend, make believe. Like most of these people around us think you are, and believe I am. Korin." She shook his arm gently. "They're actors. Some are hired, some volunteer. It's all to try and recreate the world of the Renaissance."

"But, I..."

"Please, Korin, Trust me."

"I do, endearment. But, how can I tell what is real when I am not?"

Nanceen pulled him into an embrace and whispered, "You are

real. At least to me." Soft breaths of air caressed his cheek moments before the warm press of her lips. "If you have any doubts, just ask me. Or Lara, or Iain. We'll all help. This can be confusing even to someone who's been many times before. Each time at a faire is different. Different actors, different characters, different guests."

"I understand." It was difficult to set aside his preconceived notions about humanity. In that difficulty, he discovered a new pain. How was he different than how humans thought of fairies? He forced the uneasiness aside and tried to smile at Nanceen. "I understand."

A heavy hand came down on his shoulder. He glanced at Iain's wide grin. "Come, the parade is about to start. Then, they shall be openin' the gates." Iain turned to lead the way to a clear space under a small shade tree. "This is a guid place to watch." He nestled Lara against his side. Jayse collapsed to the ground to relace one of his knee high boots. Nanceen pressed against Korin's side in a posture that mirrored Lara's. It was a moment filled with peace, one that would dissipate quickly once the gates were opened.

Even the beggers and dancing gypsies fell silent as a fanfare of brass instruments announced the coming of the king and queen of the faire. A tall knight, dressed in chain mail with a long, black feather bouncing from his helmet, led a procession of brightly dressed nobles over the crest of a hill. Under the protection of a flower-strewn canopy, a large man strutted, a buxom woman at his side.

"All hail Henry the King and his beloved wife, Anne Boleyn." Korin turned to stare at the man standing on a walkway above the gate.

A cheer and loud huzzahs rose from the crowd as they parted to let the king near the gate. He turned, held up one hand, and the crowd quieted instantly. Korin chuckled to himself. Even pretend kings were pompous and self-important.

"Welcome, good people. It is with pleasure we open this day's faire." The king's voice droned on and Korin lost track of the words. Instead, he focused again on the crowd and the variety of clothing. His fairy clothing did allow him to mingle easily with the crowd.

Gauze wings of every shape and size adorned the backs of the those who pretended to be from the fairy realm. He withheld a laugh, for many of the wings would never even lift a fairy in his true, diminutive size. Many of the false fairies were scantily dressed. A tiny smile pulled at his mouth. Few of his folk would dress in such a way, and those who did were whispered about behind the matron's hands.

The gentry maid at his side was more to his liking.

A final brassy and slightly out of tune fanfare made Korin wince. But he quickly forgot the sting to his ears when the king shouted, "Open the gates. Let the festivities begin!" Caught in the press of people surging toward the entrance, Korin grasped at Nanceen's hand, felt the reassuring touch of Iain's hand on his shoulder, and stepped into a strange, mystifying world.

T hree tiny beings knelt before the Fir Dhaerrig. The one on the king's left crawled forward and spoke. "Sire, the gentry wench returned to the Otherworld."

"Ah, good. And Korin?"

"Nay, he din't return. But, sire, she's gone again."

The Fir Dhaerrig leaned forward. His bushy eyebrows lowered over his deep-set eyes. "What? Where did she go?"

A brownie scooted forward. "Back to da human world. I's followed. They's goin' to a renaissance festival." He spit, leaving a thick wet, wad on the floor before him.

The king's brows lowered further, and a low rumbling growl rose from his chest. The brownie scrambled back to his place. When the growling continued, the brownie crawled forward on his hands and knees and used the ragged end of his coat to wipe the floor.

Nodding once, the king rose and paced the golden floor before his throne.

The three waited in silence for a span of breaths before the boggart rose to his feet and stepped close to the king.

"There be more, sire. The maid, she sent a message."

"Message? What message? To whom?"

The boggart waved two stick-like fingers through the air and a shimmering, nearly transparent copy of a sheet of parchment hovered before the Fir Dhaerrig's pointed nose. The king studied the faint writing. "So, the maid wishes to know about fairies." He laughed, and the wicked sound rang around his opulent throne room. High-pitched giggles from the brownies echoed the malice.

The boggart scratched at his belly. He disliked working with his cousins, the brownies. Disliked spying upon the gentry. The king had plans he'd not told to any others, and it worried the boggart. When he could find time away from the duties the king set for him, he would--

"Well, boys, what shall we teach her about fairies?"

The brownies glanced at each other, confusion etched deep in their dirty faces. The boggart sighed heavily and stepped to one side.

The Fir Dhaerrig rolled his gaze to the ceiling and shook his head. "This ain't gonna be easy." He moved to stand before the brownies, spread his legs wide, and planted his hands against his hips. "You allowed the message to be sent?" When one of the brownies nodded, the king grinned. "Good. Find Peg-leg Jack for me. Bring him here no matter how loudly he grumbles. Go, quickly. My plans will be formulated by your return."

The brownies bowed, scraping the floor with the tops of their heads as they backed from the chamber. The king rubbed his hands together and danced a jig until he was forced to lean upon his skull-topped staff and gasp for breath. Only then did the boggart slip silently from the room.

. . .

Why he bothered to travel the long miles to such a farce was like a knot tied deep in his belly. Memories of what he'd lost--no, what had been taken from him--burned like acid. This foolish falsehood...

Titus shook his head, moved forward in the line, purchased a ticket, and exchanged the tiny slip of paper for entrance through the tall, wooden gates.

Immediately surrounded by pretenders, he shrugged his way through the throng. His gaze darted over the crowd. He needed to stay hidden. While the others might find him familiar, he wasn't ready to reveal himself, or his purpose. Why he felt compelled to follow them to this forsaken place, he was unable to determine.

Yet, follow he did. Perhaps he would discover the reason. And discover a way to further his plans. He ducked behind a pavilion when one of the men turned and glanced back toward the main gates. Had the man sensed his presence? Fortifying his mental shields, Titus waited before he peered around the corner. It would be a trying day.

"Jack?" Showing sharp, dirty teeth, the Fir Dhaerrig grinned. The Fachan leaned heavily on his spiked staff and hopped toward the throne. Standing straight on one leg, he looked around with his one eye before focusing on the king.

"What wish you of me?" The words were surly, with no tone of respect.

The king frowned. The Fachan hated all living creatures, but nonetheless, he , as king, expected a touch of respect. Demanded it. He held his silence until the Fachan fidgeted uneasily.

"Sire." The hairy head bowed slightly.

The king was satisfied. "Sit here at my feet, Jack."

Peg-legged Jack plopped ungraciously onto a step below the throne. He settled as much as his awkward one-legged, one-armed body could and lifted his hard, one-eyed gaze to the king.

The combination of hair and feathers covering his body bristled. "Why have you called me from my mountain?"

"I have a job for you, Jack. A duty for you to perform for me."

"I need no assigned duties, sire. I am busy enough keeping trespassers from my mountain."

"And if the reward is high enough?"

"What need have I of reward? There is only one thing I desire, and even you can't give that to me."

"And what would you do with the gift of flight?"

Jack shrugged his single shoulder, an ugly, graceless movement.

The Fir Dhaerrig chuckled. The envy of flight had always resided openly in the Fachan. It was legendary. But, with only one of each limb, the king didn't think Jack would be able to achieve the balance needed for proper flight. He chuckled again. And, with Peg-leg's luck, he'd grow only one wing anyway.

"I did not come down from my mountain for you to make jest of me." The Fachan made as if to rise, but could not find purchase for his stick on the smooth stones.

"I have not given you permission to leave, Jack." The king swept his staff sideways to knock the Fachan's support to one side. "Listen to my offer. Then, decide if it brings you pleasure."

The king leaned to the side while Jack stretched his scrawny neck. As the king whispered his plan and the offered terms, the Fachan's eye glittered with merry wickedness. His thin lips pulled into a feral, delighted grin. He nodded as the king spoke. "You'll set the will o'wisps to guard my mountain, so I'm not to be bothered by invasions to my privacy. For a year and a day they shall remain."

The Fir Dhaerrig nodded and rubbed his hands together with glee.

"The one act, the spell you will give me, is all I must do?"

"Yes, yes. That's all I need. Now, Jack, won't this please you?"

"Aye, that it will, sire."

Pulling a dark bag from one of the pockets of his red coat, the king shook his head sadly. "While it is true I cannot give you the ability of flight, this spell, properly applied, will make flight an embarrassment to the victim. He shall return to me shamed and beaten. He will not have his desires--but I shall. And so shall you, Jack."

The king handed Peg-leg Jack the bag and watched closely as the Fachan slipped it beneath a woven sash. Then, he rose and generously held Jack's single arm to help him stand. "Do this well, my Fachan, and my debt to you shall be unbounded."

Chuckling, the Fachan lowered his head in a bow, clutched his spiked staff and hopped away. Jack halted with a jerk, his back stiff. "I remember, sire. It shall be done. Bother me no more."

CHAPTER THIRTEEN

By the time they stopped for lunch, Korin had seen tiny shops galore, knights jousting in a strange, ribald style, and numerous dances and plays. He was exhausted, yet exhilarated at the same time. Having chosen a small brown loaf, hollowed and filled with a savory cheese soup, he sat on the ground at Nanceen's feet and ate. She had promised him a treat, and he was anxious to try cheesecake on a stick.

He had also tried to purchase many beautiful things for Nanceen. But, stating she needed nothing, she had refused his offers. Instead insisting he was to spend his dollars on himself.

So, after eating, he planned to return to the small booth where a young man sold carved, wooden flutes. If Nanceen would not accept a material gift, then he would play for her. The tunes were already dancing in his head--lively, spritely dances and smooth, flowing love songs.

A feeling of being watched raised tingles in the center of his back and interrupted his pleasant reverie. Trying to appear casual, he set his empty paper plate on the ground and glanced around the crowded eating area. He'd not used his magical senses often since coming to the human world, then only for tricks and underwear. He lowered his gaze and grinned.

The uncomfortable feeling grew stronger, and Korin closed his eyes in concentration. Two? He blinked slowly. There were two watchers. Reaching out with a tendril of awareness, he dismissed one of the watchers as harmless. The instant his senses touched upon the other, the way was blocked. He pushed harder and gasped at the intensity of hate that returned to him.

"Korin?" Nanceen rested her hand on his shoulder. "Is anything wrong?"

The residual flavor of the strange, vicious response coated his tongue. Swallowing heavily, he tried to compose his face to calm neutrality. "No, nothing. I wish to make a purchase. Will you come with me?"

"Ah, finally. As long as it's not for me." At the shake of Korin's head, she turned to the others who were still finishing their meals. "We'll be back in a bit." She bent to grab Korin's plate, stacked it on hers, and tossed them both into a nearby trashcan.

Lara waved. "Go on. How about we meet up near the dance stage?" She glanced at her watch. "I'd like to see the presentation there in half an hour."

Closing his eyes, Korin visualized the layout of the Faire. The dancer's stage was close to the booth he wished to visit. "A wonderful idea." Without further conversation, he rose to his feet, took Nanceen's hand, and led her away.

A young man sat behind the counter, blowing a soft tune on a short, wooden pipe. He nodded when Korin approached, but continued playing. Snuggling Nanceen to his side, Korin watched the sure, swift movements of the man's fingers.

The music stopped and the man lowered the flute. "M'lord, m'lady. May I interest ye in the finest of flutes?"

Korin nodded and reached for a thick flute the length of his forearm.

"An excellent choice, m'lord, but ambitious. Have ye played prior to this day?"

"Some." Korin bit back a huge grin.

"I can allow ye to test the fingering, m'lord, but ye may not blow into the instrument--unless you make a purchase of it. Health concerns, ye understand. If ye need instruction, I am at your service." The man placed one hand over the center of his chest and bent in a courtly bow.

"I don't believe I'll need instruction." Korin turned the flute over and over in his hands and ran a light touch of his fingers over the tiny carvings that graced the wood between the smooth finger holes. It was appropriate. Mystical creatures and tiny fairies romped the length of the instrument. He held the wooden piece out to Nanceen.

Touching the wood reverently, she let a long breath pass her parted lips. Hopefully, it was a sigh of delight, or of longing. And, with her response, he knew the music from this flute would please her.

"I shall have this one."

The young man's eyes lit with delight, but he leaned forward. "The cost is high for this piece, m'lord. I carve few as intricate or finely tuned as this."

"Yes, I know. However, the cost is unimportant." With one hand Korin loosened the bag at his waist and reached in to remove the folded bills. He handed them to Nanceen and indicated with a slight movement of his head that she should make the payment. "May I try the instrument now?"

"Assuredly, m'lord." The young man hurried to reach under the counter. "The fingering is similar to the Irish tin whistle. I have fingering charts..."

His voice faded to astonished silence as Korin blew a single clear note. A series of quick scales tested his fingering on the instrument. Then Korin took a deep breath and played a short ditty, a teaching song for the young of Fairy.

The tips of the young man's ears turned pink. A flash of understanding made Korin lower the flute. He had unconsciously made the seller uncomfortable. He gave the young man a broad grin. "Will you play with me?"

"Oh, no. I--"

"Come. Chose your favorite tune and I shall follow." He leaned over the counter. "I believe our song will bring customers to your stall."

"Well...okay." The young man thought for a moment, selected a thin, short pipe, and lifted it for approval. Korin smiled; the soprano pipe would be an excellent blend with his new, lower pitched flute.

The young man lifted his eyebrows, placed the flute against his lips, and blew gently. The tune he chose was lively, with intricate fingerings.

Korin listened, nodded, and lifted his own pipe to begin a counter melody.

Nanceen leaned against the counter. She tapped one foot in time to the music. Amazed, she couldn't imagine how the two men could play so well together when they'd just met. But then, she supposed, it wasn't much different than improvisational jazz.

A crowd gathered, some listening, some dancing in tight clusters. The crowd's rhythmic clapping grew louder, drawing even more spectators.

The rapid beat of a bodhran produced another counterpoint to the dance tune. Nanceen looked around for the drummer and grinned when Jayse lifted a new drum high while he continued to play.

When the musicians drew the tune to a reluctant close, wild applause and cheers rose from the crowd. Some called for more music, but Korin raised a hand and shook his head in denial.

He moved to Nanceen's side and steered her away from the musician's booth. Stopping under a shady tree, they turned and watched as the young man grinned and bowed, laughing at the sudden increase in his business.

Jayse appeared at her other side. His breathing rapid, his face flushed with excitement. "That was great. What a way to break in my new bodhran."

Thumping the taut, highly decorated head of the drum with her knuckle, Nanceen asked, "Don't you have enough drums?"

"Ah, never, Nance. Don't have one this size." He turned the drum so he could study the head. "Or decorated quite this way. The knot design reminds me of Mom's work."

Nanceen looked over his shoulder and traced the design with her finger. "Yes, it does look like something Allyn would design." She smiled at her nephew. "A good choice."

Waving one hand broadly, the musician signaled to Korin. When Korin acknowledged the summons, the musician gestured for him to come to the counter. Nanceen pushed Korin toward the booth. "Go and see what he wants. I'll wait here."

When Korin returned to the musician's booth, the uncomfortable, physical sense of being watched grew strong. He tried to shake away the strange, shivering sensation. When he reached the counter, the man grinned at him and the tingling faded.

"Hey, man, uh...I mean, my thanks, m'lord." His smile grew wider. He leaned conspiratorially over the counter and lowered his voice. "I've nearly sold out."

"It was a pleasure to play with one so talented." Korin grinned at the man's ruddy blush. "I find my playing improves when challenged by the abilities of another. I thank you as well."

"No, I'm not that good." He lifted one hand. "However, I forgot to give you the carry bag for your pipe." Bending double, he reached beneath the counter and pulled out a long, narrow, deep blue bag.

A breeze blew softly and stirred the branches above them. Filtered sunlight danced across the bag. Iridescent sparkles twinkled at Korin. Astonished by another miracle in the drab, human world, Korin took the bag and slid the flute into the depths. "I am indebted to you."

"No," the young man chuckled, "just come back and play anytime." He reached to one side and grabbed a small, rectangular card. Holding it in both hands, he seemed to be wrestling with a decision. Finally, he handed the card to Korin. "Or, if you want to play...sometime...anytime."

Korin slipped the card into the bag with his flute. "Again, I am honored." With a short bow, he turned, intending to return to Nanceen's side.

A fierce pain slammed between his shoulder blades. He stumbled forward and bit his lip to contain an agonized groan. What was happening? He hunched his shoulders forward, but it did no good. He tried pressing his shoulder blades together; the action only increased the burning pain.

Frantic, Korin glanced around, and through the hazy blur of pain discovered a narrow passage between two squat buildings. Perhaps he could find a place of silence there, a refuge, a place other faire goers had not found.

Searing pain bent him forward and he clutched at his flute. Only once before had he felt such agonized pain, and that only a few days before on the night he transformed to a wingless, human-sized being to be with Nanceen.

Gasping, he stumbled toward the possible haven. If this pain was from his wings, would they reappear? What would he do then? Even now, the pain sapped his strength, nearly driving him to his knees. He braced his hand against a rough, weathered wall and peered around the corner.

His sigh of relief ended in a sharp, whistling intake of air.

::Nanceen.::

If his wings were indeed returning, how would she react? Would she be disgusted? Would she laugh at the folly of one of his race loving her? The agony of that thought was nearly more than he could bear, and he fell to his knees on a soft pile of leaves. The pain in his back threw him forward onto his hands.

Soft laughter sounded before him. His skin crawled as though covered with tiny insects. Forcing movement from his stiff, protesting muscles, Korin lifted his head. The sight that met his gaze stole the sparse breath the pain had left him.

A Fachan stood across the tiny cleared area, his single foot and a spiked staff planted deep in the soft earth. The crooked grin looked out of place on the creature's normally hate-filled visage. Wrapping its one arm about the staff and pressing the wood against his armpit, the Fachan pointed at Korin.

"You. You were blessed with flight. While I wear feathers, yet remain earthbound. In your arrogance, you chose to discard your precious wings, lusting not after the skies, but after a half-human gentry wench. You are a fool, Goodfellow. A fool such as your ancestor." The Fachan's one eye blinked slowly.

"Jack. I know you, Jack. Why are you doing this to me?"

What passed as a shrug lifted Jack's single shoulder.

"Why do you hate me? I've always--"

"Been kind to me? Don't bother to say the words, Goodfellow. None are kind to Jack. That's why I choose never to leave my mountain." Peg-leg Jack cackled. "But this here, this was a good cause. To see the mighty laid low."

Korin tried to right himself, but another wave of pain curled him into a ball. He clutched the precious flute to his chest. It was a lifeline, his gift to Nanceen.

::Nanceen.::

Her name streaked through his mind. What if she should see him like this? Cursing the innate frailty of his fairy body, Korin continued his struggle to stand.

"Don't worry, Goodfellow. Those pretty wings of yours will be returned to you soon. And there ain't nothing you can do to stop it. Then we shall see how the humans take to you." Jack scratched his nose and hopped back into the shadows. "Remember, Goodfellow, remember your place."

Korin stared after the disappearing creature. How had Jack found enough magic to counteract Korin's own? The skin over his shoulder blades stretched. His wings had begun to grow. Soon, they would split his skin and unfurl to their full size. Korin gave a bitter chuckle. Since he was human sized, he supposed his wings would be large as well. If the pain was any indication...

He muffled a groan against his palm. How could he hide himself? What would Nanceen do when he didn't return? Korin pressed his forehead against the cool earth and sought some comfort, some fleeting answer from the fragrant soil. His mind released one final call, one last heart wrenching sound of despair before the pain drove him to silence.

::Nanceen.::

Smiling indulgently at Jayse as he examined his bodhran and the finely carved beater, Nanceen wondered how long it would be before Korin returned. She'd glanced at the musician's stall, but Korin was no longer in sight. A tiny shrug lifted one shoulder. Maybe she shouldn't worry about him so much.

But, she couldn't help it. There were times he seemed so innocent, so playful, so...fairy. At other times, he was no different than any male. The heat of a blush crawled across her cheeks. She had to see him.

::Nanceen.::

Her name, spoken in the musical tones of Korin's voice, echoed through her mind. He called to her. He needed her. Forcing herself to be calm, she glanced back at the musician's stall. Perhaps she heard him speak only because she wished to hear him. And wished to hear her name the way he had whispered it so many times during the past night. She rolled her eyes and willed the heat filling her face to dissipate.

::Nanceen.::

Again, she heard his call. Weaker this time, with pain arching through the tones. She took three steps away from Jayse. "I've got to find Korin."

"Don't worry about him so much, Nance. He'll find his way back."

"No, I don't think so. I think...it feels like he needs me."

"You really like him, don't you, Nance?"

"I...uh...yes. Yes, I do."

"It shows. And I'm glad. It's about time."

Nanceen slapped at Jayse's shoulder. She was about to make a comment concerning his love life--or lack thereof--when the anguish of Korin's voice pierced her mind.

::Nanceen.::

The barest whisper frightened her and she turned immediately from Jayse. But which way to go?

She headed to the musician's booth and leaned straight-arme, on the counter. "Did you see which way Korin went?" she asked when the man finally noticed her.

Coming out of character, the artisan frowned. "He just kinda disappeared after I gave him the carry bag for his flute." He glanced around and pointed to one side. "Check between those two stalls. Sometimes, when folks need a bit of peace and quiet, they head back there."

"Thanks." Nanceen rushed toward the narrow passage and slipped into the dim recess without hesitation. At the end of the alley, she stopped with a jerk. Curled in a tight ball, Korin knelt on the ground with his forehead pressed into a pile of decaying leaves. She fell to her knees at his side and reached to touch his shoulder.

A ripple of movement across his back froze her hand inches above him. She watched in horror as the center of his back pulsed and the previously hidden slits in his shirt and vest gaped open.

Something dark blue and streaked with silver curled, throbbed, and stretched the openings wide. Korin didn't move, but a groan issued from his lips and sank into the damp earth.

"Korin? Korin."

He gave no answer except for another groan. Pushing his shoulders high, his back arched. The fabric twisted and a length of velvety blue poked through one of the slits. A second bit protruded from the other side, uncurled, and lay limp over Korin's back.

Nanceen stared, her mouth worked silently. As the second blue length unfurled, she realized these were Korin's wings.

"Oh, Korin."

"Nanceen. I'm sorry. I couldn't prevent it." Korin's words were muffled against the ground. "It hurts."

Avoiding the slightly fluttering wings, Nanceen stroked his arm. His head turned toward her and she gasped at the agony reflected in the dull pewter of his eyes and the tight lines straining his face. "What do I need to do?"

His eyes closed briefly and he shook his head once. "It was not so...unpleasant before. I must rest a short while. Hopefully then, I shall be fine."

"How did this happen?"

He struggled to sit. Nanceen, fascinated with the soft looking wings, could only stare at him. She longed to touch the deep blue wings to see if they were truly as soft as they appeared. Perhaps they might even be dusty, like a butterfly's wings. Wanting to trace the silvery veining with her fingers, she wondered if he would feel the touch.

"I don't know. Somehow, something broke through my magic and--" Korin sucked in a sharp breath. His wings shuddered and unfurled completely. Then he sighed and a hint of relief touched his pain-filled eyes.

"How could someone break your magic? I know only a little about such arts, but, it would take a powerful spell, wouldn't it?"

"Powerful indeed."

Graceful in his movements, Korin stood. Nanceen squinted at the fierce, determined set to his jaw. He knew who had caused the pain. Determined to know as well, she rose beside him. "Who did this?"

"I can't say." Rotating his shoulders made the huge wings ripple.

Nanceen took a step back to view the full effect. The tops of the wings reached as high as the crown of his head. Shaped fuller at the top, they narrowed past his hips and ended in swallowtail points at mid-calf. Giving her a lopsided grin, Korin showed no lingering ill effects when he spread his wings to their fullest, surrounding his face and upper body in a halo of blue. The flute case clutched in his hand matched his wings, and Nanceen had a surprising flash of vision. Korin with a circlet of twined silver and gold gracing his brow, a similar torque caressing the column of his neck, a scepter cradled in his arms.

Nanceen shook her head and blinked to clear her vision. Once again, her Korin stood before her. The wings retracted slightly to lay flat against his back. Even that simple movement created a remarkable transformation.

"Now what?" Korin asked as he spread his hands. "How do we--"

"Just who the hell is this guy?"

CHAPTER FOURTEEN

K orin and Nanceen turned toward the force of Jayse's voice. He stood, arms crossed, barely within the clearing. Lara and Iain crowded behind him in the passageway. "Or a better question--what the hell is this guy?"

"Jayse, I..." Searching for words of explanation, Nanceen stammered. Korin's shoulders slumped and he stared at his toes. She took his hand and gave a tight squeeze.

"He is of the fairy world, Jayse." Iain's deep whisper carried through the silence of the moment.

Jayse whirled to face Iain. "He's not from the Otherworld. There's no winged people there."

"I dinna say he was of our world. Ye ken, there are many worlds beyond this human world and our Otherworld. Both races have memories of the wee folk. Of fairies."

A sarcastic bark of laughter erupted from between Jayse's lips. "He ain't no wee folk, Iain. Look at him." Jayse took a step toward Korin, but the pressure of Iain's hand on his upper arm stopped him with a jerk. "Let go, Iain."

"Nae until ye calm down." Iain flashed a reassuring smile at Nanceen. "He is what he is. Arguin' about it is a waste of time."

"But, what about Nanceen?"

"Yes, what about Nanceen?" Anger flared through her, and only Korin's hand in hers kept her from marching forward and slapping her nephew. He must have recognized her anger, for Jayse took a half step back and lifted one hand in supplication.

Lara stepped around Iain and wrapped her fist in the front of Jayse's shirt. "Jaysson Allen Zeroun. Who do you think you are, questioning Nanceen's judgment? Who do you think you are to doubt someone of fey blood? Most people, even those at the faire, don't really believe in mythical creatures." She lifted her fist higher and Jayse followed to stand on the tips of his toes. "Now, you apologize. Why should the fact he has wings make him any different than the man you created music with just a little while ago?"

Using her free hand, Lara thumped the leather case protecting Jayse's bodhran. "You are part Faerie. Korin is just of another bloodline."

Korin glanced at Nanceen and cleared his throat. "I am Korin, of the family Goodfellow."

Eyebrows scrunched low over his eyes, Jayse looked confused for a moment then a deep frown cast his expression in disbelief. "Goodfellow? As in Robin Goodfellow? As in Puck?"

"Ah." Korin smiled. "You know of my ancestor."

Shrugging out of Lara's grasp, Jayse pushed past his sister and pointed an accusing finger in Korin's face. "Now I know you're a phony. Puck is only a character in a play."

"Yes, the Bard immortalized him. But he was a true being, ancient long before the Bard grew to manhood."

"I don't believe this." Jayse turned away.

Nanceen stomped her foot. "And I don't understand you, Nephew."

"Aw, Nance. I'm just trying--"

"Yes, you're trying all right. Now, we've got to figure out how to get out of here without causing Korin any more trauma."

Eyes downcast, Jayse remained silent. A disapproving cant tugged at his lips.

"We'll just have to walk out of here," Lara stated. "And hope that since so many visitors here also wore wings..." She let the words die away and glanced at the restless movement of Korin's wings. "But, none like that. This may take a miracle."

"Then, a miracle ye shall have, sweet." Iain gestured toward the narrow passageway.

A tight knot of misgiving danced in her belly. Nanceen started forward, Korin followed and, after long moments of hesitation, Jayse trailed the group through the passage and out into the throng of Faire participants.

With Lara, Iain, and Nanceen flanking Korin, and Jayse moping behind, they moved quickly through the crowds. Gasps and whispers surrounded them, but no one seemed alarmed by Korin's appearance. Even though he kept his wings tightly folded against his back, they couldn't be totally hidden.

A middle-aged woman, dressed as a peasant with tiny, rounded wings sewn to her bodice, stepped close enough to halt their forward progress.

"I'm sorry to bother you, but his wings..." She leaned sideways to peer closer at Korin's back. "They're beautiful. May I...may I touch them?"

Nanceen drew a breath to rudely deny the woman and push past her, dragging Korin with her, but Korin's soft response halted her.

"Of course."

Jealousy reared its ugly head when the woman ran her fingertips over the edge of the wing Korin extended toward her. Nanceen frowned. She should be the one touching the wing, caressing it. Her fingers twitched. Damn it, she wanted to know what he felt like, too.

"Oooh, it's soft." The woman squealed when the wing unfurled. "Oh, my God. How beautiful." Tearing her gaze away, she stared into Korin's face. "How did you make these? How do they move?"

A few more people had clustered around, and many reached out to touch Korin's wings. Nanceen wanted to push them all away, but forced a smile and pleasant response when rare comments were made in her direction.

When she could stand it no longer, she clutched at Korin's arm and leaned close to his ear. "Doesn't it hurt to have those people touching you?"

"No." He wiggled his shoulders. "Actually, it tickles."

Looking around helplessly, Nanceen wished for some intervention--anything. She didn't think she could deal with any more questions. Or any more women caressing Korin.

As if in answer to her wishes, Jayse joined them and waved to shoo the crowd away. "I'm sorry, folks. Our winged friend here needs to leave. He thanks you for your interest."

"But, how does he get the wings to move?" a tall man called. "What material are they made of?"

Jayse waggled one finger back and forth. "Nuh uh, can't tell you trade secrets. Let it suffice to say, today was an experiment. When working with special effects for movies…"

A soft clamor broke out, and the mention of movies drew the interest away from Korin's wings.

Jayse grinned at the cluster of people. "Now, I'm sure you realize I can't say any more than that. This current project is under the strictest security. You wouldn't believe the hoops we had to jump through just to try out these wings today. I'd lose my job in a heartbeat if I said anything else."

He turned to Korin and winked. "Looks like the design's a success. We'd better get this prototype back to the studio." He wrapped one arm around Korin's shoulders, shoved his drum into Nanceen's hands, then snaked his free arm around her shoulders.

Herding the group away, he bent his head and stared at the ground before him. "I'm really sorry, Nance. Korin. I have no idea what got into me."

"I'm sure the sight of my wings shocked you." Korin chuckled. "I can only imagine… I understand."

Nanceen wasn't sure she was ready to forgive her nephew yet, so she folded her arms around the drum and remained silent. Lara stepped forward and turned halfway to sidestep next to Nanceen.

"Come on, Nance. No harm was done. You know Jayse."

Sighing, Nanceen nodded. "Yes, I know. But that doesn't excuse the fact he insulted Korin by not believing."

Korin cleared his throat. "It was not that long ago--days only--that you refused to believe the truth of my origins. Or the shared past of fairy and gentry."

Heat burned from one cheek, across her nose, and onto the other side of her face.

Jayse chuckled. "Then, am I forgiven, dear Aunt?"

Nanceen nodded.

Jayse turned his gaze to Korin. "What is this gentry you speak of?"

They neared the narrow exit from the Faire, but their progress halted when a troop of dancers surrounded them. Dressed in flowing costumes and translucent wings, the dancers pranced, leapt, and twirled in a patch of sunlight. Each dancer carried a harp-shaped frame filled with tiny bells. They danced to the sounds of the bells, for no other music moved them.

Held captive for a few moments as the dancers performed, the group waited. Korin grinned in delight. Nanceen watched him. Was the only thing keeping him from joining the dancers Jayse's arm about his shoulders?

A sudden flash of emotion crossed Korin's face, and he clutched the small bag at his side. His eyes widened, then closed as if in relief. Nanceen took a breath to speak as the dancers moved on to another clearing and another dance.

"So," Jayse continued as if he had not been interrupted, "what are gentry?"

Iain led them through the exit and spoke back over his shoulder. "I have a feelin' this may be a tale long in the tellin'. We shall find one of those wonderful drive-ins, gather some refreshment, and find a quiet place to speak on it. Agreed?"

Korin's expression became wistful. "I'd truly appreciate a glass of milk."

· · ·

Titus watched the dancers, following them through the Faire until he believed it safe to leave. He had no wish to encounter any of the group he had studied throughout the long day. Not yet. As he stepped carefully across the muddy, rutted parking area, his mind wandered pleasantly.

His business plans had advanced well, and soon he would open his doors and face the competition. A pleased smile stretched his lips. Ah, the competition. Bit by bit he would destroy the company, then... then he would destroy the owner as well. And all that he loved.

He climbed into his sleek, black Pantera, changed the angle of the seat to lean further back and with the soft purr of the engine, pulled out on the road. Deciding against the interstate, he took a winding, old two-lane highway. Although the driving conditions and traffic forced him to a slower speed than he normally drove, he enjoyed the blast of wind coming through the open windows to blow the hair back from his face.

He ignored the scenery flying by and let his mind move past his plans of business takeover to consider the man who had sprouted wings. Even with dulled senses, he knew the wings were no trick, no supposed Hollywood mystique. But how they came to be... he shrugged and adjusted his sunglasses. It wasn't important.

Titus relaxed into the car's soft, buttery leather seat and laughed as bugs splattered the windshield.

A van parked in one of the old picnic areas along the highway jerked his attention from the road. He sat up straight and tapped the brake to slow his vehicle. He stared at the group clustered around a rickety, weathered picnic table.

Then, with a slow smile, he pressed on the gas and roared down the highway.

CHAPTER FIFTEEN

Lowering the third small carton, Korin cast the others a sheepish grin, "Milk is a favorite of mine."

"As we have noticed. 'Tis small wonder the wee folk clamor after the bowls once left by believers." Iain chuckled. "But, I fear we shall ne're find a drive-through with honey cakes."

Korin lifted a French fry. "These will do." He sucked the thin potato stick into his mouth and chewed with his eyes closed. When he opened his eyes, he discovered he was the focus of attention. "Oh, I..."

"That's okay." Nanceen grinned. "You've never tasted human food before, have you?"

He shook his head and popped another fry, drenched in ketchup, into his mouth. Wiping the corner of his lips with a paper napkin, Korin took a deep breath and turned his head toward Jayse.

The roar of a sports car streaking down the highway interrupted him and he peered after the retreating auto. A faint concern, like a tiny voice whispering from another room, made him pause. Then, the concern was gone, blown away like the dust of the car's passing. He turned again toward Jayse.

"You asked me about the gentry. You know of the Bard, and

his tale of a dream in midsummer." Korin's soft statement was met with a round of nods.

After a long swallow of soda, Jayse chuckled. "It's almost a family compulsion. We've seen every production of the play that comes even close to the city."

Cupping his cheek in one hand, Korin leaned on the table and glanced at the intriguing patchwork of tilled land along the highway. "And, why do you think that is?" he asked.

Jayse's eyes widened and followed Korin's stare into the distance. "I never thought about it. I suppose, for whatever reason, because it's Dad and Mom's favorite."

"I have long believed we should pay attention to what we're really interested in," Lara said slowly, as if contemplating each word with care. "Like, if you're really fascinated by a certain period in history, maybe you lived during that time." She shrugged. "Of course, you'd have to believe in reincarnation for that to happen."

Korin nodded. "Exactly. Or perhaps, we contain special memories of the past, memories of our clans and races."

"Race memories?" Jayse leaned back and shook his head. "That's just a theory."

"And we are creatures who don't exist." Silently, Korin looked at each of his friends. Realization dawned in each face.

Jayse was the first to speak. "It's not just a theory, then?"

"I don't know, but it is interesting, is it not? I have memories of happenings long before I came into the fairy world. Mundane memories that would not have come from tales or family stories. And there are dark spots, places where I have no idea what may have happened. Places I long to understand. But now, to tell you of the gentry, I must tell you some of this history. And you shall see how we relate to the Bard's tale."

"How can that be?" Lara asked.

Iain took her hand. "Why d'ye question, sweet? Much of yer life, of our life together, our love..." He paused to kiss her fingertips. "Is fact to us, fantasy to others."

Korin experienced an uncomfortable flare of heated jealousy.

Not because Iain loved Lara almost beyond reason, but that he was not allowed to love his Nanceen in the same way. He glanced at his hands. Watching Iain was like watching himself in a reflective surface--knowing if he could, his eyes would speak the same love and devotion.

Instead, Korin wadded the paper envelope from his fries and tossed it into the bag designated for trash. "As I have said, this tale, this history, takes place long before the Bard's tale. How he came to know of it may always be a mystery. The time of the tale was, however, not long after humans became the creatures they are now.

"At that time, fairy and gentry lived as one kingdom, ruled by the fair and loving hands of Oberon and Titania. Granted, the Bard was correct in telling of their occasional separations and their squabbles over the rare changeling child.

"During those long ages of rule, the king sired a multitude of children. Those whom his queen bore scattered to form kingdoms of their own. In these ages past, many have been forgotten. Of the children sired on other beings, little is known, although it has been rumored Oberon was obsessed with his children, and had records kept of each. Long ago, those records, if they ever really existed, were lost.

"Oberon and Titania tired of this world and longed for peace from the fighting between fairy, gentry and human. So, they decided to pass into another world, one unbounded by your Otherworld or the human world.

"Your gentry Otherworld remained divided among their progeny, who grew even further apart.

"Oberon had long pondered the problem of the multitudes of the wee folk." Korin paused with a grimace of disgust. "The wee folk encompass a vast variety of beings and races--from leprechauns and brownies to the bean sidhe who ride the air and mourn the passing of humans. Those who are true fairy are but a small group." Korin's disgust turned to a grin when chuckles rose at his unintentional choice of words.

"Korin?" Jayse managed a serious expression as he leaned to peer under the table to look Korin over from head to toe. "Small?"

"I'm afraid I can become defensive at times. Even within my world, the king finds reason to demean fairies."

Jayse grew serious as well. "A problem in the human world as well, although the meaning of fairy is different."

For some inexplicable reason, Nanceen had a strong urge to defend Korin. No one at the table had said or done anything to cause such a need. Except Korin. She peered at Korin from under her lashes.

He seemed self-assured, although amazed and innocent of the ways of the human world. However, Nanceen thought she saw-- deeply hidden in the depths of his eyes--the lingering pain of insecurity. She didn't know how to deal with what she saw. Maybe, if he finished his explanation, she'd find some clue.

So, what happened to the others--those not of the gentry?" she asked.

Jayse interrupted and stopped Korin's speech before it started. "You've never said exactly who the gentry were."

"Ah, the gentry. These beautiful beings were once welcomed in the human world, honored for their wisdom, sought after for healing. But, as human beliefs changed, the gentry were forced to the Otherworld, with only a few portals remaining to those who chose to believe the old ways.

"The sidhe, elves, Tuatha de Danann, the Fair Folk, Them who be, Faerie. These and others are gentry. You are the gentry."

Nanceen grinned at Jayse's stunned and puzzled reaction. "That's where our clan comes from?"

Nodding, Korin spread his hands. "The gentry of your Other-world, of Faerie, descended from that time of sadness-- when Oberon and Titania chose to leave us.

"However, they did not leave us ungoverned. Oberon chose a successor, named the one to rule after him. But who that was, even which fairy race he belonged to, is not remembered."

"How can that be?" Nanceen's senses tingled as if she were finally beginning to understand Korin's deep, innate sadness.

"Shortly after the pronouncement was made, Oberon took the hand of his fair wife and, using a magic never before displayed, opened a strange and terrifying portal. With a sad wave of farewell, they stepped together through that void. None knows where they went. Or if they succeeded in finding the peace they sought."

"That's..." Tears stung the back of Nanceen's eyes. How could she feel so strongly about so few words of an amazing story? She glanced at Lara, who was swiping away the trail of a single tear. Perhaps what Korin said about race memories was true.

Korin wiped an errant tear from Nanceen's cheek with the corner of a paper napkin. "Although most gentry do not remember the passage, or even think there could be such a happening, it affects us all, even now.

"I don't know how or why, but the one chosen to lead the wee folk..." Korin grimaced again. "Made a bet with a Fir Dhaerrig."

"What's that?" Jayse asked.

"A Fir Dhaerrig is a mean spirited creature. Small like I am, naturally, but without wings. He usually wears a red coat, so some call him The Red Man. I, however, prefer one of his other names. Rat Man is more appropriate, considering his long nose and beady eyes. But he is my king. I, and others, must do as he commands."

Korin paused and gave a sad look to those around the table. "As he commands," he muttered.

Moving his fingers as if ticking off fine points of Korin's tale, Jayse was silent a moment before asking, "If the Fir Dhaerrig took the rule from another, couldn't that happen again?"

Korin shook his head. "Many of the folk of my fairy world have either become complacent or wish no conflict. Others are solitary, often the last of their kind." The faint echoes of Peg- leg Jack's mirthless laughter caused an ache in the center of Korin's back. He unfurled his wings slightly and let the soft breeze cool his burning skin.

"Korin, be careful," Nanceen hissed.

"Aw, Nance. There's no one on the road right now." Jayse's

reprimand was met with a glare from Nanceen and a thankful nod from Korin. "Is it uncomfortable for you to keep your wings tight against your body like that?"

"No. Most humans probably consider a fairy's wings to be stiff, like a dragonfly's. Happily, since there are times when they are cumbersome..." The faint burning moved from his back to his face and Korin watched as an answering pink blush covered Nanceen's cheeks. Ah, so her thoughts ran with his. He tried to clear the rough, dry spot from his throat. "I am able to fold them out of the way. Or, I am able to spread them wide, so they lay nearly flat. It would be the only way I could lay on my back, if I so desired." The heat burned his face.

Iain chuckled. "We dinna need to see that trick here. Best we be goin'. 'Tis been a long, tirin' day, and I fear our wee bairns will be drivin' their gran and granda wild." He angled his arms high over his head in a languorous stretch. "I dinna think I care to be drivin'."

Lara took his hand when one arm came down about her shoulders. "Good."

Leaning over the table, Korin stared at the van and sighed. "Someday, I would like to try this driving. I can only imagine the feeling of movement, of power."

"Aye, 'tis all that." Iain glanced sideways at Lara. "What say ye, sweet? Shall we let him try?"

Eyebrows lifted in hopeful question, Korin sat straight and waited. What an adventure...

Lara sighed like a long-suffering wife, but grinned at Korin. "Only if Jayse sits in the copilot seat and teaches him." She curled her fingers and stretched them slowly. "I don't want to have to replace the armrest, or dig any more stuffing out from under my nails."

Once Jayse had explained the mechanics of the steering system and how to increase speed--and stop--Korin tightened the belt across his lap, glanced into the rearview mirror at Nanceen's worried expression, and pulled slowly onto the highway.

• • •

"No. Arrrgh. It cannot be."

A brownie, kneeling before the throne, shivered and backed into a far corner. He curled into a tight ball. "Tha' be wha' happin', sire,' he squeaked.

The Fir Dhaerrig pointed to the wide doorway. "Out! Get out!" He glared at the brownie as the hapless creature scooted from the throne room.

Alone, the king gave into his anger and frustration. Shining spheres popped into being in his palms, and he dashed them to the floor. As the crystal shards scattered before his kicking, stomping feet, he cursed as only a thwarted fairy could curse.

When the string of curses came to an end and the pile of shattered baubles clinked around his ankles, the Fir Dhaerrig returned to his throne and threw himself into the seat. Leaning forward, he cupped his face in his dirty hands and narrowed his gaze to stare unseeing into the distance.

How had Korin done it? Already, three of the conditions had been met, and in only as many days. The king kicked his feet and pounded the arms of the throne with his fists. A scream of rage hovered in the back of his throat, but he swallowed it back. It would do no good to vent his anger on the thin air. He needed a new plan. But what?

He closed his eyes and rested against the carved backrest of his throne. Ah, the throne, what a prize it had been for his ancestor. And now, it was his. No upstart fairy with delusions of once again joining fairy with the gentry would take it from him. So long ago, when the gentry faded to their own worlds, his ancestor had tricked the chosen king.

Satisfaction pulled his crooked mouth into a smile. If the first ruler, the ancient rat man, could trick a foolish fairy and forever rule, dealing with this--problem--should be easy.

The Fir Dhaerrig ran a thumb over the sharp points of his upper teeth and tapped a ragged nail against them. There was a plan to be found somewhere. And find it he would. Korin would never fulfill the remaining challenges. Not and live.

. . .

Exhilaration. Speed. Ah, it was nearly as wonderful as flight. Laughing after he pulled in to the parking lot of Jayse's apartment building, Korin put the vehicle in park and turned in his seat to face the rear of the van. "Are your fingers intact, Lara?"

She wiggled the digits in the air. "Didn't even have to chew off the nails."

Jayse opened his door, stretched as he slid from the seat, and turned to open the side door for the rest. "I really need some heavy exercise after that long ride. I think I'll head over to Faerie, see if I can find Macaire and do some training." He helped Nanceen fight with her long skirts as she climbed from the van. "Wanna go back with me?"

Korin's heart lurched to a painful stop. Weakened by the day's forced transformation, he feared he would be even further weakened and helpless by the simple process of walking through a gentry portal. However, he could return to his small size and slip easily through the fabric between the worlds.

An even stronger fear surfaced, and he turned away from the van to hide his reaction. If he returned to a small size, would the king somehow prevent him from regaining human size? Even though the Fachan had spoken the words to return his wings, the king was sure to be behind the malevolent action.

During the drive back to the city, Korin had tried to find the magic within him to once again hide his wings. The ability was gone. Disappeared as easily as smoke faded away on a breeze. So, he would deal with the wings. Unfortunately, he would no longer be able to move freely through the human world.

Perhaps a night's rest would strengthen him enough to endure the portal. And perhaps, when he returned to a magical world, his magic would also return. He sighed and tried to compose his face into a neutral smile. There were too many perhaps in his life.

Nanceen was speaking as he turned back. "...just stay here."

"In that case, Auntie 'Ceen, why don't you guys stay at my apartment again? Only this time, go ahead and sleep in the bed. I won't be back tonight. I seem to remember there is to be a hunt tonight."

"A hunt?" Iain's tired face brightened and he turned to Lara. "Sweet?"

"Go ahead and go with Jayse." Lara chuckled. "I'll take the kids home and see you in the morning."

Iain pulled Lara into a tight hug and kissed her soundly. Laughing, she wiggled free and pushed him toward her brother. "Just bring him home in one piece."

Korin wasn't sure if she was speaking to her brother or her husband, but both laughed and promised to return safely. He'd watched the Faerie hunts from afar, but now that he'd driven, he found no interest in the wild ride on horseback. And Jayse leaving for Faerie solved one of his problems.

Lara squeezed Nanceen's hand and headed around the van to the driver's side. Jayse dug through the pile of discarded clothing in his arms, finally pulling out a key chain. He handed it to Nanceen, then piled the clothing in her arms as well. "Will you take these up with you? I'll ride over to Mom's with Lara and use the portal there."

Wrapping his arm around Nanceen's shoulders, Korin tugged her tightly against his side. "I thank you for your hospitality, Jayse. And your help throughout this day."

"Yeah, after I lost my stupid, protective, macho attitude, huh?" With a sudden change of expression, he dug around in the back of the van and brought out the rounded drum case and the slim form of Korin's pipe. "Don't forget these. Would you take the bodhran up for me?"

"Of course. Enjoy the hunt." Korin followed Nanceen's lead and waved as the van pulled away.

Nanceen welcomed the weight of Korin's arm around her shoulder and wished she could circle his waist with her arm. But the load Jayse had dumped in her hands, and concern for Korin's wings, kept her arms before her. She looked at Korin. He grinned,

but did not turn his gaze to hers until the van was out of sight.
Then, he ducked his head and pressed a quick kiss against her
lips.

"Shall we go in? Do you think he has any milk?"

A tangle of worry lifted from Nanceen and she smiled. The
kiss had made her lips tingle and chasing the feeling, she wet her
lips. Korin stiffened, and his breathing changed subtly. The
depths of his eyes grew darker, filling her with such a rush of
promise she nearly dropped her bundle and lunged against him.

"Shall we go in?" he asked again.

"Yes." It was more than agreement. It was a single word in
which she returned the promise to him. But, this night, this night
she would be the giver. If he would not, or could not join with her,
she would still bring him pleasure such as he gave her. A wicked
thought flitted into her mind. And if Jayse did indeed have milk...

Thinking some energy would be a good thing for the night,
Nanceen found ingredients for a mandarin chicken salad tucked
in Jayse's refrigerator. However, she only allowed Korin one glass
from the fresh container of milk. She had plans, and she was
going to stick with them.

As Korin relaxed, so did his wings, and they unfurled from the
tight press against his back. The lines of strain that had formed
around his eyes lessened, and the twinkle returned to the silvery
depths. She literally ached with the desire to touch the wings, but
other than a brief brush against them as she moved around the
kitchen, she did not, for she didn't know how Korin would react
to that touch.

After they ate, she suggested seeing if there was an interesting
movie in Jayse's vast collection. Amused, she watched Korin
peruse the titles, and pick up an occasional plastic case to read
the blurb. From the jerk of his shoulders and the slow movements
as he reached for a movie, she knew he had chosen. And she had a
good idea what they would be putting in the player.

"There is truly a movie of the Bard's words?"

"Yes. In fact, many of his works have been made into movies."
Nanceen bit her lip to keep from chuckling at the astonished lift of

his fair eyebrows. She held out her hand for the movie as she rose from the couch. Korin placed it reverently in her hand and backed away.

She turned on the television, tucked the movie into the player, and gave Korin instructions. "Sit there on the couch. It's the best place to see. And go ahead and turn all the lights off. The light from the hallway will be enough. I'll adjust the sound after the movie starts."

The play light blinked, and she pressed the control button. Nanceen returned to the couch and curled into one corner so she could watch both the movie and Korin. A faint pout pulled at his sensitive lips when she didn't sit next to him, but as soon as the music began, his attention was lost in Shakespeare's dream.

CHAPTER SIXTEEN

D uring the course of the movie, Korin moved closer to
Nanceen. Although his attention seldom wavered
from the television, Nanceen cherished and delighted
in the closeness. By the time the ending speeches were said, Korin
lay with his head on her lap. She stroked his hair and let her
fingers linger in the silky strands.

"That was truly amazing. The actor portrayed the Puck much
as the tales are told of him."

"There have been many productions of the play, and even
though every actor brings his own idea to the part, most are quite
similar. Maybe it's how humans imagine fairies to be."

"Or, mayhaps, this human ideal comes from the true behavior
of fairies." Korin closed his eyes as Nanceen stroked her fingers
over his light eyebrows. "That's nice. Will you do it again?"

A smile tugged at Nanceen's lips and she ran her fingertips
over the smooth angles of his face and along the thick fringe of his
lashes. This was what she wanted. After giving his face loving
attention, she slid her hand over his shoulder, rubbing softly.

"Umm." Korin turned slightly, angling his shoulders to allow
her free access. He curled one hand under his cheek and over her
thigh. "Good."

The time since Korin's wings reappeared seemed days long to Nanceen. How long had her fingers ached to touch the shimmering blue and discover the true texture? This time she could indulge herself. Hesitating only a moment, she lifted her hand and carefully touched the edge of a wing.

Soft as a baby's powdered skin, yet not powdery, the wing surprised her. She stroked the smooth texture. She didn't know what she had expected, but this wasn't it. The wing was far from the fragile butterfly texture, nor was it leathery as a bat's wing might be.

The edge of the wing curled around her finger and she gasped. A repeat of the sensual caress lifted goose bumps along her arms. She glanced down at Korin's face. His eyes were closed, but his lips formed a mischievous, knowing smile.

Was the area where his wings grew from his body still sensitive? She trailed her fingers over the blue and silver span of the wing and through the slit in his shirt. When her hand made contact with the skin at the base of the wing, she jerked her fingers away. The skin burned hot.

A brief memory flashed through her mind of a time when Bryce was a baby, and had become ill. She had sneaked into his room and touched his tiny belly. Barely six years old herself, she had cried at the dry heat wracking the body of the baby Lara brought back from a trip through time. Somehow, she had known how dangerous the fever was, and how ill the small boy had become. In fact, he had barely survived those first few days.

Was Korin ill? Would he--die? The suddenness of the frightening thought brought another sharp gasp to her lips.

"Endearment?" Korin moved from under her hands, turned slightly and rose to his hands and knees on the couch. Inches from hers, his eyes were filled with questions--not with the haze of fever and illness. She lifted her hand to touch his cheek. It was warm, but only from where he had lain against her thigh. "Nanceen, what's wrong?"

"Your skin, your back--is so hot. I was afraid... afraid you were ill."

A sad, crooked grin only partly eased her concerns. "No, I am not ill. I believe the heat remains from the return of my wings." He unfurled his wings to their fullest, let them flutter down close to his back, then ease into their partially closed position. "I don't feel any abnormal heat."

"But, your skin between your wings is burning. Almost like a bad sunburn."

"If I burn, endearment, it is for other reasons."

Oh, how she understood those reasons. Her entire being burned with desire. The desire to join completely with Korin. But later, when he was ready. Tonight, she would continue with her hastily formed plan.

Before she could take action, Korin leaned toward her and captured her lips in a gentle kiss. As his lips moved over and with hers, a burn of determination replaced the heat of embarrassment. Twisting slightly, she broke the delightful contact with Korin's searching mouth, smiled softly and rested her palm against his cheek.

"Come to bed with me."

The pain filling Korin's expression at her words nearly broke her resolve. Instead, she spoke quickly, both to convince him-- and herself. "I know there must be some prohibition against... against..." She bit at her lip and tried again. "I won't do anything you don't want me to. I promise. But please, please Korin. Let me try to return some of the pleasure you gave me last night."

Korin sat back on his calves. "You do please me, endearment. Ah, my Nanceen, so well do you please me." He took her hand, lifted it to his mouth and sucked the tip of one finger into the warmth. Releasing her fingers, he whispered, "If that is what you want."

"I do, Korin." Rising, she returned her hand to the strength of his fingers and tugged until he rose and followed her. She felt a slight twinge of guilt as she thought of her plans to make use of her nephew's bed. A deep breath calmed her. Jayse had offered...

Jayse's bedroom was small, and the large, high bed filled most of the space. Korin held back in the doorway. A border of thin, intricate knots topped the walls, and a single, elaborate knot painted on the wall served as a headboard for the otherwise simple bed. He let his jaw drop. "Beautiful."

A nervous giggle preceded Nanceen's words. "It is. Allyn, Jayse's mother, is an artist who specializes in knot designs. It's how my brother met her. She's done at least one room in everyone's home." A faint pink touched the crest of her cheeks. "Usually, the bedrooms."

"I am honored to view such a wonder."

The intensity of Nanceen's gaze upon him had Korin looking away from the beautiful designs and into her dark brown eyes. A slight frown darkened her expression until she blinked. The frown was gone. "You're serious?"

"How could I not be, when faced with genius such as this?" Korin swept his arm from side to side to indicate the room. "This is as the world should be, any world. A haven of peace and beauty. A place of safety." As he spoke the words, he understood the truth of his speech. Whether there was magic in the knotted designs, or simply the magic of his gentry maid, he would be safe here. No tricks of the Fir Dhaerrig could touch him here.

Nanceen's throaty laugh sent shivers of anticipation coursing over him. "So, you think you'll be safe here?"

"With you. Yes."

Her eyebrows lifted and she took half a step back to stare intently at him. "I'm not so sure, Korin. We shall see."

She moved in front of him, wrapped her arms around his neck, and pressed tight against him. The longing he'd buried so carefully sprung to life in full, painful force. As did the physical evidence of that longing. When he gasped, Nanceen held him tighter and offered him her mouth.

Gladly he took her offering, but let her direct the kiss. Moving from sweet and tentative to possessive and fiery in the passing of a heartbeat, the kiss made him gasp again. Nanceen took his breath into her mouth, heated it, and returned it to him.

But when her hands moved from the back of his neck and across his shoulders to the edges of his wings he nearly collapsed from the sheer glory of the torment. Only the movement of her lips against him and the way her fingers sketched patterns over his wings kept him upright.

His lips trembled, cold and empty when she broke the kiss and pulled back. "Come to bed with me." Her words were airy, breathless. All he could find the strength to do was nod.

Walking backwards and taking him with her, Nanceen drew him toward the bed. Korin ached, longed, fought with himself not to take control and love her as he had the night before--and more. "But..."

"Don't worry," she whispered close to his ear. "I promise not to do more than you wish me to. Not that I don't want to." Her voice dropped lower until he wasn't sure if he heard, or only felt the words.

She kissed him again and traced his lower lip with her tongue before dancing it into his mouth. The thrust of her satiny heat pulled a corresponding movement from his hips. She sighed. Her hands slid slowly down his sides until she grasped his hips and held him firmly against her. They groaned together at the capture of the expanding length of his desire between them.

"Will you take off your shirt?"

"Yes." And anything else she wished. Unwilling to let even a breath of air between their bodies, Korin eased back to shrug out of his loose tunic.

"Uh, how do you get it off over your wings?"

His harsh chuckle brought a new light to her eyes. He wanted to explore the meaning and the emotions behind that expression, but had promised himself that this was her night. Mayhaps, should all go well, he would have a long Otherworld lifetime in which to discover that--and more--about her.

Korin half-turned from her while keeping his gaze locked with hers. "Watch, endearment, and see." With only a brief thought, his wings curled inward. The fuller tops curved down slightly. He was then able to easily slip the tunic from his body. It fell to a rumpled heap at his feet.

Nanceen reached for the small leather bag tied at his waist, but he stopped her hands and shook his head. He quickly untied the strings and laid the bag carefully on a narrow bedside table. Then, he spread his hands and turned back to her. Expectation trembled through him.

She pointed to the bed. "Will you lay on your stomach? This has been a stress filled day, so I thought I might give you a real back rub."

Ah, another new experience. Fairies seldom touched the backs of their partners, and rarely caressed another's wings. His mind worked feverishly, imagining what a delight it could be to have Nanceen's hands against his bare skin. The simple strokes of her fingers on his wings had already nearly driven him mad. Withholding a shudder so filled with emotion he thought he'd collapse into a quivering mass, he crawled onto the bed, dug his hands under a thick pillow, and rested his cheek against the cool, cotton material.

Nanceen followed him onto the resilient surface and straddled his hips. Korin turned his face into the pillow to stifle the groan he could no longer deny. Only one thought filled his mind-- turning to his back and burying himself in the sweet heat now pressing against his buttocks. The thoughts and the tactile sensations were exquisite torture.

"Can you spread your wings, so they go out to the sides? It will be easier for me to reach your back." Did he imagine it, or was there a catch in Nanceen's voice, a huskiness not present only moments ago? He did as she asked and held his breath. Waiting.

At the first touch of her hands on his shoulders, the air whooshed from his lungs in a rush of delight. His hips lifted from the bed, pressing tighter against Nanceen.

She giggled and rubbed against his buttocks as if settling herself more comfortably. Her weight, forcing his firm length into the mattress, intensified the torture. "Endearment," he groaned.

With only the sound of their shortened breaths filling the room, Nanceen leaned onto her hands and began a slow, deep massage. Her nimble fingers kneaded, coaxed, and loosened the tight muscles of his upper back. She worked the small of his back

and ran her hands low along his hips, curling the tips of her
fingers under the waistband of his breeches. She caressed his
sides with long, sure strokes that reached under the spread of his
wings.

It was glorious. It was torment. He didn't ever want it to end.
Yet, there was a missing piece to her touch, an emptiness that
begged to be filled. Korin arched his back as her hands skimmed
his skin.

"Oh, Korin," she gasped. The trill in her voice confirmed she
was aroused as well.

Then she touched him in a place no other before had touched
him. A spot that sent shards of agony and ecstasy through his
blood stream, heating and freezing him both.

Her palms lingered at the exact center of his back. Her fingers
splayed so they touched the places where his skin turned into the
fabric of his wings. A place so sensitive, so erotic...

His wings lifted stiffly from the bed and curled back. Nanceen
leaned forward to replace the touch of her hands with the caress
of her lips. His wings flowed over her, encased her, touched and
caressed her as she lay along his back.

"Oh, yes," she purred. The hot, hot tip of her tongue traced the
juncture of wing to back. Korin fought to remain still, but his
wings quivered and trembled as violently as his body.

She sucked a tiny bit of the juncture into her mouth. His body
jerked and arched high off the bed. The pull of her suckling made
his wings convulse even more tightly around her. Crushing the
pillow to his chest, Korin threw his head back and let the weight
of Nanceen's hips press his loins tight against the bed. The
achingly soft cry of her name echoed in the quiet room.

The soft cocoon of dark wings held Nanceen and she smiled
against Korin's heated skin. A light sheen of sweat covered his
back and she inhaled deeply, taking in the rich, earthy, masculine
musk of his release. She eased her hands around his waist and
hugged him tightly.

A tremor ran through the wings that surrounded her and they
eased open. The air was cool and she missed the security of his

unusual embrace. When his wings were out of the way, Korin rolled to his side, angled her, and molded her to him. Then he rolled to his back and held Nanceen tightly to his side. He blew out one long, slow breath.

"I'm sorry, I didn't even let you take your pants off." Nanceen sighed, then giggled.

"It doesn't matter, endearment. Perhaps..." He took her hand and by holding his palm flat against the back of her hand, pressed her palm against the rise below his waist. "...soon."

She cupped her hand over him. The fact he was aroused again so soon gave her a rush of sensual power. She was ready as well and stroked the firm bulge under her hand. The feel of him was... dry. Surprised, she jerked her hand away. "Korin? I thought you... I mean, the way you..."

He cradled her face between his palms and gazed into her eyes. The confusion in the silvery shadows of his eyes faded slowly and he gave her a soft smile. Keeping one palm against her cheek, he used his other hand to return her hand to his groin. He moved her palm slowly up the ridge of his erection, then tucked her fingers under the waist of his breeches. His hips bucked once when she slipped her hand under the material and filled her hand with him.

"Yes, endearment. I have heard a phrase used by humans, although I long discounted the possibilities. So, yes Nanceen, the earth moved for me." The sound of his chuckle was loud, rough, and choked off suddenly. "The pleasure was... intense."

"But, shouldn't there be some evidence?" Her face burned. "Unless fairy males are different than humans or Fae--gentry."

"There is no difference." Korin tugged on her shoulder until she turned toward him. Then, he grasped her hips, held the hand caressing his length captured between them, and rotated his hips. He could not hold back his low, needy moan. "For how else could the races mix, and children be born?"

Nanceen countered the movement of his hips with firm caresses of her hand. She panted, she wanted him, and she didn't care about prohibitions. But, if this was all she could have... She squeezed her fingers tight around him.

"I can do no more, endearment. Not yet."

She loosened her fingers just enough for his length to slide against her palm. Two quick tugs on the front of his breeches freed his erection. Allowing herself a delighted sigh, Nanceen wrapped him in her hands' embrace. Rhythmic contractions of her fingers played along the satiny skin. Korin gasped, clutched at her hips, and thrust hard into her hand.

Nanceen altered her grip so her thumb touched the damp tip. The tiny bit of moisture was slick, heated, and she spread it down his length. This was a pure, male response, one Korin could not hide nor deny. So she encircled him, listened to the sounds of his abandoned thrusting, and watched his face.

Korin's eyes were tightly closed. His head shook slowly back and forth as if he denied the primal actions of his body. Sharp points of desire surrounded his fingers where they pressed into her hips and buttocks. Small spasms kept her tightly against him. Nanceen freed one hand, stretched to reach around him, and touched the place on his back that had first brought him so much joy.

His cry was low, harsh, guttural. The length in her hand throbbed, expanded, and pulsed to the beat of her heart. Korin grew rigid. With a sharp thrust, he called her name, then relaxed against the pillows. His eyelids slipped open and he licked his lips.

"I am no different than males of other species. Except, mayhaps in one respect."

Nanceen eased her hips from his and glanced at his groin. There was no moisture, no physical evidence of his second orgasm. She frowned. What was she doing wrong?

"There is nothing wrong, endearment." Korin's fingers shook when he lifted her chin. He ran the back of his finger along her jaw and over the fullness of her cheek.

She slid her hand from his groin and covered the fingers against her cheek. "Then, what?"

"I will not share my seed until I am joined with you. Only in the heat of your body will I allow the seed to flow."

"But, doesn't it... I mean..." She shrugged. "I don't know what I mean, Korin."

"Don't try to understand, endearment. It is as I have said. Take the pleasure I am able to give you now. And dream, dream of the pleasures of our joining. For it will come to pass, my Nanceen."

She believed him. And as she let him tug the clothing from her body, and she pulled his breeches over his hips, she showed him how she believed in him. And how impatient she was with the waiting.

CHAPTER SEVENTEEN

W hat good was it to be the king of Fairy if he couldn't control his subjects? The Fir Dhaerrig grabbed a haunch of partially cooked meat and lifted the greasy, dripping mess to his mouth. He snarled his frustration as he twisted his head to rip off a chunk of meat. Juices dripped from the corners of his lips as he chewed open-mouthed.

His family had long expected an upstart like Korin Goodfel-low. Expected, but they had not truly planned for the possibility. Now it was up to him to deal with the situation with little infor-mation and less support from his family history.

Tossing the half-chewed haunch to the hound at his feet, the king belched, then cursed loudly. "Damn 'em all. Every one of my forbearers was fools. Damn 'em." He shoved dishes across the table, sending some of the gilt pottery crashing to the floor. The hound whined softly and backed away, dragging the heavy haunch.

"Fools. Why didn't anyone keep track?" Even his own linage was clouded with blank periods of history and lost records. Sure of his right to rule, a gift from the long dead Fir Dhaerrig, the king still fought his own mindless uncertainty whenever he confronted Goodfellow.

The king picked at his teeth with the tip of a large dagger and paused a moment in unaccustomed, serious thought. Watching the hound tear at the meat with sharp, pointed teeth thrilled the Fir Dhaerrig, and he imagined his own pointed teeth ripping the flesh of one Korin Goodfellow.

A sad sigh flowed from the king's chest. Long gone were the days when he could take such actions against a foe. Gone were the times when any means were used to obtain the desired object or a position of power. The fairy had become too civilized for his taste. Now all he was left with was trickery. A smile twisted his lips into a grimace of delight.

Trickery had won his family the throne of the fairy folk. And it would be trickery to once again solidify that rule. Best of all--he clapped his hands--it would be trickery that would rid him of the thorn in his family's side.

He clutched a spoon in his fist and attacked a sweet concoction his cook had undoubtedly prepared in hope of lifting his spirits. The Fir Dhaerrig grinned around a huge mouthful and wiped the dribbling excess from his chin with the sleeve of his red coat.

Now, what trick, what chicanery would create the most havoc for Goodfellow--and the most pleasure for him? And, if it destroyed the last of the Goodfellow line...so much the better.

As the king chewed and contemplated, a brownie slipped through a small side doorway of the dining hall. He fell to his knees, bent to touch his forehead to the stone floor and waited.

Watching the brown and gray clad creature dispassionately, the king finished his sweet. After he licked the plate clean, he tossed the metal container at the quivering brownie.

"What news?"

"Sire, may I approach?" The brownie's high voice was muffled by the arms he had wrapped protectively around his head.

"Yes, yes. Be quick with your words, brownie."

The small creature clamored to his feet and scurried to the king's side. "My lord. A message comed back from the gentry maid's sister. We gots it afore the maid comed home."

"She has returned?"

The brownie's dark, shaggy hair shook as he gave a negative answer. "Nope. She still be in the human world. We knows where, but we ain't able to see her, ain't able to get to her. Or the other."

"Magic?"

"Don't know, sire. If 'tis, we din't unnerstand it and ain't able to break it."

Roaring in his ears like a storm upon the ocean, anger filled the king. Just as suddenly, the anger faded. He tossed a bit of a sweet to the brownie, who scrambled after it much as the hound chased after the bone. "Never mind the maid right now. What's in the message?"

"Here it be, sire." The brownie took a tiny scrap of folded paper from a deep pocket and carefully lay it on the table to unfold it. Then, with a swipe of his hand across the page, the paper expanded to its original size. The sheet was as long as the brownie was tall and covered the king's dining table.

The Fir Dhaerrig stood and moved to the end of the table to read the flowing cursive writing. The brownie lowered his gaze to the floor and stepped back.

"Hmm, interesting." The king smiled. "So, the sister believes she has found some pertinent information on fairies and will return to the Otherworld in four day's time." A frown lengthened the king's pointy face. "How can I use this?"

"Lots can happen in a fourday, sire." The brownie cackled and the brittle laughter lifted the sparse hair on the back of the Fir Dhaerrig's head. "You makes the best plans, sire."

"You confidence overwhelms me. Now be quiet and let me think."

The brownie backed away and sat in the corner with the hound. He started a playful tug of war with the canine's bone and growled back when the dog protested. The king rolled his eyes to the ceiling. There were few better places for a brownie than with other mindless creatures.

He turned his attention back to the paper before him and traced a word here and there as he thought.

Straightening with a jerk, he clenched one hand into a fist, shook it at the page, then bent backwards to shake it at the ceiling. His laughter rose and he danced around the table.

"That's it, that's it. How we'll get the Goodfellow. And end it now. Forever." He stopped and leaned over with his dirty hands pressed against his knees. Unsure exactly how his plans might play out, the ending would still be glorious. And ultimately satisfying.

There was something very intimate about sharing space--and breakfast--at a small table. Barely large enough for two placemats, the table was cozy and allowed Nanceen and Korin to entwine their fingers as they ate. With their knees pressed together under the wooden tabletop, they talked softly, muttering things only a night of passion understood.

There was a knock at the door, but before Nanceen could rise the door swung inward and Jayse stuck his head through the opening. He grinned when he spotted them at the table and stepped into the apartment. "Oh, darn. I was hoping to interrupt something."

Korin lifted his glass of milk in salute. "Mayhaps, if you had been a bit earlier." He squeezed Nanceen's hand. "Or mayhaps later."

"Korin." Nanceen tugged her hand away from his and lifted her napkin to hide her face. She wasn't that much older than Jayse, and often had lively discussions about sex with him and Lara. But Korin's simple statement embarrassed her. It wasn't like Jayse had no idea what might happen when he let them stay at his apartment... told them to use his bed. But, still.

A hand appeared at the top of the napkin, and fingers curled around the edge. A more intense heat flared across her face as the action reminded her of the caress of Korin's wings. Everything would remind her of him now. And, strangely enough, she didn't mind.

After letting Korin tug on the napkin, she lowered it back to her lap and grinned at the two men. A shrug lifted one shoulder and she lifted her cup of tea to forestall any further questions or comments.

"How was the training?" Korin asked.

Jayse pulled a third chair from a corner of the kitchen and crowded between them at the table. Nanceen gave him a dirty look, and he returned an innocent smile to her. "Macaire discovered a new technique and spent a lot of time trying to teach me. For some reason, I was really awkward yesterday. Finally, we just gave up and joined the hunt. The Queen rode with us last night, and Granda, too. I don't think he's ever gotten used to the horses, but Noid loves it so much, he goes anyway."

"Noid? What is noid?"

Jayse and Nanceen joined in laughter. Korin glanced back and forth between them and his brows lowered in confusion.

Nanceen took pity on him and rested her hand against his arm. "The short version of the story is that my da--Jayse's granda--had a dog. A big, black, goofy dog he named Noid. Some-how, Noid discovered the Faerie hunts and how to pass between his human world and the Otherworld. Da followed him and met Mother. They fell in love. I guess you could say the rest was a true fairy tale because Da gave up his life in the human world and remained in Faerie with Mother."

Nanceen smiled fondly. "Noid protected us all when we were children. Without him..." Her smile faltered and Jayse's expres-sion grew somber as well.

Jayse took a breath to continue the story, and Nanceen gave him a grateful glance. "Without Noid, my father would have been murdered. I never would have been born. Without the deter-mined love of our canine protector, Nance and her sister would have been sent God knows where through dangerous portals."

"How could this happen?" Korin took Nanceen's hand, but directed his question to Jayse.

"An evil Faerie decided Dad wasn't fit to be the Queen's heir because he's half human."

"There are many in the fairy worlds who carry mixed blood,"

Korin interrupted. "Why should it matter? As long as the blood of Oberon and Titania run through him--"

Jayse started to chuckle, but choked on the sound and cast Korin an incredulous look. "The blood of... Korin, what if what you told us yesterday is true?"

"It is."

"Then, that means Dad's descended from--"

"Yes." Korin nodded happily. Nanceen gulped for air as she realized the implications. Korin turned his smile to her. "Ah, endearment. Now you understand as well."

"That means... means..." Jayse continued to sputter, unable to get a full thought past his lips.

"Us, too?" Nanceen asked. "You mean we're descended from Oberon and Titania?"

A simple smile gave Korin's answer.

Jayse slumped back in his chair with a whoosh of expelled breath. He shook his head. "I don't believe it."

Nanceen tapped the back of the hand Korin had pressed flat against the tabletop. "He means he's just amazed. So am I. My god, Kae will have a field day with this information."

Silence filled the small kitchen. Finally, the tension left Korin's hand and he slipped his fingers from under Nanceen's. After a sip of milk, he took her hand and returned to their earlier conversation. "What happened? What punishment did the evil one receive?"

Jayse paused, sat forward and shrugged. "He was caught in his own trap and was sent through a time portal he'd created for Nance."

A shudder passed from Korin to Nanceen. The story of the defeat of Fiedhlim was well known, for the Queen had made it part of the clan's verbal heritage. And she supposed Kae had written it down somewhere to add to her collection of truths and myths.

She turned her fingers to squeeze Korin's hand. Kaelea could now move fairies from myth to truth. Her fingers clenched convulsively and Korin gave her a quizzical look. Smiling, she nodded toward Jayse, and Korin returned his attention to the young man as he told the family history.

Nanceen studied Korin's profile. The flashes of anger and pain passing through his expression, the tick of a muscle along his jaw, told her the tale affected him a great deal.

He was a strange combination--innocence and strength, power and vulnerability. Not really the type of man she ever thought she'd choose to love.

Yes, that was it. She loved Korin. It went far beyond the physical desire that now constantly resided low in her belly and high across her breasts. She wanted everything from him--everything for him.

Was she being greedy? She didn't care. If this was greed, then she'd gladly be so for the rest of her life.

One of Korin's wings fluttered stiffly, drawing her attention. And a fresh bit of sorrow tickled her nose with the possibility of tears. There were some obstacles to her love, and, while those of her family who had met Korin accepted him--

"Then, it's good no one knows the where or when of that portal."

Jayse shook his head. "No one did, until Lara went back in time and found Iain. She also found Fiedhlim--using a new identity. Once again, he nearly destroyed Dad, and possibly would have, if not for Iain."

"The evil one still causes pain?"

"No. This time he was captured and returned to the Otherworld. The Queen stripped him of magic, made him totally human--and mortal. The Alastronia--members of the clan who are the defenders of mankind--sent him somewhere, somewhere in the human world. Somewhere far from this time and place."

The stiff quivering of Korin's wings eased and they folded back against his body. Did anger make them react so? Nanceen let a deep breath fill her lungs. Not only did she have the joy of learning normal nuances to Korin's behavior, but the subtleties of his wings as well. Her skin tingled... his very expressive wings.

"I've got to take a shower." Jayse planted both hands on the tabletop and rose. "Oh, I forgot. I passed by your cabin and noticed there was a message waiting for you." He patted the side pocket of his loose, gauze shirt and slipped out a folded page. "Sorry, I meant to give it to you sooner." He handed the message to Nanceen.

"Don't worry about it." She glanced down and grinned at the flowing cursive of her sister's handwriting. "It's from Kae." Jayse gave them a brisk wave and walked away. Moments later the faint sounds of the shower filtered to the kitchen.

"What is your message, endearment?" The now soft edge of a wing tenderly touched her face.

Carefully, she pressed her palm against the velvety blue and held it to her face. She rubbed her cheek against the wing and smiled with seductive pleasure at Korin's sharp intake of breath. How amazing how sensitive, how expressive, his wings were. The erotic responses of the wings during the night had even surprised Korin.

Reluctant to leave the feelings, she pressed her lips against the wing and lowered her hand. Korin gave her one more soft caress before he retracted the wing and leaned toward her.

"The message?"

"Oh." Would he be angry she'd asked Kaelea for information about fairy folk? Would it seem like she was 'checking him out,' not trusting him or believing in him? She opened the message slowly, smoothed the page that had been crumpled by its confinement in Jayse's pocket, and lowered her gaze.

Nance,
Great news! I've found a source for what you wanted and--can you believe this--there may actually be histories there that will confirm my other theories and my study. Dear sister, I thank you for inadvertently steering me in the right direction. I'll be home with what I have for you in

A smudge marred Kae's normally precise, clear writing. Nanceen let a small chuckle escape past her lips. Kae was so much a perfectionist; she'd never let a smear blur a message. Instead, she'd rewrite the entire page. Nanceen turned her attention back to the sheet in her hand.

in one day. Meet me if you can. This is so exciting, Nance. I feel as if I am at the edge of a wonderful discovery.
Soon, Kae

"Korin?" Nanceen lifted her gaze and was jolted by the intensity of the liquid silver eyes that met hers. For a moment, she was unable to speak.

His gaze caressed her. "Yes, endearment?" The words continued the sensuous caress and she nearly lost her nerve. By taking a deep breath, she was able to gain control of her emotions and speak without the quiver threatening her voice. "I asked my sister to find out anything she could about fairies."

"Knowledge is a beneficial thing."

"But I don't think I truly believed in you when I did. It feels like I went behind your back, I didn't trust you--trust in you."

"And now you do?" Korin's question was asked with obvious concern and curiosity.

"Yes. Now I do."

"What problem does this cause, Nanceen?"

"I... I don't know. I just wanted you to understand. I didn't want this questioning to stand between us."

"What does your sister say?" Korin tapped the paper with one finger.

"She'll meet me in the Otherworld. She says in one day's time. That could be either today or tomorrow."

"Then you must return to learn what she may have discovered. Perhaps, it will answer questions for both of us."

Nanceen stilled his tapping finger by wrapping her hand around it. Then she lifted his hand and kissed the pad at the tip of his finger. The passage through the portal worried Korin and concerned her as well. Should she ask him to return with her? She wanted him with her when she learned Kaelea 's findings, but didn't want to risk his strength with another painful passage.

Her thoughts and concerns were clear to Korin. Although he dreaded the gentry portal, he tried to ease those concerns with a smile. Nanceen's brows drew closer and the corners of her full lips flattened. He'd failed. There was nothing he could do but pass through the portal with her, and hope the experience would not be too costly.

"We must return," he stated in what he hoped was a matter-of-fact manner. "I believe we both need to know anything your sister may have discovered. Mayhaps, she has found information to fill in the gaps in my history."

"But what about the portal? Is there any way you can go between the worlds like you usually do?"

"I don't believe I would be able to find a large enough tear in the fabric between worlds to accommodate me now."

Nanceen hesitated. He dreaded the question she would ask next. "Can't you become smaller for the transfer, then..." She held one of her palms low to the floor before she lifted it to his shoulder height.

His magic had been blocked and twisted over the past days, so Korin was not willing to attempt such a dangerous transformation. Afraid he might become stuck in one size--with or without wings--he'd much prefer the size he was now.

So he shook his head. "I'm afraid it may be dangerous."

"And the pain you experienced the last time we used a portal wasn't?"

Korin pushed back his chair and stood. He walked toward the narrow window above the sink and peered out into the midmorning brightness. He would endure that pain, at any time, to be with Nanceen. But how to convince her of that, and keep the worries from consuming her? He spoke without turning to her. "Yes, there was pain. But it passed quickly."

"But..."

Korin turned and spread his hands. "There is pain for me in any magical transformation."

"And you did this for me?"

"Yes. And do so would again. For the joy I have gained with you far outweighs the pain." He told the truth, but wasn't sure Nanceen would understand it in the same light. "Perhaps within your sister's findings will be an answer to this problem, and we shall find a way to move easily between the worlds. Ah, if there were only a way I could show you my home, the world of the fey races."

After taking a deep breath, Korin made a pronouncement. "We should go to the gentry Otherworld now." It was best to take action quickly, while he felt strong.

"Okay?" Nanceen's reply was hesitant and questioning. "But we don't have to rush off. Is there anything else you'd like to do in this world before--"

Korin fluttered his wings in long, slow strokes and opened them to their full glory. "I believe my options are somewhat limited." He grinned to soften the irony of his tone. "Let us return to your world. And solve some of our mysteries there."

He held out one hand and, thankfully, she took it immediately, stood, and moved into his embrace.

"If you're sure."

His answer was a quick kiss. To linger over her lips would have meant a delay that might cost him his resolve.

"We'll use the portal here in the apartment."

"A good plan. Nanceen?" When she looked up and their gazes locked, Korin forgot his concerns, forgot the previous pain, forgot everything.

"What, Korin?"

"I... forgot. Do we need to wait for Jayse?"

"Wait for me for what?" They turned together at the sound of Jayse's voice. Rubbing a small towel over his wet hair, he entered the kitchen. He stopped mid-swipe, dropped the towel to the counter, and adjusted the tie of his robe. Giving them an intense look, he grinned. "Taking off? So to speak."

A rumble of laughter shook Korin. "I don't even know if I can lift this body now. Perhaps the strength of these large wings has grown proportionately, or it has not. But yes, we are to return to your Otherworld now."

"I'm afraid your wings will cause quite a stir there as well." Jayse shrugged helplessly.

Nanceen leaned against Korin, and he willingly gave her strength and support. "Kae says she may have some leads on information about the fairy races. If she does, maybe it will be the beginning of bringing the fey folk together again."

"So, you believe what Korin told us about a split between our races sometime in the past?" Jayse pulled a carton of milk from his refrigerator, shook it, and poured a few drops into the sink. His raised eyebrows brought another chuckle from Korin.

"I beg pardon. I just can't resist certain things." Korin tightened his hold on Nanceen and glanced at her. The heightened color across her cheeks was one of those things, and he longed to touch her skin and taste the heat of her blush.

Jayse cleared his throat. "Ah, I can see that. Let me know the next time you want to stay here and I'll stock up... on milk." His contagious laughter even made Nanceen giggle.

"We should go," Korin announced reluctantly. He enjoyed the easy camaraderie he'd found with the gentry; it was far more acceptance than he felt with his own people. And he hated to leave, not knowing when--or if--he would ever find it again.

Jayse moved forward and held out one hand. Korin looked at the offering, then lifted his gaze to meet the dark brown of Jayse's eyes. There were questions there, concerns and promises. Korin nodded once. "All is safe with me, Jayse." He wrapped his hand around Jayse's forearm. ::*You need not fear for Nanceen.*::

The tight grip on his forearm reinforced the silent communication. Jayse nodded once as well before he stepped back. The intensity fled from his expression to be replaced with his normal, happy go lucky demeanor. "Take it easy, 'kay?"

He glanced at the clock on the stove. "Yikes. I've got to get going. Dad has me helping plan a gathering for the architect Bryce's been working with. Some company expansion thing. If I'm late, somebody'll have my hide--and it won't be pleasant."

His deep laugh followed him down the hall as he jogged toward the bedroom.

Nanceen pulled on Korin's arm. "What was that handshake thing all about?"

Unable to express the intensity of communication, Korin shrugged. "A guy thing?"

"Where'd you hear that phrase?" Nanceen rolled her eyes and shook her head. "It doesn't matter. I should go. Are you sure you want to go with me?"

Forever. Wherever the winds take us. Instead of speaking his fanciful words, Korin nodded.

Nanceen moved toward a blank wall at one side of the great room. Disturbing the still air of the apartment, she sketched a design with her fingers. Korin held his breath as the sparkling portal formed against the wall. A softly spoken word set the portal, and he saw the sylvan glade before Nanceen's small cabin.

"We'll go straight home." She spoke without turning from the portal. "Then if there's any problem, we'll be... you'll be..." Korin pressed against her back and wrapped his arms around her, just below her breasts. The weight of her breath pressed against his arms. He blew softly over her ear and tenderly sucked the lobe between his lips. Gasping, Nanceen covered his hands and pressed her body back against his. The softness of her buttocks against his groin sent shudders up his spine, and his wings quivered with response. If they didn't go now, they never would.

"We shall continue this when we are home, endearment. A way to pass the time while we wait for your sister." He pried his body from hers and made a motion for her to precede him through the portal.

Nanceen gave him one quick, seductive look, blew out a soft sigh, and passed into the Otherworld.

Steeling himself for the pain sure to assail his body, Korin straightened, kept the image of his Nanceen before him, and took jerky steps forward...

... into pain so searing, so hot and piercing, he was unable to cry out his agony.

. . .

Even though she spent time both in Faerie and in her brother's human world, Nanceen always felt a great sense of homecoming whenever she returned to the glen where she and her sister lived. But, this time, this time she was bringing the man, the fairy, she loved, home with her. How would things change?

Kae and she had often talked about what would happen when one of them found a lover, or perhaps a mate. But she never thought she would be the one--it was always Kaelea who had the plans, the ideas, the dreams.

Until she had dreamed of Korin.

Nanceen paused after stepping through the portal. Korin was reluctant to use the convenient transference, and she understood how there could be magical prohibitions to prevent his comfortable passage. But the pain? His smiles and assurances did little to reassure her. However, she wouldn't question his decision to follow her to the Otherworld, and she would do what she could to ease the transition.

He should have been beside her by now. Unless he couldn't force himself into the glowing portal. Nanceen turned, ready to return to the human world. Let Kae find her there with the news.

A rending, a horrible ripping reverberated through the glen, bounced off the cabin walls, and returned to surround her with mind numbing cold. Wind whipped leaves and twigs against her face and arms, stinging, blinding her. She lifted one arm to cover her eyes and tried to peer around the minimal protection. A maelstrom spiraled in the center of the portal opening, a swirling darkness that stole the light.

The wind growled and a huge, misshapen, vaguely man-shaped form hovered in the center of the maelstrom. The head coalesced into a huge, heavy, bestial face. The creature laughed, its lips stretched to thin, sharp lines. Pointed teeth glinted in the fading light. Below him lay a motionless, winged...

"Korin!" Nanceen screamed and tried to rush forward, but an invisible force kept her from reentering the portal. "Korin!"

Korin barely lifted his head to shake a denial. She didn't care if he didn't want her to come after him, save him she would. The creature was unknown to her, for beings had never been reported within the portal. But she would face any danger for Korin.

She forced one foot forward, and a blast of icy wind pressed her back. "No! Let him go! Leave him alone!"

The creature turned its head toward her. Something dark and slimy dripped from its fangs. It grinned and winked at her. It drew back one foot. With another wink it shoved at Korin's inert form.

"Take him, wench. What's left--not much." The creature's gravely voice held her frozen until a limp figure rolled to her feet. "Foolish wench. I'll wait for you, too."

One gust of wind howled behind her, then whooshed into the portal. The sudden quiet of the glen was loud in her ears. She covered her ears with her hands, but the ominous silence continued in her mind. Until the soft brush of something against her leg somehow brought sound back to the present.

Nanceen fell to her knees beside Korin and peered closely at him. Afraid to touch him, she held her hand inches from his back. "Korin?"

Long, jagged rips shredded one of his wings. The other, lying limply on the ground, had an 'x' torn through the center. "Oh, Korin. What am I going to do?"

Curled in a tight ball, Korin remained silent. Only the widely spaced, shuddering movements of his breathing indicated he lived. Nanceen gasped in horror, covered her mouth, and screamed Korin's name.

CHAPTER EIGHTEEN

"I didn't tell you to destroy him completely. I wanted to take my own satisfaction on Goodfellow." The Fir Dhaerrig stomped back and forth, but the world of the Bocan, the place between waking and dreams, wasn't solid enough for his stomping to make any noise. Still, he stomped and gained some satisfaction from the rigid movements of his arms and legs.

"It's still alive."

"But you damaged him a great deal, Bocan. What if he doesn't recover?"

The creature shrugged. "Don't care--one way or another. It was fun. When can I do again?"

"Maybe never. If you had done as I directed--"

"Did. Held it in portal. Hurt it. What more do you want?"

"I want it--him--alive. So I can destroy him."

The creature shrugged again. "Maybe recover."

The Fir Dhaerrig scowled. "And if he doesn't?" He jammed his hands against his hips and faced the creature. "What should I do to you if he dies?"

The sound of rocks grating together became the creature's laughter. "You do nothing to me. Can't. You not of my world. My king, but not my world. Go now. Tired of you."

A flash of darkness surrounded the Fir Dhaerrig, and the king found himself standing in the center of his throne room.

"Curses on ye, Bocan." Echoes of the creature's laughter rose to the high ceiling, lingered, then faded into silence.

Although the ringing sound of his footsteps filled the silence, the Fir Dhaerrig took small pleasure in stomping to his throne. Plopping onto the cushioned seat, he rubbed his temples. Had he made a mistake using the Bocan? Had he loosed the evil--only to be unable to control it? The forces he felt behind the creature's power, its delight in creating havoc and destruction, worried the king--frightened him--and he didn't understand how to deal with the feelings. Until now, he had always been the one in control.

"Aiiee... what have I done?" He feared the creature would haunt his dreams and hover at the edge of his mind--always waiting. "No. It shall not be. If I can handle the Goodfellow, I can deal with the Bocan."

He shook his fists at the ceiling. "You can't control me, Bocan. You won't take refuge in my dreams. I am king--and king I shall remain." His shouts lowered to a whisper. "For I am king."

The Bocan's image appeared behind the king's lids when he closed his eyes. There, at the same time, Korin Goodfellow's face was superimposed over that of the Bocan. The king gasped, rubbed his eyes, and cursed. When his vision cleared, only his increasing and frightening concerns remained.

Nanceen bent over Korin's crumpled form. Her tears fell to darken the golden strands in his hair. One of her hands rested near the center of his back, her fingers still to feel the slight lift of his breath. She was helpless--he might be dying and she didn't know what to do. She could think of nothing but her own guilt. For if she hadn't insisted on returning, if he had not followed her, this wouldn't have happened.

"Oh, Korin. I'm so sorry. Please, don't leave me. Tell me what I need to do to help you."

Fingers pressed into her shoulder. She jerked away and leaned further over Korin to protect him. A tall body crouched next to her and hesitantly touched her arm. "Nanceen?"

When she lifted her head, Derrik's face was blurred by the tears hovering on her lashes. She grasped at the strength he offered and clutched his hand. "Derrik. Do something. He needs help."

Derrik glanced down at the twisted body. One of his eyebrows lifted, but he showed no other indication of surprise at Korin's appearance. He must have seen something, some pleading in her face, when his gaze returned to Nanceen, for he turned his head to the Alastriona standing behind her.

"Macaire, fetch the healers. I'll be takin' this one to Nanceen's cabin. Hurry." He watched for a moment until the younger Faerie nodded briskly, turned, and rapidly formed a portal. When the Alastriona was gone, Derrik returned a questioning gaze to Nanceen. She wasn't ready to answer questions. She shook her head.

Derrik smiled gently. "We detected a disturbance within a portal, but could not pinpoint the location. I'm sorry we were too late to save yer friend."

"He's not dead, Derrik."

"Aye, but verra badly wounded. Come, I will be carryin' him to yer cabin. When he has been cared fer, I have some questions fer ye."

"Yes, defender." Nanceen answered automatically. Derrik's other eyebrow lifted, and she lowered her gaze. "I'm sorry, Derrik. I don't know what happened to Korin, but there was something, some creature in the portal. I... I don't think it was from any world we know."

"An' this one?" Derrik canted his head toward Korin.

"He's..." How could she quickly explain the difference in races with the same name? "He's one of the wee folk. A fairy."

"Aye? I dinna think he's verra wee." Derrik chuckled. "But, small enough for me to carry. Lead on, Nanceen. Macaire will be returnin' soon enough with the healers."

Reluctant to lose even the slight contact of her hand against Korin's back, Nanceen rose slowly. If she didn't touch him, he wouldn't be real, and he'd disappear like he had in her dreams. It was an unreasonable fear, but she couldn't persuade herself otherwise. When she forced herself to stand back, Derrik took care to turn Korin and lift him easily.

As she led the way the short distance to her cabin, Nanceen couldn't help looking back to reassure herself Korin was still there. Some faint memory, perhaps some tale told when she was a child, pressed to return. Would Korin fade from existence, leaving her alone and forever lonely? Or would he simply die, the life leaving his body an empty shell?

Nanceen berated herself. She would not think this way. She would not let Korin die. He would not leave her--not like this. She had more than enough will to keep him alive and with her.

Healers waited at the cabin door. Nanceen led them into her bedroom and directed Derrik to lay Korin on her bed. A soft, barely heard moan passed his slack lips when his back touched the soft mattress.

The healers stood around the bed, silent questions filled their expressions. They didn't voice those concerns, but later talked among themselves as if Nanceen and Derrik weren't in the room. But not one of them touched Korin.

Finally confessing to having no knowledge and no thoughts of what to do for the wounds in the dark, crumpled wings, the healers suggested only turning Korin to his stomach and trying to keep him comfortable.

Nanceen bit back angry, spiteful words and escorted them to the door, shooing them from her home. Leaning her forehead against the door jam, she let hot tears fall. Helplessness was not a feeling she had often experienced, and was definitely one she would gladly never feel again. Strength was what she needed, and strength she would find--somewhere. Strength to care for Korin until he was well and whole.

Wanting to be sure she could face Derrik without collapsing into a fresh bout of tears, she waited a few moments longer.

Leader of the Alastriona, Derrik was responsible for the safe passage of any through the gentry portals. She smiled sadly. How easily she claimed Korin's name for her clan. It did make it easier to keep the races clear in her mind.

After blowing out a long, heavy breath, Nanceen returned to her bedroom. Derrik stood over Korin, tenderly spreading the tattered remains of a wing flat against the bed. He had turned Korin to his stomach and arranged his hands to rest on the pillow at each side of his head. The torn edges of both wings were pressed together but the pale sheet peeked through the tears. The bare expanse of Korin's back and a pile of material at the foot of the bed gave evidence that Derrik had removed Korin's clothing. A thin coverlet had been pulled up over his hips.

Nanceen gave a soft cry and knelt beside the pile of clothing. She dug through the fabric until she found the small bag Korin protected so carefully. Somehow she knew even in his unconscious state, he would be concerned for his belongings. So she tucked the bag under one of his palms and closed his fingers gently around the worn leather.

Derrik gave her a compassionate look and nod of understanding when she stepped back and shrugged.

"Thank you for taking care of him, Derrik. I never would have been able to do this by myself."

"'Tis only one part of me duties, Nance. Yer brother would no' be so pleased if I dinna help one ye cared fer. This happened within the portal?"

Nanceen sat next to Korin, and carefully arranged herself so she was close, but kept herself still so she didn't touch his wounded wings. Korin had not mentioned a creature the first time he passed through the portal. And this time his reluctance was not great enough to indicate he knew what might await him. "I believe so. And I don't think Korin expected the attack."

"Describe the creature who did this. What did you feel?"

"I came through the portal from Jayse's apartment. It was like any other time I've crossed from one world to the other. Korin was reluctant--"

"Why?"

"When we first entered the human world through a portal a few days ago he experienced pain."

"An' you dinna think it was from an attack?"

"No," Nanceen shook her head and glanced down at Korin. A pattern of dark bruises formed on his fair skin, his back and arms were covered with welts as though a whip had struck him repeatedly. Bright red patches like sunburn covered his cheek and nose. She traced a finger along the short fringe of hair that curled over his forehead, then pushed it back from his face. She returned her attention to Derrik's patient waiting.

"No, not an attack. Korin thought it was because of some prohibition against a being with his magic using a gentry portal."

"Gentry?"

"Umm hmm. That's what the fairies call those of our race. It's a long tale and stems from Shakespeare's play."

"Ah, yer brother's favorite?"

"Yes. I'm sure everyone will want to know more. Can I save that story until later so I don't have to repeat myself too often?" She cast him a pleading look and was rewarded with a warm smile.

"I dinna think that will be a problem. My concern now is with the danger in the portal, no' an unconscious fairy."

"Korin says his people find minute tears in the fabric between the worlds, and that's how he normally would travel. However, when he became larger--to be with me..." Heat flushed over her skin and she lifted one hand to cover her cheek.

Derrik chuckled. "'Tis oft the way of things, Nance. Of love. Dinna worry. So, yer fairy friend grew large and..."

"And so was too big to fit through the little tears. He had to use a portal, even though he thinks that perhaps the prohibition was set in place to keep fairy magic from escaping into the human world. Then, when we were at the Renaissance Faire, something happened--some magic he couldn't explain. His wings grew back."

"Grew back?"

"He had managed to hide them somehow. When they reappeared, it caused him a lot of pain." Nanceen bit at the inside of her cheek. Because of her, he had suffered so much pain. And now...

Derrik crouched before her and took her hand. "I will examine the portal. We shall speak soon on this." He let his gaze slip to Korin and Nanceen felt the intensity of his curiosity. "Take care of yer friend, Nanceen. I dinna ken what else we can do fer him now." He rose and placed a quick kiss on her cheek. "I understand yer feelin's. 'Tis a strange business, the attraction of one to another."

Nanceen rose and hugged him. "Tell Tommy hi for me, okay? And, thank you."

Once Derrik had gone, Nanceen pulled a gliding rocker close to the bed. Before she sat, she wiped Korin's face and back with a cool, damp cloth. His skin was heated, and burned through the folded terrycloth and into her palm. Immobile, silent, torn and bruised, the love she finally found lay beyond her help. There was little hope that any of Kae's information would help her now. She sat, rocking slowly, and waited.

T ime grew to have no meaning. Everything revolved around Korin's care. Although, somewhere in the depths of her mind, she wondered where her sister was.

Through the rest of the first day, a long, dark, hopeless night, and long into the second day, Korin barely moved. Afraid she would further damage the tattered wings, she hesitated to turn him from his stomach. So, she gently rubbed the places on his skin that reddened from the pressure of laying still and carefully moved his arms and legs. Sick with worry over his lack of response, Nanceen tried unsuccessfully to dribble tiny spoonfuls of milk between his pain-tightened lips.

Weary and frightened, Nanceen knelt on the floor beside her bed and rested her face next to Korin's hand. He still clutched the

small bag. What did he protect so diligently? She would ask him--
when he woke.

The sting of tears burned, and she closed her eyes to ease
them. Hot tears escaped from between her lashes and dampened
her hand where it rested under her cheek. "Oh, Korin. You
promised not to leave me. Don't let that dream come true.
Please?" She opened her eyes and inched her fingers closer to
Korin's hand. When her fingertips touched his, she sighed.

A light touch on her shoulders felt inordinately heavy.
Nanceen jerked upright and scrabbled to her feet. Hands raised
and fisted, she was prepared to fight to protect Korin. She slowly
lowered her hands, sobbed once, and stumbled into her sister's
open embrace.

CHAPTER NINETEEN

"I got here as soon as I could," Kae whispered after they settled into chairs across the room from the bed. Nanceen angled her seat a few inches further to one side in order to see Korin clearly. "But if I would have known it was an emergency, I would have left my findings and been home in one day."

Nanceen sniffed back tears and crumpled the soft square of cotton Kae had pressed into her hands. "But your message said one day."

"No, my message said four days. I wanted to take a little time to close down the current phase of research because I was afraid I would lose sight of my findings. Nance, what happened?"

"When Jayse brought me your message--saying one day--I knew I had to return home to wait for you. Even though it caused him pain to travel through a gentry portal, Korin wanted to come with me."

At the word 'gentry,' Kaelea's dark brows arched high on her forehead.

"Kae? What is it?"

"Strange you should say a gentry portal. I had just found writings that mentioned our race being called the gentry."

"Yes. After the split between the folk once ruled by Oberon--"

"The tiny fairies and other fey creatures and those like we are? Nance, how do you know all this? I just barely discovered the texts."

Nanceen nodded once toward the bed. "From Korin." Following her sister's gaze, Kae stared at Korin for a long moment. Uncomfortable with her sister's scrutiny of her lover, Nanceen began to squirm. Despite her unFaerie-like, studious ways, Kae had enjoyed the pleasures of many lovers, and had even taken a few to bed before Nanceen could admit to possible feelings of her own toward them. The nausea caused by the thought Korin might find her sister more appealing churned deep within Nanceen's belly. Fiercely protective, she wanted to rise and place herself between Korin and her sister. Only the press of her nails into the hard wood of the chair anchored her in place.

"He's a...fairy?" Kae's gaze returned to Nanceen. Her eyes revealed nothing but the curiosity a new subject of study created in her and Nanceen relaxed.

"Yes."

"But he's so...he's not...well, tiny."

A bitter laugh threatened to turn to a sob and ripped from Nanceen's throat. If he had been tiny, they wouldn't be there, watching his silent struggle for life. "No. He wanted to be with me, and somehow magiked himself larger. For a while, he even made his wings disappear. But someone, with greater magic, I guess, made his wings return. Then, when we came through the portal, that happened."

"But how?"

"A creature of some sort--a monster. I came through the portal first, and Korin followed. The monster attacked him. It was...it was horrible. I turned and saw how the creature laughed as it beat Korin and tore at his wings. Then, with a rush of dark, cold air, it tossed Korin into Faerie. He hasn't moved or anything since Derrik brought him here."

"Good. Then the Alastriona are investigating. What about the healers?"

Nanceen hid another snort of laughter behind her hand.

"They did nothing. Wouldn't even touch him. Derrik put him in my bed, and I've been trying to keep him comfortable. How long has it been?" she asked, not really expecting any answer.

"Do you still have my last message?"

Nanceen blinked at the change in subject, nodded, and pointed to a tall chest. Kaelea rose, found the parchment, and settled back into her chair. Holding the paper up to the dim light from the window, she squinted, frowned, and shook her head. "I didn't make this change. Someone tried to erase my four and has written in a sloppy attempt at a forgery." She lowered the page to peer at Nanceen. "It would appear we have been tricked. Perhaps it was meant for your fairy to be attacked."

"But, why? Who would do such a thing? No one in Faerie knew about him until this happened--except Lara and Iain." Nanceen leaned forward and clutched the growing pain in her belly. "Who?"

Kae studied her message closely. "Maybe it wasn't anyone from the Otherworld. Could he have enemies in his own world? Maybe someone who doesn't like the fact he's taken up with a member of the gentry? According to what little I found, the separation was sudden and complete. Maybe distrust plays an important a factor. I don't know. In any case, we have to find out, before anyone else is hurt."

"Yes, that's what Derrik said, too. But if Korin said anything like that, I don't remember. And I really can't imagine him having enemies."

"Ah, my sweet, innocent sister. I think everyone has enemies. Who'd think our brother would--and look at the evil he's had to face since he discovered his Faerie..." Kae grinned and amended her words, "... his gentry heritage."

"Korin says the story behind A Midsummer Night's Dream is true." Nanceen gave Kae a small, sad smile when one of her eyebrows rose in question. She'd always admired her sister's ability to raise only one brow; it was something she could never do. Jerking her shoulders slightly, Nanceen continued. "In fact, he claims to be descended from Puck."

Watching Kae bite back a chuckle made the protective ire rise again. Kae must have seen some flash of anger, for she lifted her hands in apology and leaned forward to take Nanceen's hand.

"I'm sorry. But, you must admit, this is rather difficult to believe. As a race, we thought fairies to be myth. Even since I've discovered more mentions of them in ancient ballads and songs, to find one lying in my sister's bed... well, I'm sure you can understand. Can't you, Nance?"

"I'm sorry too, Kae. I guess I'm a bit protective."

"A bit?"

Nanceen shrugged. "You've called me innocent. But Korin... ah, he knows so much, and yet so little. To watch him discover the human world..." Nanceen's words faded as fresh tears burned their way down her cheeks. "If he wouldn't have gone there with me, this wouldn't have happened."

"And you take all the blame, don't you?"

Nanceen nodded and bent forward to hide her hot cheeks in her hands. She'd often taken the blame for Kae's misadventures as well. That may have been out of sisterly love and devotion, but this--this nearly cost Korin his life. She peeked through her fingers at the bed. Korin's torn wings lay limp across the surface. Had it been only a few days ago that those wings had cradled her and touched her in such sensuous ways? Would they ever again? How would they heal? Would Korin blame her for the pain and destruction?

Her sister's hand cupped her chin and lifted her face. Compassion and curiosity were the only emotions in Kae's dark eyes. Kae brushed stray hairs back from Nanceen's forehead. "I always wondered why you cut your hair, but it suits you. Go to my room and rest, Nance. You'll do him no good if you exhaust yourself to a comatose state."

"But--"

"No buts. I'll stay here with him and call you if anything happens."

"But--"

"I have a book to keep me company."

Nanceen's laugh was part sob. "Of course you do. Don't you always? Thank you, Kae." Silently, Nanceen stared into Kaelea 's face. With the communication only those of a single birth know, she shared her love for Korin.

Kae nodded solemnly. "I know. I'll watch him. Did you know Da and Mother have been here all along? And an Alastriona guard as well? We won't let anything else harm him. Or you, either. Now go. Rest. Mother has been waiting to coddle you a bit."

"Why didn't anyone tell me?"

"They've been in this room many times, but your attention has been elsewhere, darlin'. Now go. Ease some of Mother's worry. I'll move my chair close to the bed. One peep from our guest, and I'll let you know."

Kae took Nanceen's hand, rose, and pulled her to her feet. She waited while Nanceen paused by the bed, stroked the back of her fingers across Korin's cheek, and bent to kiss his forehead. "He's so hot, Kae."

"Ask Da to bring me a fresh basin of cool water, and I'll bathe him."

"I can't ask you to do that."

"Who needs to be asked? Now go. The sooner you rest, the sooner you'll be back at his side."

Those were the only words that could have prompted Nanceen to leave. She hugged Kae fiercely and turned away before she found another reason to stay. As she reached the door, she heard Kae carefully slide a chair across the floor. With one hand on the doorknob, she glanced back over her shoulder to see Kae settling cross-legged in the chair, a large volume spread open on her lap. Kae looked up, lifted the one eyebrow, and gestured toward the door with a jerk of her head.

Dragging her feet, both from exhaustion and reluctance, Nanceen entered the cabin's main room. Tipping his chair over, Stephen rose and caught her in a solid embrace.

"Da. I didn't know you were here."

"And where else would we be, daughter?"

"How?"

Derrik cleared his throat. "The Alastriona have no' been able to discover what attacked yer friend. So, I thought it prudent--"

"To protect us, defender?" Nanceen smiled at Derrik. "I'm sorry, I didn't know. I'm sorry, I've caused so much trouble." Her mother moved to take her hand and lead her to the table.

Kelene pushed her into a chair and placed a bowl of her favorite fruits in front of her. "You must eat something, Nanceen."

"Yes, Mother."

Kelene leaned to peer into her daughter's face. "None of that false submission, dearling. I know it will be difficult. When your Da returned to the human world, I thought I would die. I would not eat, would not join the hunt, did not enjoy the dances. I understand how you feel." She pressed her lips to Nanceen's cheek and whispered, "Truly I do. Eat then, if not for me, if not for you, then for him. Be strong and he will return to you."

"You can't promise me that, Mother. No one can."

Kelene crouched at Nanceen's side. "No, I cannot. Not even our Queen could promise such." She lay her hand over her heart. "But I feel it here." She brushed her fingers over Nanceen's closed eyelids. "And I see it here. If he loves you half as much as you love him, nothing will keep you from each other." Kelene picked up a piece of fruit and pressed it into her daughter's hand. "Eat just this one if it is all you are able to manage. Then, you shall rest. We must care for you, so you may care for your love."

No force of will could hold back the tears her mother's belief brought to her eyes. With a choking cry, she wrapped her arms about Kelene's neck and cried on her mother's shoulder. Soft, stroking circles of her mother's hand across her back helped ease the tears, and Kelene patted away the resulting hiccups.

Silence filled the cabin as Nanceen struggled to chew and swallow the juicy piece of fruit. When she was done, Kelene urged her to her feet and walked with her toward Kaelea's room. Nanceen hesitated at the door, covered her mouth and turned back.

"Kae needs some cool water--for Korin's fever. I've got to--"

Kelene's hands held her back. "Your da has already taken the basin. You will rest."

Although she was sure she would never be able to sleep, Nanceen allowed herself to be tucked into the bed. Her mother slipped silently from the room, but left the door cracked open. The low rise and fall of conversation from around the table was a strange comfort to Nanceen. Her family would help protect Korin. Maybe they could even find a way to completely heal him. She turned on her side and faced the door. Korin had no family, so maybe her family would truly accept him. She closed her eyes and images of Korin's reassuring smile filled the darkness of her vision. *::Korin.::*

A trio of boggarts kept under the cover of downed leaves and wildflowers and tried to creep near a small cabin centered in a tiny glen. Under orders from their king, even the presence of the gentry defenders didn't keep them from attempting to reach their goal. They were partway across the glen when the young gentry male who guarded the cabin door froze and turned to face them directly. The tiny, dirty men dropped to their hands and knees and tried to cover themselves with their camouflage of leaves and twigs.

The gentry defender frowned and took a step forward. At a signal from the leader of the three, they separated and skittered away in different directions. The gentry's head swiveled as if he tried to follow the progress of each tiny creature. His eyes narrowed and he returned to his position beside the doorway.

The leader sat back on his haunches and took a deep breath. To either side of him, companions were doing the same. How were they to spy on the Goodfellow, if they couldn't even get near the cabin? Making a decision, the boggart created a noise like the sound of wind through the grass and waited as his companions retreated to the heavier cover of the surrounding forest. He wished to use some trickery to ease his frustration, but that would anger the king more than the failure. The Fir Dhaerrig would have to send another to discover the fate of the Goodfellow.

Rejoining his companions, the boggart whispered urgently to each and sent them back to their homes. He was unhappy he would have to take all the blame, but his fellows would crumble pitifully under the king's anger. Taking a deep breath, the boggart slipped through the fabric between worlds.

T itus had waited long hours in the park, waited to see her. As he waited he focused on a new phase of his plan. Frowning, he left the shadows of the picnic shelter. She would not be there that day. Perhaps she was not the key to satisfy the plan after all. Long, swift strides carried him from the grassy green of the park to the concrete area designated for vehicles.

The faint, musical beep that announced his door was unlocking irritated him, and Titus growled low in his throat as he slipped into the leather seat. The roar of the engine echoed his frustration as he sped through the city streets.

Time was upon him, time to take action and bring down his competition.

D arkness. Piercing light. Nothing. Then the feel of a silk-covered pillow beneath his cheek. Oblivion. Pain. Korin chose the light, the feeling, and the pain and forced open his eyes.

With his vision blurred and watery, he couldn't focus on the space around him. He tried to blink, but the pain was excruciat-ing. So, he stared at the silk near his face until the blurriness solidified into the fine weave of the cloth. He tried to listen, but only the rush of emptiness filled his ears. Concentration tore his brain asunder, but he bit his lip and tried to focus on something--anything.

The soft crinkle of a thick page turning registered through the pain and he tried to smile. But his muscles wouldn't obey his commands. He tried to speak. His vocal cords were frozen along with his muscles. Only by sheer will was he able to move the fingers of one hand.

The rustling stopped and a face appeared close to his. A face he knew.

"Na...nc...een."

"Oh, my god, you're awake."

It was his Nanceen, but it wasn't. Long hair fell about her face and hid the identical features. But the look in her eyes, that was different. His brow wrinkled in confusion.

The voice, so like Nanceen's, whispered, "I'll go get her. She's been beside herself with worry over you." As each word was spoken, his mind registered the differences in the voice and finally, he realized this was Nanceen's sister.

"Ka...lee."

"Yes, I'm Kaelea. Hush now. Let me get Nance. Don't move."

"Can't."

Kaelea grinned and gently stroked his forehead. "Since you're awake, I'm sure you'll be moving about soon. Be right back."

With a whoosh of air she was gone, and Korin closed his eyes. It took too much energy to stay awake, to push away the oblivion. His fingers spasmed. He clutched something in one fist. By fiercely concentrating, he recognized the soft leather of his small bag. He squeezed his fingers together. There was a satisfying rustle of parchment within the bag. She had given it to him, placed it where he could keep it safe. Ah, his Nanceen.

As if his senses were suddenly opened, a cacophony of sounds rushed around him. With the return of those senses came the return of intense, burning pain. Korin bit his lip against the cries rumbling in his dry throat. He'd never experienced such agony, couldn't imagine it existed. Why did he hurt?

Raucous laughter rang loud from the oblivion still hovering at the edges of his consciousness. Now that he heard it again, he would never forget the sound--or the creature who laughed as it tore through the sensitive tissue of Korin's wings.

His wings! Korin took a deep breath and tensed his shoulder muscles. There was no response from his wings. He tried again, and again a third time. Finally, a tiny jerk lifted one wing from the mattress. He could not hold back the moan of pain the effort cost him.

A door slammed open, and feet pounded in a rush across the wooden floor and around the bed. A figure dropped to its knees and reached over the width of the bed to touch his face. The hand jerked away when he gasped in pain.

"Korin, what can I do?"

That was the voice he waited to hear; the voice he now realized was there even in the oblivion. "Nan...ceen."

"It's me, Korin. Oh, thank goodness. You're awake."

"Barely." He tried to smile to ease the worried frown from her face. Even with her reddened eyes, gaunt face and lank hair, she was beautiful to him. But she had not cared for herself. "How long?"

"Forever. You've been unconscious four days. I didn't know what to do. I was so--"

"Shh, endearment. I heal. Slowly, I fear."

"I was so afraid, Korin. So afraid my dreams would come true." Her gaze slid to one side. "I was afraid you would leave me."

"No." The force of his denial surprised him. "Stay, always." With the effort of speaking what little strength he had garnered left him. Even the pain faded as darkness caressed the edges of his vision, his hearing, his mind. "No, must... stay."

"He needs sleep, Nance." A deep, masculine voice sounded from across the room. Korin didn't recognize the timbre, or the flare of unusual accent, but understood the caring within the words.

"Yes." His lids lowered slowly, reluctantly blocking Nanceen from his view. He sighed once when a soft caress stroked the sweat from his face and he returned to the oblivion.

. . .

K nowing the slightest movement would bring a wash of fresh pain, Korin hesitated before opening his eyes. The room was silent, but when he cautiously extended his senses, there was a low murmur of voices from nearby.

The silence was comforting, and knowing Nanceen was near eased the tension that settled across his shoulders and upper arms.

He took a long breath to carefully expand his lungs. A tight twinge, centered in his back, kept him from breathing deeply. A bitter grin touched his lips. Helplessness was not a condition he easily accepted. And he had been helpless far too often of late.

Determined to leave the bed, Korin clenched his fists in preparation for moving. His eyebrows lifted as his fingers closed around his small, leather bag. Slowly, he dragged his hand closer to his face and his grin stretched with pleasure. Then, he frowned. Only Nanceen would have known to protect his belongings in such a manner. Had she looked inside the bag before she placed it in his hand? Had she seen the agreement he'd made with the Fir Dhaerrig? Would she have understood his written language? If she had, how did she feel about him now?

The worries gave him more reason to rise from the bed and discover the extent of the damage done to him within the gentry portal. No, it wasn't the portal that caused him the pain this time. Rather the strange creature lurking there.

He'd never heard of evil stalking users of a gentry portal, and with a sinking in his heart, he knew somehow he was to blame. His use of the portal brought the beast.

The rustle of parchment within the bag when he clutched it reassured. Softened by the folds of his human money, the agreement was safe.

Korin took another long, slow breath, steeled his quivering muscles, and inched his chest from the mattress. Long minutes later, he was on his hands and knees, panting from the exertion. Sweat beaded on his forehead and covered his chest. At a loss for how to gain a seated position, he tried to calm his harsh, agonized breathing. He had no wish to collapse back to the bed, and had no desire for Nanceen to enter the room while he struggled with his uncooperative muscles.

The minimal weight of his wings lay heavy over his back. He attempted to lift the weight, but there was no response. Closing his eyes and concentrating only focused pain in his wings. Korin angled his head and peered back over his shoulders. A length of one wing lay limp across the surface of the bed. Korin gasped and bit at the inside of his cheek to keep from vocalizing his despair. A large tear, an 'x' that showed the bedding through the membrane, rendered his wing immobile.

"No. Not this." He turned his head to the other side. The tattered remains of the lower half of the second wing brought tears to his eyes. "How?"

How the wings had been destroyed was not his question--but rather how he would survive without them. Although he had enjoyed his wingless time in the human world, the wings were part of him, of who he was, what he was. He hung his head, but refused to give in to the mental agony. Anger replaced the pain and he clenched his teeth, grinding the surfaces together until his jaws ached. How? How would he repay the Fir Dhaerrig for this desecration?

Korin flopped to his side and let a low moan vibrate his tightly clenched lips. With his legs hanging over the edge of the bed, he pressed against the mattress with one hand and sat. Panting from the exertion, he let his shoulders slump and his head hang wearily. He pulled the sheet over his lap and rested his leather bag in the hammock formed between his spread knees. He wanted to peer into his bag, but feared doing so would be a violation of the tentative trust Nanceen had bestowed upon him.

Instead, he reached behind him and gently touched the ragged, trailing ends of a wing. After sliding his fingers under the light membrane, he lifted, drew the edges forward and onto his lap. Until the night he and Nanceen had learned of the erotic capabilities of his wings, he had not thought them to be so sensitive. Now, as he touched the tears, he felt jarring, burning pain in every nerve ending, and each torn fiber.

Looking closely, he noticed areas where the tears seemed to be healing. Faint raised lines of strange, flexible scar tissue covered some of the smaller rips. A heavy breath filled his chest and pushed away some of the dull, lifeless ache centered there. Perhaps the rest of the wounds would heal as well. He tried again to force movement into the lifeless wings. There was nothing but pain for his efforts.

"What are you doing?"

Korin attempted to put a neutral expression on his face and turned his head and shoulders toward the door. Even through his pain and despair, he smiled at the sight of Nanceen framed by the doorway, a look of displeasure hard on her features.

"You shouldn't be sitting up. Not moving around like that. We don't know how badly you were hurt."

Korin shrugged. "Bad enough."

Nanceen moved into the room, circled the bed, and stood before him with her arms crossed under her breasts. "Korin, you were unconscious for four days." Her expression softened and her eyes sparkled with unshed tears. "I don't want anything to happen to you, just because you think you feel better."

The world spun around him so Korin closed his eyes and willed himself to stay upright. "I don't think I feel better." He sank slowly to his side and grunted with pain when his body crushed the wing folded beneath him.

"See?" Nanceen leaned over him and lifted his shoulder. After spreading the wing flat, she helped Korin to lay on his back. "You stay still. I think your wings are starting to heal, but if you move around too much, you'll re-injure them."

It felt as if he had a mouth full of cotton when he tried to answer Nanceen. The words formed in his mind, but couldn't quite seem to make it to his lips. The cottony haze crawled into his mind and obscured his thoughts, and when a sharp bolt of lightning-like pain shot through him, he welcomed the retreat into nothingness.

. . .

Trying to match the edges of the tears in Korin's wings was like putting together a nearly solid-colored puzzle. Nanceen's frustration rose, but she tamped it down ruthlessly. It was her fault he had been so severely wounded, and if there was anything she could do to repair the damage... She sighed, straightened and placed her hands at the small of her back so she could arch her spine to work out the kinks.

Lines of pain still crinkled around Korin's eyes, but the deep furrows lining his forehead had lessened. Dark shadows marred the fair skin of his face and bruises still covered his chest and shoulders. Nanceen smoothed the light blanket higher on his chest and frowned. After nearly five days the bruises should have begun to fade. She closed her eyes and sent a silent curse after the healers. Afraid to do anything themselves, they had even persuaded her brother to wait, and not use his healing powers.

There must have been more behind Jaye's refusal, for when his dark eyes met hers in apology, there was a true sadness there, hiding some other emotion she didn't have the strength to read at that time. Maybe it had something to do with the Queen.

Nanceen shook her head. No, she really didn't think so. Her aunt would never be so cruel. It had to concern the creature that attacked Korin. Her additional silent curse, her condemnation of the creature, halted suddenly when dark laughter filled her mind. There, within the laughter were words she could almost hear, almost understand. When the laughter faded, she shivered. And knew the words--*I already am.*

A light tap on the door brought Nanceen's attention back to the room. She opened her eyes just as Lara entered. "He's still unconscious?"

Nanceen nodded. "He was awake for a little while and tried to get up. Obviously, it was too much for him to try so soon." She glanced down at the still body on the bed. "The healers won't help him."

"So Iain told me. That's why I'm here." Lara stood on the

opposite side of the bed and shook her head as she glanced at Korin's injuries. "I can't do anything about the bruising--boy, he looks terrible."

"Thanks."

Lara chuckled softly at Nanceen's sarcasm. "I see you are also returning to us." She dug in a deep pocket. "I brought something that might help with his wings, though."

"It looks like they may be starting to heal in places. But I can't keep the edges together. There's no way to bind them, no bandages that will work."

"This might." Lara held up a small bottle. "I get this at the drugstore near Jayse's apartment. It's some sort of a liquid bandage. I use it all the time on the kids. Belle, especially, is always getting some little cut that needs attending. Now, I don't know if it will work on these wings--who knows what they're really made of. But I think we should try, don't you?"

"Lara, you're a lifesaver. It has to work."

"Korin's wings aren't dusty--like a butterfly's--are they? I don't know if this stuff would stick then."

"No, they're... they're... different." Heat flooded her face and she turned away.

"I see. Pretty sensitive, huh? Can I touch one?"

A rise of jealousy further heated her face and forced Nanceen to take a few long breaths before she could answer. This was her niece, for goodness sake. Her deliriously happy, married niece. What was there to be jealous of anyway? Only the touch of his wings, his hands, his mouth.

The heat fled her face and pooled low in her belly. Nanceen struggled internally to get control of herself. "Yes, of course."

Nanceen could barely watch as Lara's hand paused inches from an uninjured spot on Korin's wing. Did Korin feel the touch when Lara stroked the thin membrane? A faint downward tip of his lips made her think he did, and did not find enjoyment in it. "Well?"

"Interesting. Not at all what I expected." Lara pulled away and her face settled into a no-nonsense, business-like expression.

"How about if you fit the tears together and I'll brush on this liquid bandage? I don't think the wings are that much different than skin--only softer and more flexible."

Nanceen moved around the bed to stand beside Lara and looked at the tiny bottle. "I hope there's enough there."

The tinkling of tiny bottles sounded when Lara patted her skirt pocket. "I've got more."

CHAPTER TWENTY

D ark laughter echoed through Korin's subconscious, tickled his memories, and wrapped a new sense of unease into a tight knot. There were no words to the laughter, no source he could detect in his weakened state. He knew the laughter, knew the evil, but not the intent behind the sounds.

Struggling to rise from the darkness of his mind's healing protection, Korin fought against the hands gently pressing on his wings. He moaned, and the sound covered the echoes of laughter. He was burning, and he cried out for water. Cool, damp, a cloth stroked his cheeks before covering his forehead. Soft words, whispered close to his ear brought comfort, but no release from the pain and darkness.

As he sank back, deeper into the darkness, there was the laughter. Always the laughter.

N early a week had passed, and Derrik was no closer to solving the riddle of the creature in the portal than he had been the day of Korin's attack. Use of the portals was kept to a minimum, and each passage was monitored and escorted by Alastriona. Yet none experienced even a hint of evil, and each passage was concluded safely. Frustrated, Derrik paced before an open portal.

Somewhere in there, somewhere between the worlds, was a danger. He could not even determine if the danger had been only to Korin, or if future passages would be in jeopardy. Derrik wanted desperately to question Korin, both about the portal and about the fairy races, but the wounded fairy barely regained consciousness before sinking again into a personal oblivion. Even with his strong, magical touch, Derrik could not keep Korin awake, centered and coherent.

He tried to comfort Nanceen, but did not know if the fairy would ever recover. His physical wounds had begun to heal, but there was an emptiness in his spirit. Something that kept him from fully healing. If only the healers would have been willing...

Derrik shrugged. The healers were so enmeshed in age-old traditions, none were willing to experiment, none dared to bend the strictures of their calling. Thankfully, the defenders found courage and joy in growth and change. Once the mystery of the portals was solved, there would be much to learn from Korin.

Now, he had to depend upon Kae and her skills of research. She haunted the historian's chambers and had already discovered hidden scrolls and ancient books of which the old Faerie claimed no knowledge. Now, Kae studied those writings and had found additional mentions of the split between fairy and gentry.

"Derrik?" As if summoned by his thoughts, Kae crossed the clearing to stand beside him at the swirling portal. The faint electrical charge lifted stray hairs from around her face and waved them about with a life of their own. He smiled a welcome.

"Have ye found anythin' new?"

"Yes and no." She sighed and rubbed her eyes with the heels of her hands. "Yes, I have found mention of the fairy races, but no indication as to why there was a split between our peoples. And no, I haven't found any mention of a creature that lives within a portal."

"I have been thinkin' on that. Might it be the creature dinna actually exist in our portals? Might it have come there, perhaps been placed there, for a reason we dinna ken?"

'What makes you think that?"

"As the Alastriona guard the portals, many pass between the worlds. None have been harmed. None before Korin, none after. Only Korin. 'Tis no' even a sense of danger now, or of evil within the portals."

"Will you allow unguarded passage?"

Derrik grinned somberly at the concern hovering in Kae's dark eyes. "Nay, I willna. No' until we ken what attacked Korin. An' how to defeat it."

"I'll get back to work. It would be easier if I had some description to work with, you know." Kae took a deep breath. "But, I suppose I won't get one until Korin can stay awake long enough for someone to talk to him."

"Aye. 'Twould be of help. I think 'tis time to be speakin' wi' yer brother. Jaye can no longer follow the healers' mandates. He must try an' heal Korin. We canna be forced to cower from somethin' we dinna understand."

"I agree, Derrik. Do you want me to try and talk to him?"

"Nay. I think yer needed more at Nanceen's side. I canna guarantee I can convince Jaye to try and heal him, or that his healin' will work."

Kae lowered her gaze to the ground and kicked at tufts of grass with the tip of her soft, leather boots. "I'll go right home." Her eyes were wide when she lifted them. "I hope we can solve this soon--for her sake."

"Aye. She cares much fer the fairy."

"Aye, she does, defender. She does."

"Aiyyyeeee!" Korin bolted upright and the cry died on his lips. Gone was the comfort of the darkness and, to his surprise, gone was most of the pain. He opened his eyes warily to a semi-circle of faces, some familiar, some he'd never seen. His eyes widened and he searched for Nanceen. A sigh passed his lips when he found her. "Endearment?"

Fat tears spilled from her eyes as she knelt beside the bed and took his hand. "How do you feel?"

"I feel..." Korin searched for the words to adequately explain his sudden recovery. "I feel... alive?"

A sob that tried to become a laugh burst from Nanceen. Korin opened his arms to her and she rose, sat carefully on the edge of the bed, and collapsed into his embrace. The feel of her was a healing touch, more medicinal than any concoction he could imagine. But this was not what had brought him back from the darkness. He glanced up and found the face of a man.

The man's eyes were similar to Nanceen's, dark and expressive. Was this the brother she had spoken of with such tenderness? The questions must have shown on his face, for the man took a step closer.

"I'm Jaye. Nanceen's brother. I've tried to assist in your healing." He grinned with satisfaction. "And it appears to have helped. Welcome back, Korin."

"You are father to Jayse and Lara?"

"Yes." Jaye's brows drew low over his eyes. "We need to talk, soon. Unfortunately, my business in the human world is in need of my presence."

Nanceen sniffed and rubbed the wetness from her face as she turned to look at her brother. "Isn't it something Tommy could handle? I'd appreciate it if you could stay longer, just to make sure--"

"He'll be fine, Nance. And no, Tommy needs help with this. Some new caterer has started up and is using some smear tactics to try and discredit Zeroun's. Nothing we can't handle, but I do need to be there to tackle the damage control."

"Titus." Nanceen shuddered and Korin adjusted his hold on her. This Titus, the man from the park, was threatening her family? It was small wonder he felt unease around the man.

"That's the man. Came out of nowhere." Jaye shrugged. "Perhaps a little competition will be good for business. We haven't had any serious competition in quite awhile." He turned and crossed the room, but stopped at the door. "But don't hesitate to call me if there is anything else I can do. And please, Korin, answer Derrik's questions as best you can. We need all the information we can get about the creature that attacked you."

"I shall."

"After he rests." Nanceen insisted as she shrugged out of Korin's embrace and stood to face the doorway.

Lara giggled. "Ah, Nance, he's been asleep for seven days. How much more rest does he need?"

A sevenday had passed while he fought the darkness? Korin rubbed at his forehead in disbelief.

"Are you okay?" Nanceen's concerned face appeared in his vision.

"Yes, I believe so. I've been here a sevenday? I... it doesn't..." His shoulders lifted and he felt a twinge as a slight spasm traveled through one of his wings. He remembered--the pain. Unwilling to face the destruction of his wings, Korin closed his eyes. "My wings?"

Lara sat at the foot of the bed and touched his foot. Afraid to see the sorrow in her face, he opened his eyes slowly. But, her expression was clear and hopeful. "Nance and I tried to repair as much of the damage as we could--since the healers wouldn't even try. I had some liquid bandage from the human world and it seems to have worked fine on your wings. We fixed most of the rips." Silent, her eyes begged for forgiveness and, if she had done so much for him, Korin couldn't understand why.

Nanceen lifted one wing carefully and spread the width so he could see. Two long slashes formed an 'x'. The ends of the slashes had barely begun to knit. "We can't get these edges to stay together. I don't know if it will ever be whole again."

Korin chewed on his lip, afraid to ask his next question. "And the other?"

It took Nanceen ages to reposition the limp fabric of his wing. Finally, she lifted her gaze to him. "There were lots of rips. We were able to mend most of them, and they're healing. But... oh, Korin. There were pieces missing."

Missing? The violation and mutilation threatened to rise as thick bile in his throat. Mutilated? Would he ever fly again? He concentrated and tried to move his wings. There was a slight movement, but the strain that popped beads of sweat onto his forehead was hardly worth the tiny reward. He was handicapped. A fairy without flight. He laughed bitterly. Now he was no better than Peg-leg Jack.

Then, he sighed. There were many of the fey races who survived well without flight. And so, he could as well. As long as his other magic remained to him. As long as Nanceen...

He looked at her. Tenderly, he brushed the tears from her lashes with shaking fingers. That she cried for him told him much. He stared into her face, stroked her cheek, and pushed the short curls back from her face. At the back of his awareness, he heard Lara shoo the rest from the room. The door closed with a soft click.

"If my wings do not heal, I will not be whole. I will be crippled. Perhaps I will be an outcast among my kind. Such loss is not common among the fey. And not understood."

The tips of Nanceen's soft fingers stopped his speech. "You are always welcome here. No matter whether your wings function or not. I... I love you, Korin. And I want you to stay with me."

Nanceen watched Korin's eyes as she spoke then held her breath as he absorbed her words.

His hands lifted and captured her face. Leaning close, he pressed his forehead against hers. "And I love you, my Nanceen, my endearment. But I cannot stay... yet."

"Does this have anything to do with why we can't make love?"

"We have made love, endearment."

"Yes, but..."

"Was it not enough?" He leaned back and smiled sadly at her.

If she asked him the same question, his answer would be the same as hers.

"No. I will always want more."

Korin nodded. "As will I. And now, now I don't even know if the prohibition means anything any longer."

"Then we could... when you're stronger?" The thought of sharing her body with him, of loving him as she'd imagined during the long days of sitting at his bedside, brought heat to her body and a tingle to cover her skin. She reached out tentatively and touched his firm mouth with her fingertips.

Korin's lips parted and the tip of his tongue ran across her fingers. Nanceen gasped in delight, and swirling passion settled heavily at the juncture of her thighs. No hint of pain, or sorrow, remained in the sparkle of Korin's eyes.

"I do believe your brother has done much to heal me. I am strong--strong enough to love you as you desire--as we desire."

"Oh, yes." Nanceen drew back from the temptation of his lips. "But the others."

"Listen, endearment." Korin paused and Nanceen listened to the silence settling in the house around them. "They have gone."

"Yes." She kissed him lightly. "Gone. Korin?"

"Yes, my love?"

Nanceen reached around him to spread his weakened wings to one side, then pressed a hand gently to the center of his chest. Korin lay on his side, and a willing smile graced his lips. Nanceen sat beside him, staring. When Korin licked his lips, she sighed, leaned over, and took possession of a kiss so tender, yet so passionate, she was lost in the myriad sensations.

At the gentle insistence of Korin's hands, she lay beside him, and molded the length of her body to his. Already burning with need and desire, she pressed closer and slid one knee between his legs. When he lifted his leg over her hips, the hard ridge of his sex pressed against her through the thin blanket. That blanket and her clothes were the only things between her and...

Korin tugged at the blanket behind him, pushed it down his

hips, and silently encouraged Nanceen to help kick the material to the end of the bed. Now, only her clothing...

Korin was methodical in removing her skirt and tee shirt. His grin filled with wicked seduction and he refused to touch her skin until she lay naked beside him.

Whether the sigh of pleasure when his hand rested lightly on her hip came from him, or from her, didn't matter. The flexing of his fingers drew her closer and he wrapped his leg over her hip once again. The hard heat of him pressed against her belly brought tears to her eyes.

"Nanceen? My endearment? Why do you cry?"

"I love you."

Korin chuckled. The rough sound moved him against her and the laugh ended in a sharp gasp. "Is it so terrible that you must cry?"

Nanceen wrapped one hand behind his head and tangled her fingers in his short, silvery gold hair. "No, not terrible. Wonderful. So wonderful, I can hardly believe it."

"Believe, my love. Believe." Korin's mouth upon hers silenced her words, but not her moans and soft cries of pleasure. Korin placed gentle, tiny kisses along Nanceen's jaw line and whispered syllables in a language she didn't recognize. Shivering under the tender ministrations, Nanceen stroked his hair, the angle of his cheek, the masculine curve of his neck. "What are you saying?" she gasped when he tugged her earlobe into the heat of his mouth.

A caress of his tongue preceded his answer. "It is only a song."

"What song?"

Korin angled above her and kissed the center of her forehead. His lips lingered, and moved as if passing the words directly to her mind. "A song of love insatiable."

"Insatiable?"

"Only you, my Nanceen." Korin gathered her in his arms and held her tightly. By the desperation of his touch, she understood the hopes, the joys--the song.

Her kisses matched his desperation. The touch of his hands on her skin ignited her and brought lightning storms of feeling to her body. He caught her vocal responses in his mouth, tempered the cries with silky strokes of his tongue, and delved deeper and deeper into her senses. All the while continuing his soft, whispered song.

Nanceen couldn't sense where she ended and Korin began. Stroking his shoulders made him smile, touching at his waist brought soft gasps to his lips, and when she wrapped her arms around him and caressed the sensitive skin between his wings he arched his back and cried out. The movement pressed the pulsing heat of his erection firmly into her belly and her cry joined his.

Nanceen squirmed against him, rubbing against his captured sex. Korin realized the prohibition set upon him by his king was wrong. Being with his endearment was right. The only thing right in any of the conjoined worlds, the only thing right in a long life of wondering where he belonged, how he mattered. Gently, he pushed on Nanceen's shoulders and she lay back willingly. He cupped one breast and teased the firm, rosy nipple between his thumb and finger. Her heavy lids covered the sparkling brown of her eyes; her lips were swollen and pouty as she gasped for breath. Watching her face carefully, he grazed her nipple with his teeth before he sucked the peak into his mouth.

Nanceen lifted her hands to run her fingers through her hair and tossed her head back and forth. When her eyes opened to his, he drew on her nipple with increasing pressure. The desire swirling in her eyes tightened to a dark spiral. Korin traced one hand down her side and over the curve of her hip. He nipped at the peak in his mouth at the same moment he touched the swollen bud of her need.

Nanceen's fists slammed to the mattress on either side of them and she clawed at the sheets. Moving his attentions to her other breast, Korin stroked her and circled the twin evidences of her desire with finger and tongue. Her soft cries grew vibrant and her hips moved against the circling of his hand.

Ignoring her cry of dismay, Korin lifted his head. Lost in the sensations of giving pleasure, he was barely able to remember the words of his song. He returned his attention to her body and the movement of his lips against the taut skin between her breasts burned like icy fire through his veins. It was a pain, a pleasure together. He sang to her, and drew the song into himself, until he felt her breathing, knew the beating of her heart as his own. His passion was hers and hers his. It was one. Insatiable.

Caressing her hot, wet core with his finger, he covered Nanceen with his body and positioned himself between her thighs. Her arms and legs wrapped around him, holding him, encouraging him, begging him to bring the song to climax.

"Nanceen?"

She opened her eyes to concern, questions, and the strain of desire. There were so many questions in his speaking of her name, and yet, there was only one answer she could give. "Sing to me, love."

The deep, shaking breath that interrupted his already ragged breathing pressed their bodies together. His hand slid from between them to hold her hips.

"Korin." She sighed, slid her hands beneath his trailing wings and cupped his buttocks. "Korin, finish the song."

Korin leaned his forehead against hers, and soft musical tones accompanied the unusual words. His rigid desire pressed against the heat of her, and she adjusted her hips minutely. Arching, she took the tip within her. A gasping hitch in his voice interrupted the song and instinctively, Nanceen waited.

"I love you, my Nanceen."

One long, slow stroke filled her and she cried out the intensity of the pleasure. "Oh, Korin."

He gave her a shaky grin and began at a leisurely pace, letting her feel his entire length with each stroke. Lifting her shoulders, she pressed her mouth to his and matched the stroke of her tongue with the rise of her hips to him. She lifted her legs higher, wrapped them around his waist, and opened herself fully to him. He touched her deeper, until the sweet friction clenched her inner muscles around him.

His pace increased. Now the hot, wet meeting of their bodies

drew her tighter. It was almost unbearable, but the most wonderful, most sensuous moment she'd ever experienced.

Korin lifted himself high on hands planted close to her sides.
His lips moved with his song, and it reverberated through her
body. The joy, the strain of his expression delighted her, and she
met his increasing thrusts, stroked his trembling arms with her
hands, and dried the sheen of sweat from his face with her
fingers.

With a strangled cry he jerked and burned into her. The
pulsing throb pressed against her inner muscles until they
contracted around him, and her own release burst over her with a
suddenness that pulled a wild keening from her soul. Their cries
mingled, rose, quieted and rose again as a second climax shook
her when Korin leaned forward and whispered a final syllable to
her forehead.

Korin held Nanceen tightly while the shuddering controlled
her. He let the pulsing response of his body wash over him. The
song echoed through him. He'd never imagined... never
dreamed... never experienced--until Nanceen. When their bodies
calmed, he rested carefully against her and sighed deeply.

"Uh, Korin." As if the honey of their passion rested in her
mouth, her words were slightly slurred.

"My sweet endearment." His own voice was muffled as he
nuzzled her neck.

"Korin, what's going on?"

There was confusion and a taste of fear in her question, so
Korin arched back to look into her face. The movement stroked
his length against her inner warmth and he grew firm, expanding
to fill her again.

"Umm, that's nice, Korin. But something's happening."

"I don't understand."

"We're not in the bed anymore."

"We haven't fallen to the floor, have we?" Korin chuckled. The
sensation surrounding his growing erection was unbearably
delightful, and he gasped.

"Uh, not exactly. Korin, I can't feel anything beneath me."

He gave her a wicked grin. "That must be a testament to my lovemaking."

"Wonderful, delightful, more than I ever imagined. But I don't think so. Korin, look down."

He didn't want to pull his gaze from her face, from the sated heaviness of her eyes or the soft, welcome swelling of her lips. She gave him a worried smile and he tore his eyes away to look beneath him.

It took a moment for his eyes to focus and his mind to grasp the fact they were floating a man's height above the bed. He made an inarticulate sound and Nanceen giggled.

"How'd you do this, Korin?"

"I did nothing, endearment." He tried to force enough movement into his wings to create flight, but only a dull, aching pain answered his mind's summons. "I cannot fly." He tried to hide his dismay at the flat statement. Nanceen stroked his face and her eyes filled with compassion. And love. Suddenly, flight no longer mattered.

"Then why are we up here? How do we get down?"

He shook his head. "I don't know."

"Well, then maybe we should take advantage of the moment and not question it."

"Endearment?"

Nanceen wiggled her hips and he groaned. "Since there's no mattress to press into your wings, how about if we..." She wiggled again and rolled them through the air until she straddled him. "Interesting. There's nothing beneath us but air. Still, I can do this."

Leaning forward, she lifted her hips until he was nearly free of her, hesitated a moment, then lowered herself to take him even more deeply. She stroked his chest and lingered over the tight buds of his flat nipples. Pressing against the length of his body, she rubbed her breasts over his chest and whispered words of her own against his lips. The rhythm of their joining flowed over them in silence, only the soft sounds of flesh against flesh echoing within the room.

Until the tightening spiral became too much. Korin held her hips with tense fingers and plunged upward to hold himself against her. Nanceen arched back and cried as a second wave of release shook her and Korin spilled his heat, his life into her.

Only for her, always.

CHAPTER TWENTY-ONE

Nanceen lifted her hips and let Korin slide from inside her, but she couldn't prevent her small moan of disappointment. She stretched beside him, wrapped one arm over his waist, and rested her head against his chest. The mattress pressed against her sensitized skin and she sat. "Oh, how'd that happen?"

Korin reached out and tugged her back to his side. "Mayhaps, only when we are joined..."

"Hmm. I could get used to that--flying without wings." She kissed his chest.

Korin jerked to a sitting position, leaving her alone and cold against the solid mattress. "What did you say?"

She brushed damp curls back from her face and shrugged. "Flying without wings?"

Korin laughed. His wild, free laughter was contagious and Nanceen found herself joining him. "What's so funny?"

He sobered but still smiled, and took her face between his hands. "I cannot tell you just yet, endearment. Not until I'm sure..."

They leaned together, lips drawn as if by a fierce magnetic

force. Before their kiss began, a distant claxon sounded. The frantic ringing of the bell brought a wide smile to Korin's face.

But the unusual sound jerked Nanceen from his arms. Sudden fear rose like a tsunami wave in her, and she shuddered.

Korin's joy was gone in a blink of his eyes. "What's wrong?" He had to give Nanceen a slight shake and ask her again before she focused on him.

"Something's happened. That's an emergency signal. I've never heard it used before." She struggled from the bed. "I have to go."

The force of her fear settled around Korin like an unwelcome captivity. This sounding of bells concerned him as well. More than the fulfillment of one of the conditions, this was evil. Had the creature somehow left the portal? Had someone else been attacked? He stumbled weakly as he crawled from the bed. "We shall go."

Nanceen paused in dressing and turned to him. There was denial on her lips and in her eyes. He let her speak the words. "No, you're still weak." Bright pink flushed her cheeks. "I used too much of your energy."

"No, Nanceen. I will come with you." He held her hand. "This has to do with me, with the attack within the portal, mayhaps."

She took back her hand. "Then hurry."

He was dressed moments after she finished. They started toward the door when he remembered his small bag. A niggling presence in his mind told him to leave it behind would be dangerous, so he tugged on Nanceen's hand as he turned back.

"Korin?"

"I must bring my bag. Do you know...?"

"It's on the stand beside the bed. Hurry."

The claxon sounded, the ringing a counterpoint to their frantic footsteps in their race from the cabin.

· · ·

T he claxon's chime vibrated through the boggart's hands and into his sensitive ears. He bit his lip against the pain and crouched beneath a sturdy bush at the edge of the clearing. How could he do anything with that noise? He couldn't even think clearly.

Before he could force himself to action, the gentry maid and the Goodfellow rushed from the cabin and ran down the opposite path. The boggart frowned, scratched his belly, and slapped his hand back over his large ear. There was nothing more to be done here, nothing to see. He hadn't been told to follow the Goodfellow--and the Fir Dhaerrig's throne room would be much easier on his ears.

So, he turned in a tight circle and disappeared through a tear in the fabric between worlds.

There were no ringing bells in the throne room, but it was far from quiet. The boggart stood under an ornate archway and stared at the king.

Belly bouncing, the Fir Dhaerrig danced a wild jig in the center of the room. Raucous music poured from another archway. The din grew louder as more musicians arrived and joined in the fracas.

The king paused in his dance and leaned heavily on his skull-topped staff. Panting, he gestured for the boggart to come to him. "What news?"

"Sire." The boggart removed his orange-red cap and bowed his head. "There be great commotion, noisy clanging in the gentry world. The maid and the Goodfellow, they runned to the clanging. Hurt me ears, so I comed back."

Clapping the boggart on the back, the king grinned, showing pointed, dirty teeth "Good, good." He grabbed the boggart's upper arms and spun him into the dance. "Celebrate with me, friend. My new plan."

"What plan be that?" The boggart gasped and struggled to release himself from the king's fierce grip. Something strange was happening, something that began to frighten him.

"Why, I took something from the gentry world. Something to bring Korin Goodfellow to me and to secure his future compliance with all my wishes."

The boggart froze. "What be that, sire?" There was nothing he could think of that would tempt the Goodfellow away from his gentry maid. The boggart licked his lips and grinned. She were a comely thing.

"Ah ha. Look, gobber, look at my triumph." Using his staff, the king pointed to a heavily guarded alcove.

The boggart took an astonished step backward, then another. His hands lifted in a protective gesture. Small twigs and bits of dried leaves fell from his shaggy hair as he shook his head. "No," he whispered. "Oh, no."

The Fir Dhaerrig had gone much too far.

T he clanging bell peeled over and over to force their running feet into a matching rhythm until a sudden silence froze them in the center of a widening of the path. Nanceen clutched Korin's hand and tried to draw a deep breath into her burning lungs. Beside her, Korin's chest heaved. He shouldn't have come; it was too soon after his attack, too soon after a healing.

As if sensing her concern, Korin lifted their joined hands and brushed the back of his fingers down her cheek. "I'm fine. What now?" Then, his eyes grew wide and he turned toward a side path, a path so familiar to Nanceen she could walk it in her sleep. "Do you feel it, endearment?"

When she let her concern for him fade, the magical pull of the silent claxon was a tangible ripple in the air. She reached for it with her free hand and the shimmer retreated, beckoning her toward the path. "Yes, the call. We'll find the reason for the summons if we follow the call."

She took a step forward, but jerked to a stop, both hands lifted to keep a wild, anguished cry from escaping her lips. Korin's eyes mirrored her fear. "Oh, God, no. Not at Lara's."

Her feet rooted to the Faerie soil and she shook her head in denial. No. Nothing could have happened to Lara or one of her family. Not here. If she didn't go to the cabin, then nothing would be wrong. It would be okay if she didn't know. If she--.

"Nanceen." The authority in Korin's voice drew her slowly back to his side. "We must go. Lara will need you."

"But what if something happened to Iain?"

"Then she will truly need you. Come. We must hurry. There isn't much time."

"Time?" Nanceen held back as Korin tried to pull her forward. "Why do you say that?"

"I..." Confusion filled his expression. He glanced from her to the path. "I don't know, but we must hurry. There is an urgency not present before. I am needed."

Without further words, Korin left her standing alone in the clearing and trotted down the path leading to Lara and Iain's cabin. Nanceen reached one hand after him, but could not bring herself to call him back. She closed her eyes, drew a deep breath and, lifting her skirt to keep the hem from catching in the bushes and tall grasses lining the path, followed his swift passage.

Korin allowed himself a grim smile when he heard Nanceen following. He didn't understand the strange pull or the urgent summons he believed only he felt, but didn't comprehend. Concentrating as he ran, Korin fought to bring some controlled movement to his wings. But, other than being able to fold the partially healed remains close to his back, the wings could do nothing. Now, more than ever... now, when flight would take him quickly to where he was needed, he mourned the loss. Not allowing himself the luxury of self-pity, he soon entered the glen surrounding Lara's cabin.

Nanceen stumbled behind him and he caught her to his side and swiftly studied the scene before him.

Held tightly by her husband, Lara stood in the center of the yard. Korin allowed himself a small sigh of relief--they were safe. On the porch, Antin huddled on the lap of an older woman in a rocker. Kaelea sat at the woman's feet. The man who had healed him stood behind her, resting one hand on her shoulder as he spoke to a tall Faerie with a warrior's stance. Korin gave a sharp nod. He had often sensed the warrior at his bedside.

Except for the stricken expressions filling each face, nothing seemed amiss. All were unharmed.

Nanceen touched his hand, left his side, and rushed to envelop Lara in a tight embrace. Korin frowned. He was missing something, something important. A faint, malevolent chuckle sounded deep in his mind, followed by the clear laughter of a child.

Belle. The small girl, the dark haired beauty who called him her bu'fly man was gone. The surety he had caused this tragedy sank him to his knees. But why would anyone wish to harm the darling child?

A memory of her sweet laughter curled through him, followed by a surge of heat rising from the bag tied to his belt. It had been her laughter, the sound of Belle that had alerted him to the fulfillment of the first of his king's conditions. The king--he dared to...

The tall warrior stood before him and Korin rose to meet his gaze.

"I dinna believe yer well enough to be here."

"I think I know where Belle is."

"Aye?" Skeptical, the man rested one fist against his hip, as if he reached for the weapon strapped there, and canted his head to one side.

"Yes, warrior, I do."

The man's lips twitched. "I am Derrik, leader of the Alastriona, the defenders of mankind. And of Faerie. D'ye believe Belle's disappearance has aught to do wi' yer attack within the portal?"

Korin thought for a moment. "Mayhaps, though I don't think there is a direct link. However, I do believe both incidences have been orchestrated by a single being."

"Aye?" The defender visibly reigned in his impatience and waited for Korin to speak again.

"It is the Fir Dhaerrig."

The man who healed Korin joined them. "I'm Jaye, remember?"

"I do. You are my Nanceen's brother."

The man's dark brows lifted at Korin's choice of words. "I'm also Belle's grandfather. What do you know about this?"

It would be difficult to explain to these intense men, but Korin felt the rising of a corresponding strong intensity within himself. It was within him to fight for those he loved. And within him to challenge his king. "The Fir Dhaerrig denied my petition to court Nanceen. To be with her, I made a foolish bargain with my king."

Jaye took a threatening step forward, his hands lifted. Korin stood firm against the frustrated aggression, willing to accept the assault if it would bring an end to the agonizing situation. Anger flashed through Jaye's dark eyes, then faded swiftly away to be replaced with determination. "You think your king took my granddaughter?"

"Yes."

"To what end? She has nothing to do with you and Nanceen."

"No, but the Fir Dhaerrig knows I will return to my world to find her. It is often the way with stolen children. I do not believe he will purposefully harm her."

"Harm?" Jaye's voice rose an octave and drew the attention of the others in the yard. Lara, Iain, and Nanceen joined them.

Iain's tightly controlled anger vibrated around him and Korin took a step back. Iain growled, low and feral. "My darlin' girl's been harmed? And you know where she is?"

Korin nodded.

"Take me."

Derrik lifted his hand. "He shall take us all."

Shaking his head, Korin stared at the ground. "I cannot. Unless you have the magic to shrink to a hand's height. I can return to my natural size, but I cannot magik you as well. I shall go alone, deal with the Fir Dhaerrig and return with Belle."

"Yer no' strong enough."

Korin gave Derrik a wry smile. "I shall have to be." He glanced around the tight group. "I don't believe it will be a physical fight.

The king wants me. For some reason, my love of a gentry maid threatens him. I have always threatened him." Korin shrugged. "I will bargain with him again, with the release of the child as the only condition."

One arm about Lara's shuddering shoulders, Nanceen listened silently. Until Korin spoke of a bargain.

"Korin, you can't. You won't be allowed to return."

"That is always a possibility, endearment."

Nanceen stepped from Lara's side and wrapped her arms about Korin's waist. "You can't leave me. You promised."

"Is not the life of a child, and the joy of those who love her, more important than my life? As much as I love you, Nanceen, I must right the wrong my love has caused." He angled his head to brush his lips against hers. "I have been selfish enough to have caused this pain. Now, I must--"

Nanceen pulled his face down for another kiss. The love, pride and concern in her kiss humbled him. He would do anything, and everything to prove her emotions were well placed.

"I'll wait for you here," she said when she stepped back from his embrace. "Don't be too long." She would see him again--she would.

Derrik rested one hand heavily on Korin's shoulder. "'Twould be better if I could go wi' ye."

Once again, Korin shook his head. "I see no way. I'll return to my natural size and create a tear in the fabric between worlds. I cannot make a tear large enough for you."

"I shall follow ye through a portal."

"There is magic, ancient magic, that prohibits a portal passage from your world to mine. Traveling through a portal from here to the human world causes me weakness and disorientation. I don't know what traveling between two magical worlds would do to you. Perhaps the prohibition is an ancient geis to keep the worlds separate. Besides, I'm sure I will find the Fir Dhaerrig within his throne chamber. You wouldn't fit. There's nothing you can do."

It was taking far too long to convince the angry gentry males he was the only one who could enter the domain of the Fir Dhaer-rig. Intervention by Nanceen and Lara finally ended with their grudging agreements.

As he moved away to find a more private place for his transformation, Nanceen grasped his upper arm. "Korin, be careful."

"As always, endearment."

The shy lowering of her lashes over the pink blush of her cheeks would be enough to keep any man from duty. Her fingers stiffened and relaxed around his arm. He touched his lips to the heat of her cheek. "I must do this, Nanceen."

"I know." The whisper was barely audible above the beating of his heart. He pulled her into a rough embrace and she clung to him. There was a desperateness to her touch, a fear he shared but dared not name. "I love you, Korin."

"And I you, my love." He whispered the words against her forehead, kissed her worried brow and stepped back. "I must go." He turned and, without looking back, slipped into the surrounding forest.

In the dim light of a heavy overhang of tree branches, Korin slowed his pace. When he could no longer hear the voices from the cabin, he stopped, leaned forward with his hands on his knees, and struggled to make his breathing even. He was weaker than he had admitted to the others and feared he would not even be able to make the transformation, let alone deal with the king.

Although he would have liked to delay the transformation until he was stronger, he would not cause his friends additional anguish. Every moment away from Nanceen lay like a stone within his heart. He could only imagine the pain and the emptiness caused by a missing child.

Without further thought, he spoke the tight, abrupt syllables to return his body to his tiny, fairy size. Thankfully, the transformation was not as physically powerful or pain filled as those dealing with his wings. But as the Otherworld grew around him, Korin's hopes and dreams shrank smaller than a pebble he could hold in his now tiny hands. Would he be able to return to

Nanceen in a size where he could love her? Would he be able to return at all?

He settled into his fairy form and sought to use his wings. There was no functioning, although the discomfort faded to a dull ache. With a slash of one hand, he formed a tear, focused on his destination, and stepped through to stand at the wide gilt doors leading to the Fir Dhaerrig's royal domain.

J aye paced from one side of the clearing to another. Slightly offset from his path, Derrik crushed the grass across another part of the yard. Iain strode in a small circle, from Lara's embrace to where his son sat wide-eyed with his grandmother, and back again. If the situation weren't so serious, so dangerous, Nanceen would chuckle at the absurdity of the men's actions. With her own nerves worn to a rugged frazzle, Nanceen stepped in front of her brother. "Pacing isn't going to help."

He looked down at her. Stark pain etched deeply in his dark eyes and pulled tight lines across his face. His fear was reflected in each of the faces around the clearing. And it was up to Korin, a being new to them, a man they didn't know, to return Belle to them and erase the anguish. There was nothing she could do, nothing more she could say to help ease them. Or to ease her own pain.

The sudden painful depths of being of alone nearly collapsed her to her knees. She glanced around the clearing. She wasn't alone, and would never be alone within the closeness of her family. But it was different now. Korin was her family. And she didn't know if she would ever see him again.

Taking Jaye's arm, she led him to the porch and pulled on his hand until he sat on the single, low step. As heir to leadership of the Clan, he took Belle's disappearance as a personal affront. And, as a loving grandfather, he was helpless. Nanceen had a flash of understanding. How hard must it be for him to rely on that unknown man for the safety of his family? Somehow, she had to try and distract him, and in doing so, herself as well.

"You said there was some problem over in the human world? Something wrong with the business?"

"Are you trying to distract me?" The words were harsh, but the slight grin he gave her when her gaze jerked to his was soft and understanding.

Nanceen shrugged.

He wrapped one arm around her shoulder, tugged her against his side, and kissed her cheek. "Thanks, sis. I think we both could use some distraction." He glanced at the others clustered about the clearing. "We all could."

"So, is there anything I can help with?"

Jaye tugged a folded paper from his shirt pocket. "There's a new caterer in town."

"Yes, I've met him." Nanceen gave Jaye a guilty grimace and continued. "In the park. One day this guy just came up and started talking to me. Said he was new in town and wanted to start a business. He thought catering would be interesting. But it wasn't that long ago I met him--he couldn't have gotten a business going that fast."

"No, he probably was ready to go when you met him. I wonder if he knew who you are, and your involvement with Zeroun's. Having competition is not the problem. The city's been growing and perhaps there would be enough business for both companies. Lord knows, there are times we can barely cover our obligations."

Nanceen gave him a playful shrug. "That's because you're a perfectionist."

"And look where it's gotten Zeroun's. The problem with this new caterer is his underhanded business practices. Take a look at this." He unfolded the paper. "I printed this off the Internet."

Before Nanceen looked at the page, she stared into the surrounding woods. Drawn to the exact spot where Korin disappeared, her gaze lingered and grew blurry with tears.

"He'll be fine, sis. There's something about Korin, some quality, some--something that lets me trust him. With Belle's safety. And with yours. Kae's told me what she knows about the supposed split between our races. It could be that now is the time to mend that split."

Derrik folded his tall form into a cross-legged position on the ground near them. "Aye. I canna explain, but I feel it as well." He fingered the long knife he'd tucked into a leather scabbard at his side. "I dinna care fer this waiting."

"Nor do I." Iain's stark declaration startled Nanceen as he and Lara joined them.

Concern and comfort flowed around the tight family group. Antin left his grandmother and crawled into his father's lap, lay his head on Iain's chest, and slept. The adults lowered their voices, trying to keep their fear tightly to themselves.

Nanceen sniffed and rubbed at her eyes with the hem of her skirt. "So, what about this usurper caterer?"

Jaye jerked at her words, then turned his attention to the paper. "Smear tactics. He's trying to undermine Zeroun's, trying to discredit my business." He poked at the paper repeatedly with one finger. Nanceen snatched it out of his reach before he ripped holes in the much crumpled and folded page. Jaye scraped his hand through his hair. "I can't believe the rumors he's trying to spread."

"Nothing I can't handle, Dad." All eyes turned to the deep voice. Jayse took another step forward, followed closely by Bryce. "We've taken care of damage control for Zeroun's. Now, what can we do here?"

Bryce leaned against the porch railing. "Pop's just finishing up. He'll be here soon."

"Good. The family needs to hold together now, and Tommy's always been there for us all." Jaye sighed, scooted slightly to one side when his wife joined him on the step, and sighed again. "And now... now we wait."

CHAPTER TWENTY-TWO

Titus chuckled while a newly constructed page loaded on the Zeroun's web site. So, they didn't waste time in responding to the opening of a new catering business. Or his rumor mongering. Passing information that even the matrons of the city found suspicious had been a tricky undertaking, but lucrative. He already had three contracts stolen from the other company, and was following up on a growing list of other leads.

The new web page would do little to affect the growth of his business, but it proved he had Zeroun's worried. Good. The anticipation of bringing down the arrogant Jaye Zeroun wound like a tight spring in his chest. It would be a satisfaction like none he had known.

Wringing a red-orange cap in his hands and muttering to himself, a boggart stumbled past Korin. As if suddenly recognizing the presence of another, the dirty creature jerked to a stop and turned slowly. His nut-brown eyes grew wide and the cap fell from limp fingers. "The Goodfellow."

"Aye. And is our good king within?" Korin took one step toward the boggart, but the smaller creature backed away, shaking his head. Korin's eyebrows lowered and a nearly visible knot of tension grew between them. "Well?"

"Oh, sir, yes, sir. But, don' go in there. He's waitin' fer you. It be not safe fer you." The boggart sunk to his knees and groveled before Korin. "I din't mean nothin' by spyin' on you, kind Good-fellow. I only do'd as my king commanded. I din't mean no harm. I din't know he'd do what he did. He be wrong, sir. Very, very wrong. I no be followin' him no more."

Korin waited with barely restrained impatience while the boggart continued his pitiful tirade. When the tiny man took a deep breath, Korin lifted one hand to stop his speech. "What are you talking about?"

"We's been talkin'."

"Who's we?"

"The boggarts, the brownies, all the clans of the Sidhe. We's not like the king no more. We's don' want him no more."

"I don't understand." Korin had his own problems with the king, his own reasons for not approving of the actions the fairy ruler had often taken. But he had no idea there were others-- entire clans who now claimed dissatisfaction.

"Even some of the solitaires, they no like 'im either. I din't know about others. A new king be wha' we need. A new ruler. This last--this stealin'. It be too much. Me, I kinda like the gentry. They be mostly kind folk. Lots agrees with me, sir. Lots. What can we do?"

The mention of the gentry pulled Korin from his own list of grievances against the Fir Dhaerrig. So, his suspicions were correct. The king had been involved. "I don't know what you can do. Me? I must face the Fir Dhaerrig."

The boggart scrambled eagerly to his feet. "Yes, yes. You mus' fight 'im."

"No. I don't want to fight. I just want the return--"

"He'll no' give up his prize. He wants to fight you. He hates you, Goodfellow, sir."

"Yes. I know that." Korin's shoulders slumped under the weight of his lifeless wings. Despite any good intentions he may have, what good could he do against a being who was whole and complete? His eyes closed against the defeat and hopelessness that stormed through him.

A bright memory, like the soft touch of a lover's caress, prodded at the defeat. He had felt incomplete before Nanceen. Now, she had filled him to overflowing. She loved him--without his wings. He straightened his back, squared his shoulders and gave the boggart a twitching grin. "Yes. I know that."

"What you gonna do?"

Korin didn't know what would happen once he entered the throne room, so he shrugged his shoulders. "Face the Fir Dhaerrig and let the fates fall where they may."

The boggart nodded as if it were the most intelligent answer Korin could have given him "We's be wi' you, Goodfellow. Support you, anyways," he finished quickly after Korin raised his eyebrows. The boggart took a backward step. "Luck t' you, Good-fellow." He turned and scuttled away.

Giving a single dry chuckle at the retreating figure, Korin let his worries fade for a brief second. So, others were unhappy with the king as well. It could put a different light on the outcome of this confrontation. As long as these hidden others continued to oppose the way the Fir Dhaerrig ruled if he lost.

No. He couldn't afford to lose. The life of a child was held in balance, and he delayed too long with the boggart. Refusing to let the doubts and weakness return to haunt him, Korin faced the wide doors. Standing spread-legged, he concentrated and pulled his wings closer to his body. The ragged pain caused by the move-ment held him frozen for the space of many breaths.

Then, he placed his palms flat against the wooden doors and shoved them open.

The banging of wood against the stone walls caused the musi-cians to lose their places within the dance, and silence followed the ringing impact. The few fairy folk who had joined the Fir Dhaerrig in his dance jerked to a halt and faced the door. When the king finally joined his subjects in peering into the brighter outdoor light, Korin stepped into the hall.

"Return the child to her world."

"Eh, Korin Goodfellow." The Fir Dhaerrig snickered. "The broken winged one. Ah, welcome." He glanced at his followers with a frown that slid to a grin as they dutifully began to laugh.

"Return the child."

"But I find I enjoy her company. Perhaps it is time to begin again the practice of bringing changelings to our world."

"You would not."

The Fir Dhaerrig stormed across the floor to stand before Korin. "Wouldn't I? You underestimate me, Goodfellow. Like my ancestors, I will do anything to obtain what I want."

"And what is it you want, sire?" Sarcasm dripped from Korin's words. The battle of words was one he thought he could win. A physical battle would be difficult, especially if the Fir Daeerig's followers joined him.

"What do I want? Why, you, of course. I want you home, here in the fairy world, where you belong."

Korin narrowed his eyes and let disbelief color his expression. "You no more want me here than you care about the child. Where is Belle?"

"The brat's name is Belle? Now I understand. I had wondered how the fulfillment of the first two conditions was sounded. Ah, but no matter. No more of the conditions will be filled. No longer will you court the gentry maid. No longer will you have contact with folk outside the fairy realm. Do you understand me, Goodfellow?"

"Where is Belle? Return the child to me and we shall be gone. I will not return."

"Again you seek to bargain with me, Goodfellow? So, do you think you can do better than your ancestor? The original Goodfellow--The Puck--bargained with my many times great grand sire.

And lost. As you shall surely do should you bargain with your king."

Silent, Korin stared at the king with consternation. What was the Fir Dhaerrig talking about? What kind of a bargain had been made so long ago? A bargain that the king knew, but he did not? Admitted, much of his family's early history was lost.

The Fir Dhaerrig swept his hand to one side. "But see, Goodfellow, in good faith, I shall show you the child. Be at ease, Korin. The child is safe. I would wish no harm to a new member of my kingdom."

Before Korin could deny the king any right to Belle, a partition opened to one side of the hall. Curled in the cramped space, Belle lay with her eyes closed, her small mouth lax in sleep. Korin took a step toward her, but was halted by the swift rising of the Fir Dhaerrig's staff into his path. The sharp point of the skull's snout poked into Korin's shoulder.

"I didn't give you leave to be with the brat, Goodfellow." After shoving the staff to one side, Korin fisted his hands and held his arms stiff against his side. "I do not need your permission to take the child back to her family."

"You must obtain permission from me for everything, Goodfellow. Gone are the days you may do as you wish. Gone are the moments you flaunt yourself before me. Once and for all, I shall break the family Goodfellow. And you, Korin Goodfellow, shall be mine to do with as I desire." The Fir Dhaerrig's face crinkled with wicked merriment as he repeatedly poked Korin with the skull-tipped staff. "D'you hear me? You are mine."

Korin bore the king's taunting silently, took the abusive blows without flinching until a vicious jab caught in a nearly healed tear of one wing. His neck arched back until his tightly closed eyes faced the ceiling. His mouth formed a tight, straight line as he bit his inner lip keep from moaning. The pain seared through him, bringing sweat to burn his face.

"So the broken wings are still a bit tender, eh?" The king danced to Korin's other side, jabbing his staff, but not touching Korin.

Feeling the charged air swirl around him as the king feinted first one way then to the other side, Korin struggled against growing weakness and diminishing hope. How could he fight the king, or anyone, when he couldn't even defend himself against taunting words and the jabs of a simple staff?

There was a faint whistle near his left ear. He lifted his hand and caught the staff in his fist before it landed on his shoulder. One jerk pulled the wood from the Fir Dhaerrig's hands. Korin opened his eyes and smiled grimly at the king's surprised expression. "What do you know of the attack?"

Surprise turned to feigned innocence. "What attack do you speak of, Goodfellow? There have been no attacks in the fairy world."

Korin poked the butt end of the staff into the king's ponderous belly. "The attack upon me within the gentry portal."

Chuckling, the Fir Dhaerrig waggled his finger back and forth. "You know better than to enter a gentry portal. It's your own fault if you were… um… discouraged from further use."

Resisting the urge to swing the heavy wooden pole against the king's hairy temple, Korin took a deep breath. "What creature did you send into the portal? Will it harm others?"

"No one but upstart, uppity fairies, who believe they're better than the rest. Your precious gentry are safe." The king snatched at his staff and jerked it back into his possession. Korin stumbled forward with the force and landed on his knees before the king.

"Now, that's what I like to see--obedience and veneration from a fool. Get you from my sight, Korin Goodfellow. Hide like your ancestor did after his fall before my clan. Forget the gentry maid, forget the existence of other races. Follow the decrees of your king and all will go well. Disobey me with the smallest of infractions, and the consequences will be severe." The king leaned close and lifted Korin's chin with the skull end of the staff. "Do not tempt me, Korin."

Wincing away from the king's fetid breath, Korin waited a moment before he lifted his gaze. The smile he had for his king, the determination he forced into his features, made the Fir

Dhaerrig take a step back. "Return the child to her folk, then mayhaps I will bargain with you."

The staff clattered to the floor and the king stomped one foot, then the other. "No. There will be no bargains. It is the time of my clan, my rule. It is not to be challenged by the likes of a Goodfellow. I will keep the child, make her my fairy changeling. She shall serve me as you will not."

"I will not allow it." Unsteady, Korin rose to his feet.

"Allow?" The king clutched his belly with one hand and laughed. "You can do nothing. Allow? Be pleased I allow you to live after this display of rebellion. Rejoice I allow you to remain within the fairy world, broken and humiliated as you are. Find a mountain like Peg-leg Jack and hide yourself away, Goodfellow. Do not dare to come to my court again."

At the mention of Jack, Korin nodded. Another confirmation. The Fir Dhaerrig had been involved in the return of his wings--as well as the portal attack. Everything that had happened had been designed to prevent him from fulfilling the conditions of the agreement. He slipped his hand to his side, felt the parchment through the leather of the bag, and took comfort from the crinkling presence. But Nanceen's love made it possible to thwart the Fir Dhaerrig's machinations. And, even though she was far from him in the gentry Otherworld, her love would continue to strengthen him.

Korin squared his shoulders and with an effort that nearly cost him his remaining strength, spread his tattered wings wide. After a moment to gather the remnants of his determination, he turned in a small circle, meeting the gazes of each of the gathered fairy folk. "See what the king has caused."

The low whisper of a moan traveled around the chamber as the fairy folk were shown the ripped and shredded remains of Korin's large wings. The murmur of comment followed the moan and filled Korin with the strength of the grudging support of his fellows.

"No. This is all the Goodfellow's doing," the king shouted. He snatched up his staff and stomped along the edges of the gathering. "I've done nothing but protect our fairy world. It was him." The king stopped before the throne and slid onto the high seat. He lifted the staff slowly until it pointed, shaking, at Korin. "He demands congress with the gentry. He wants to merge the worlds and bring back the degradations of the gentry."

Harsh laughter burst from Korin's lips. "There are no legends of strife between fairy folk and the gentry. Tales are only told of the gracious rule of Oberon and Titania. When they passed the veil to an unknown world, only then did problems begin. It is our history."

"History?" The Fir Dhaerrig chuckled. "What do you know of our history, Korin Goodfellow?" The king swung his staff to indicate the others in the room. "Out, all of you. I find I must educate this young fairy."

Korin stood solidly in the center of the floor. What a fool the king was, sending all the others from the room. While Korin had never perfected any fighting skills, he thought his quickness would be to his advantage. And the life of Belle, the happiness of his gentry friends, was worth any price he had to pay. He would win this day. And prayed Nanceen would forgive him for his foolishness.

"I need no education from you, Fir Dhaerrig."

Bushy eyebrows rose over the king's dark, beady eyes. "Oh, but I think you do. Have you never wondered why Oberon would give over the rule of fairy folk to one who would bargain with the Rat Men?"

Korin shrugged. "I would imagine the great Oberon determined who was the best suited to rule after him and chose that fairy."

The brush of eyebrows rose further until they were lost under the shock of dirty hair falling over the king's forehead. He snorted with laughter. "You are rather uneducated in the ways of our world, aren't you? Rest assured, Oberon did make a choice, the other? He made a bargain."

"Your clan has fallen far since those days."

"Not really, Goodfellow. Now listen, upstart, and hear the

history of the clan of kings, of the Fir Dhaerrig." The king pounded his staff twice on a large, crystal studded stone next to the throne. At a sharply spoken word, the stone cracked and a thick, hide-bound volume rose, hovered in the air a moment, then settled to the floor at the king's feet. "See here, here is the true history of the clan of kings. Begun by my many greats grand sire, each king since then has recorded his rule. As have I."

"What interest do I have in a journal?"

"You will find this enlightening." The king used the staff to open the cover. "See. Here is copied the proclamation Oberon made before he ran from his responsibilities. Hear the words of our first, great and glorious king."

The hard sarcasm created a boiling anger within Korin. To speak so about Oberon was--

A low, melodious voice rose from the book, stealing Korin's anger. The voice was beautiful, forceful, a leader's voice. Korin's eyes burned. The sounds of Oberon's voice filled him with a great longing to know the ancient king, to pledge himself, forever, to such a king. He tried to clear his head. That king was long gone. He had to face the current king, a far, far cry from what a leader should be.

"I know the words of the proclamation. They are spoken often at celebrations. I have read them within the archives."

Rubbing his hands together, the Fir Dhaerrig leaned forward. "Wait. There is more, words none have heard these many centuries. Words you need to hear."

Korin took a deep, calming breath and listened. It was difficult to retain his anger as the wordy proclamation flowed over him. However, a new, strange strength gathered within him. If it helped him in the coming battle, he would wait. And listen.

And lo, my beloved peoples, as Titania and I linger not upon this world, we would not leave you without leadership. The fair ones, the gentry have chosen to live as clans, separate but together, led by the children of Titania, ruled over by the sons and daughters of Oberon. This is our decree, our wish, our hope for the future.

To the wee folk, charming fairies, the dryads of the trees, nymphs of

238 · LIZZIE STARR

lakes, howlies of the skies, dwarves of mountains deep--to all these and more--we have no children to lead you.

Korin sighed and angled away from the throne. Belle slept, innocent and alone within the alcove. Listening to a proclamation learned by all young of the fairy world before their right of passage to adulthood was a waste of time. He folded his arms across his chest, turned back to the king, and glared at the smirk on the Fir Dhaerrig's pointy face.

The king lifted one finger. "Wait," he whispered. "There's more."

More? The proclamation ended with Oberon's lament. No one knew who was chosen as king, nor how the Fir Dhaerrigs had stolen that rule from the appointed one. Korin snorted in disbelief. How could Oberon have been such a fool? Or mayhaps he was no fool, and it was the Fir Dhaerrigs who had changed. Either way, Korin was finished with the abusive rule. He would take Belle and return, somehow, to the gentry Otherworld. There would be a life for him there, even if he remained the size of a man's hand.

"I said listen." The king's shout intruded on Korin's thoughts and he returned his attention to Oberon's voice.

We have thought for long days, forgone the pleasures of the hunt and dances for many long nights. Now, my queen and I agree and shall anoint the one chosen to lead the fairy folk. It is by our will, by our word, the new king is chosen. He has long been with us and has learned to temper his foolhardiness with understanding and wisdom. He shall rule you honestly, with a fair and loving heart. Honor him as you would Titania, follow him as you would Oberon.

Comes now before you the chosen of Oberon and Titania. Behold the Puck. King of the fairies, Robin Goodfellow.

The ringing of the voice faded high into the chamber's stone ceiling. Korin blinked twice. He hadn't heard correctly. He blinked again.

"Oh, you heard the words right, Goodfellow. Your ancestor-- one prankster named Puck, the idiot Robin Goodfellow--was proclaimed king after Oberon. Just because he kissed the hem of the king, fawned over his bitch of a queen. And so, he was king. But not for long."

"I don't understand."

"Of course you don't. Puck didn't want it known what a fool he had been, so he hid the history of what happened from other fairy folk. Have you never wondered why your family always stayed so far from court? Until you, foolish boy. You would have done better to have stayed away as well."

There was too much for him to understand. After taking Belle back to her family, he would return and learn the truth. He had been away from the gentry Otherworld too long already and concern over his friends' fears rose strong within him.

The Fir Dhaerrig rose to his feet, adjusted his belt, and moved to stand directly before Korin. "Listen to me, Goodfellow. Leave now, and we'll forget this ever happened. Go back to your secluded life. Leave me my changeling and bother this court no more. I promise you--you will not find a welcome here again."

"I will not leave without the child. Belle must be returned to her family."

"I..." The king thumped his chest. "... am her family now."

A sneer twisted Korin's lips. "You are no king." The hiss of his words surprised even him. "How did you...?"

"Become king? Why, I inherited the throne from my sire." The Fir Dhaerrig chuckled. "Oh, I am sorry. You meant how did my clan become the clan of kings? It's all in the book, if you'd care to listen. But, no. I see you are too impatient for that. I will tell you." The Fir Dhaerrig stepped away from Korin, spread his legs, leaned his staff against his side and tucked his hands behind his back.

"I suppose Puck was a good enough king, but he had one flaw. Well, I take that back, he had many flaws." The king jerked and lifted his staff across his chest in a warding gesture when Korin took a step forward. "But the flaw of which I speak was his love of betting. He would do anything for a gamble. He gambled once too often. And lost. He lost the kingdom, Goodfellow. Not caring enough for the fairy folk, he took a challenge, was unable to fulfill all the conditions, and failed."

Sharp, pointy teeth glistened wetly when the king grinned at Korin. "Much like you did."

"He would not have done so," Korin muttered.

"And who would have thought you would bargain your freedom, lose your wings, and fail--all because of a woman? And not just any woman--a gentry maid. A woman you could never, in your wildest dreams, seduce and hold."

The anger holding Korin's wings spread flushed from him, and the wounded appendages slumped about his shoulders. The rat man was correct. Much had been wagered, and much lost. The parchment at his side crinkled. And much had been gained. Any losses had come from trickery. The king's trickery.

"What artifice did your clan use to keep Robin from a honest win?"

With his face settled into an expression of wounded pride, the Fir Dhaerrig rested one hand on his chest. "Chicanery? You accuse my clan of trickery?"

"Yes, your clan. And you. My wounds are a result of your treachery, your plans, and machinations. What did you hope to gain from this?"

The king returned to his throne, used his staff to close the book, and sighed. "It was always feared a Goodfellow would come again to challenge my clan's rule. So, we hid the true proclamation and it was forgotten. Until you showed up here, begging to court a gentry maid. What a fool you are, Goodfellow. With you ends your family. And any threat to the clan of kings. I should just kill you now."

"I doubt you have the courage for it." Korin rolled his shoulders, tensed, and tried to relax his muscles. So, it would come down to a physical fight. Whatever the outcome, Belle must be safe. "You seem to love the challenge and the bargaining as well as you say Robin did."

The king grinned. "Ah, yes. It's a fine day when I can best someone."

"Then bargain with me."

"That parchment at your side is the only bargain I make with you, Goodfellow. And, as with your beloved ancestor, you have fallen to the Fir Dhaerrig. The clan of kings remains unchallenged."

"No, it does not. If you will not bargain, you will fight. For the return of the child."

"The child? You wish nothing else, Goodfellow?" The king waggled his eyebrows at Korin and lifted one hand, palm forward, and a figure took blurry form--two figures--locked in a passionate embrace. "Hmm, Korin. Is there nothing else you would bargain for?"

Closing his eyes against the writhing figures, Korin shook his head. "For the freedom of the child. Nothing more."

"Eh, you've lost the desire? I make no bargain with a fool."

"Fight, my one time king. I follow you no more."

CHAPTER TWENTY-THREE

The passage of time held no meaning as Nanceen and her family waited for Belle's return. Even the chittering songs of the birds were silent. The family gathered in tight, supportive clusters, then separated, each to deal with the waiting in their own way. Then they would come together again and dry each other's tears in a flowing dance of sorrow.

The youngest of the Alastriona, Jayse's friend Macaire, hovered at the edge of the clearing, waiting to carry messages or assist his leader in any way. The Queen sat with Kelene and Stephen. Although the support and nearness of the rest of the Faerie clan was tangible in the clearing, the fey themselves left the family alone in their despair.

Nanceen sat with Kaelea at one end of Lara's porch. Kae had spread a fragile, tattered scroll on a blanket before her and leaned close to study the faded writing.

"Kae? Do you think I'm being foolish?"

Touching her index finger to the scroll to keep her place, Kae glanced up at her sister. "About Korin?"

Nanceen nodded. She looked out over the clearing, then stared at her tightly clasped hands. She wrung her fingers, tightening her grip until the tips of her fingers turned white.

"Love is..." Kae gave a mirthless chuckle. "I was gonna say love's not foolish, but I suppose there are times it is. At least, it makes us foolish. But no, I don't think you are, Nance. Just how deeply do you love him?"

"More than I understand. More than I can keep bound up inside me. If I could rush into his world and bring him back, I would do it in a heartbeat. If he would ask me to remain in that world with him, I would give up my life here to be with him. There's no words. I love him. I love Korin. No matter what happens."

Kae straightened. "Ooh, you've got it bad, sis."

"But--"

"And that's good, Nance. So wonderful. So beautiful. He'll be back. I'm sure of it."

"How can you be sure when I have so many questions?" Nanceen forced herself to loosen her cramping fingers. "All I know is when he's with me, I'm not lonely. I'm home."

"I know." Kae tapped her chest. "I feel it here. Like I've always known your feelings, understood how you felt. Like you know me. I'm so happy for you, Nance. So happy, I could just burst."

"Kae?" When her sister looked at her expectantly, Nanceen shook her head. "Oh, nothing. I'm sorry. Go back to your reading. I'm sorry I interrupted you."

"You know you can interrupt me anytime." Kaelea returned her attention to the parchment.

Starring into the blurry distance, Nanceen attempted to clear her mind. But all she could do was wonder what was happening in Korin's fairy world. Was he safe? Had he found Belle? When--?

"Oh, my." Kae's startled exclamation drew the family to her side. They waited as she traced words with her finger and mouthed them silently. She flattened her palm over a large hole in the scroll and glanced up at the family clustered around her.

"This part, right here..." She pointed to a long passage. "This is the transcription of a speech. A speech--I don't believe this--a speech given by a fairy king. It's Oberon. And, he explains how the gentry clans were to be ruled by his children--and Titania's."

Jaye leaned over the scroll, but unable to read the arcane language, only shook his head and straightened. "How old is this?"

"Ages, Jaye. This was written a millennium before Shakespeare. And written by a fairy scribe." Her eyes grew wide. "This might be more than legend."

Nanceen closed her eyes. "Does it say anything about a separation of gentry and fairy? Could this be the time Korin told us about?"

"Nooo... nothing directly. No. Wait. This says wee folk... we have no children to lead you. Then there's this huge hole, almost like someone ripped out a part of the scroll. I have no idea what that means."

Derek cleared his throat. "It means the tale Korin tells is true."

Unwilling to take his eyes from the Fir Dhaerrig, a few steps backward took Korin to the center of the hall. The Fir Dhaerrig remained on his throne, expressions of glee, dismay, and confusion racing across his face. When the king didn't immediately join him, Korin moved toward the alcove where Belle slept under magic he hoped gave her happy dreams. He brushed his fingertips across the child's softly rounded, pink cheek. The soft spikes of her sooty lashes tickled his hand and the tense lines of his face relaxed into an honest smile.

"Never fear, little one. I'll return you to your family soon."

The small, rosebud mouth puckered and relaxed, and a soft breath of air passed over Korin. "Bu'fly man." The whisper, dream words only, increased the intensity of determination within Korin, and he leaned forward to kiss Belle's cheek. She giggled in her sleep. "Tickles."

The child could hold him in her hands, and he would appear as no more than a doll, or a broken winged butterfly. And he was her protector. He would do what he must to see she was safe. And home.

There was a family resemblance about the slight almond tilt to Belle's eyes. Nanceen's dark eyes also tipped up at the corner, and Korin took a deep breath to hold in the memory of the softness of her eyelids against his kisses. Time grew short.

He turned with a jerk and startled the stealthy advance of the Fir Dhaerrig. The king stopped dead in his tracks, his staff lifted high above his head and now shaking in his hands.

Korin rested his fists on his hips and planted his legs apart. It would anger the king, so he laughed. "More tricks, rat man? Can't you even fight fairly?"

The staff lowered slowly. "You want a fair fight, Goodfellow? Fine." A sharp, awkward motion created a stir in the air before Korin. A long, dark staff appeared and hovered at shoulder height. "My choice of weapon, since you offer the challenge. I have no need of a blade to defeat you. My staff will beat you down, my staff will break yours, and my staff will subdue you. By my will alone shall you live or die." He paused and grinned, showing his sharp, pointed teeth. "I think the latter."

The Fir Dhaerrig strode to the center of the hall. Planting the butt end of the staff against the stone floor, he kept his back to Korin and waited.

Using strength he didn't think he could spare, Korin struggled to fold his wings against his back. The movements brought fresh stabs of pain that added stronger focus to his determination. With his wings tucked away, Korin reached for the staff, twirled, and swiped it singing through the air, to test the balance. Surprised at the perfect length, he balanced the smooth wood against his palms and grunted with satisfaction.

The king turned to him. "Shall we? Although it would be better to have witnesses--"

"There be witness, sire."

Both the king and Korin turned toward the sound of the rustling. A tight group of boggarts, followed by a small representation of fairy folk inched back into the hall. They sidled along the walls until the open area was ringed by bodies.

The king grinned. "Ah, good. Now none can accuse me of

trickery. Master Goodfellow? Are you at last ready to meet your fate?"

Korin grunted again, lifted the staff into a defensive position and waited. Fighting with a stave was common training among the fairy folk, for the weapon, sized to each individual, equalized strength, stature, and ability. Korin trusted his ability.

The suddenness of the king's attack pushed Korin back half a dozen steps before he was able to do more than defend. The skill with which the king fought brought numerous stinging blows to Korin's body as he studied the Fir Dhaerrig's fighting style.

With a grim nod, Korin judged the speed and distance needed for his attack. He adjusted his position to face the Fir Dhaerrig squarely, one hand lightly gripping the center of his pole, the other resting halfway to one end. He twirled the stave once, lifted one eyebrow to mock the king and, with a flourish, returned to his original position.

The Fir Dhaerrig leapt forward and thrust his staff toward Korin's belly.

A simple twist to one side and a lift of the rear of his pole caught the king's staff. The thud of wood against wood echoed loud, and the king screamed a challenge, pressing forward, trying to force Korin's stave to one side.

Slipping to one knee, Korin pulled his stave back just enough to thrust, alter his grip to the end of the cool wood and swing the length at the Fir Dhaerrig's ankles. When the king jumped over the whistling wood, Korin rose, took three steps back, and focused again on a forward facing position.

"Foolish actions, Goodfellow," the king panted. He turned to the assembled fairy folk. "See how he stands? See how he leaves himself unprotected? Any child's attack..." The king's staff whirled through the air, coming down with a hard, two- handed stroke. But, the whoosh of attack fell to the stone floor missing Korin by a hair's breadth.

Returning a sharp thrust to the King's upper arm, Korin danced lightly to one side. As the fight progressed, his strength grew. He didn't understand how that could be, but wouldn't question it until later. After he defeated the rat man. Korin spun in a circle and jabbed his staff backwards into the king's soft belly flesh.

"Oomph." Recovering from the blow, the Fir Dhaerrig silently thrust and feinted with his staff, changing his grip rapidly so the blows came from one side then the other without pause.

Korin ducked, twisted, and slid from side to side to avoid the blows. The insane urge to laugh was knocked away when he misjudged a thrust and the tip of the king's staff landed squarely in the center of his chest. The pain forced him to double over and struggle for air.

"Ah ha. A point for me." The Fir Dhaerrig turned toward the folk lining the walls, lifted his staff high above his head and cackled. "See how the Goodfellow fails yet again?"

Straightening slowly, Korin lifted his own staff high and twirled it horizontally above his head. Faster and faster the wood spun. He stepped toward his opponent. The whine of air as the stave sliced through it alerted the king and he turned just as Korin leapt into the air. Using the weight of the stave to carry him forward, he kicked out at the king's face, flew over him, and landed, facing the astonished Fir Dhaerrig. Letting the spinning slow vertically before him, Korin lowered the stave.

The Fir Dhaerrig rubbed the side of his face. "A fine trick, Goodfellow. Now, let us end this."

Ducking under the slowly spinning stave, the king swept out with his staff, caught the side of Korin's knee, and laughed at the sickening crunch of wood against shattering bone. A low moan accompanied Korin's fall to the floor. A triumphant shout rang as the king pressed one foot into Korin's chest to hold him steady and held the pointed skull against Korin's throat. He leaned onto the staff until the skull punctured the skin and drew a thin rivulet of blood.

The new pain twisted Korin's leg into an unnatural position. He fought the agony as he fought pressure of the Fir Dhaerrig standing on his chest. He fought the hot, damp feel of his flowing blood. But he could not fight the failure sinking deep in his belly.

Why had he thought he could fight the rat man--and win? Why did he think he could rescue a changeling child? Why had he imagined he, a broken-winged fairy, could bring happiness to a gentry maid?

::... *love him. I love Korin. No matter....*::

The words, the broken sentences, touched his mind with a soft caress. No. She could not love him. He had failed. And would probably die for his efforts.

::... *no matter...*::

The pressure against his neck lessened, and the Fir Dhaerrig stepped from his chest. But before Korin could draw a relieved breath, the king kicked his broken knee. Korin could not withhold the cry that rang throughout the chamber. He curled into a writhing ball of pain.

The Fir Dhaerrig's face appeared close to his, and the hot, fetid breath made Korin's bile rise. "And now, Goodfellow, I grow tired of you. No longer do you have the option of returning to your family's seclusion. No longer will you pass the doors to my chambers. Once you are carried from this room--dead--you shall return no more. I will even erase the memory of you from the world of fairy. You, and your ancestor will be no more."

Korin tried to twist his face away, but the king grabbed his hair, pulled it tight in his fist, and held Korin in place. "You look at me. Let my visage be the last you see."

::*Endearment, I'm so sorry. I couldn't save Belle. I wasn't strong enough. Forgive me*::

Closing his eyes, Korin waited. He gave no thought to the method the Fir Dhaerrig would use to end his life, and it truly didn't matter. Mayhaps the gentry warrior would discover a way to save the child. Mayhaps Nanceen would find love with another and forget him. Mayhaps, in the oblivion of death, he would forget her as well.

He doubted it.

· · ·

Nanceen stood, jerked, and tried to catch her balance against the porch railing. Panic settled in her chest, restricted her breathing, and made her tear at the loose neckline of her shirt. Wild with fear, she turned away from her family. "I... I need to take a walk... or something. I'll be back soon." Their gazes burned into her back as she stumbled away from the cabin and into the woods. When she was out of sight, she fell to her knees and pressed her hands against the cool, damp earth.

Something happened to Korin. She felt it within the fiber of her muscles, the marrow of her bones, the very cells of her body. But how? She sat with her back against the rough bark of an aged tree. The word how blazed across the inside of her closed lids as she tried to calm herself.

Her brother and his wife had an unusual connection. Sparks flew--literally--when they touched. She'd heard of couples who developed some sort of a psychic connection, one that grew stronger as they spent years together. Was this what that kind of a relationship was like? Similar, yet so completely different from the twin's connection she had with Kae.

A sudden jolt of agony doubled her over and she clutched her stomach. She choked back a strangled cry. ::*Oh, Korin. What's happening?*::

Black doubt careened through the agony. Was the doubt hers, or Korin's? Hot tears burned her eyes before squeezing between her lashes and trailing down her cheeks. It didn't matter. She had to defeat the doubt. Only then would Korin return to her.

::*Be strong, my love. I'll be here when you return, when you bring Belle back to us. I promise. Promise....*::

She lifted one hand to her chest and made a motion from her childhood. ::*... cross my heart.*::

CHAPTER
TWENTY-FOUR

T he Fir Dhaerrig loosed Korin's hair, shoved his head to one side, and spit on his face. "Bah, You're hardly worth it, Goodfellow. I thought you might offer me some challenge after all. Now, bid farewell to life, Korin, bid farewell to your dreams." The king laughed and lifted his staff. "I think a single blow to the temple will suffice. As easily as I broke your knee, how hard can your head be?"

Korin closed his eyes and fought the pain and desperation to bring an image of Nanceen behind his closed lids. She would be the last beautiful vision of his life. He didn't believe in any afterlife. There would be no travel through the veil to another world for him. It was the end of Korin Goodfellow. At least he had known his endearment's love. "Nanceen," he whispered.

Listening to the sounds of the Fir Dhaerrig taking a firm stance near him, hearing the way the king tested the swing of his staff, gave Korin strange comfort. At least the pain would be gone. But how could he leave Nanceen alone? Despite the dread, he sighed. At least she had a supportive family.

"Now, Goodfellow. The anticipation is over." After tapping the staff three times close to Korin's head, the Fir Dhaerrig lifted the heavy wood and grunted as he forced it downward.

Korin smiled, the sad stretch of his lips a relief.

"NO! This one mine."

A loud groan sounded, followed by the clatter of wood against stone. Korin's eyes popped open in surprise.

A dark shape floated between him and the king. The Fir Dhaerrig cowered on his knees, his head covered by his splayed fingers. The tremor in his voice showed his fear. "Return from whence you came, Bocan."

A Bocan? Korin urged his tight muscles to slide away from the formless being. There had never been a witness's account, no descriptions ever made, so the Bocan was thought to be mythical. Was. Now, if this were a Bocan...

"I not have 'im before. Liked the taste of fairy. Want more. Always more. I take... and later take more."

The Fir Dhaerrig's hand shook as he lifted it toward the Bocan in denial. "No, return. I command you."

"No foolish little creature commands me. I want, I take."

The king struggled to his feet. The fear and panic filling the pointy face gave Korin a small sense of satisfaction. Struggling to raise himself on his arms, Korin dragged his useless leg away from the cold presence. He stopped, shivered and gasped. The cold, the voice, the enmity. This was the creature that attacked him within the portal. A Bocan, a creature, whose only delight was to attack and mutilate travelers, was free within the gentry portals. And now in the fairy world as well.

But what could he do? He couldn't even fight one Fir Dhaerrig, couldn't even save one child from becoming a changeling. Better just to let the Bocan take him.

Korin stopped his struggles and angled so he could see Belle. She still slept the magical sleep, and would know nothing of the terrors of the Bocan. Taking a deep breath, Korin closed his eyes.

The Bocan was within the portals? He jerked to sitting, gasped back a cry of pain, and clutched his knee. How many gentry would the creature take? The worth of his own life was less than nothing. But the lives of his friends, of Nanceen, were in danger.

He couldn't defeat the Bocan, but perhaps he could wound the creature enough that the gentry warriors could subdue him.

When he scooted toward his fallen stave, the ragged bottoms of his wings caught against the flat stones of the floor. Pain turned to anger, and anger to rage. He ached to howl at the unfairness of it all. He'd wanted nothing more than to change the course of fairy history. Now he knew loving a member of the gentry would do that. The howls died in his throat, he wrenched the wing tip from under him and stretched to reach the staff.

Bracing the end of the tall, wooden pole against the floor, Korin lifted the free end and held it at an angle that he hoped would pierce the Bocan when the creature came for him. It was a last desperate act, but mayhaps a redeeming one.

The Bocan moved closer to the Fir Dhaerrig. Its slobbery breathing rose in pitch, the wavering form solidified into lifted arms, a thick, dense body and shaggy, overlarge head. The king shouted, but the sound was lost as the darkness of the Bocan closed around him. The surprise and terror filling the king's face was barely visible through the darkness.

"You no rule me, fool king. Banish me? No. Banish you." The Fir Dhaerrig's mouth moved, his eyes grew wider, and his head shook back and forth. The Bocan's wild laughter brought pain to Korin's ears. The king looked frantically around the throne room. Korin followed his gaze. Only one boggart remained crouched behind a tall, golden coffer. The rest of the fairy witnesses had fled. There would be no help.

Before Korin drew breath to issue a challenge to the Bocan-- although why he thought it important to save a king who had grievously wronged him--the creature swung one arm in a wide arch. The wild-eyed glare of the Fir Dhaerrig followed the move- ment. He was caught unaware by the punch from the other direction.

The Fir Dhaerrig flew backwards, but instead of landing heavily against his ornate throne, a halo of light flashed once around his body and a swirl of darkness took him. The echoing screams stopped abruptly when the darkness caved in upon itself and was gone.

"Good. No trouble Bocan no more. Now, where my fairy lunch?"

Blistering cold engulfed Korin when the Bocan turned toward him. He could see the creature's face--and wished it was still a formless being. Long, black teeth, dripping with yellowish slime, glistened in the creature's evil smile. Orange rimmed, lidless eyes stared at him. "Oh ho, there be you."

Korin tightened his grip on the staff and settled his face into what he hoped was an expression of calm defiance. He vowed silently to show no fear as the creature took him. ::*Sweet endearment, my Nanceen. I do love you. Farewell, darling one.*::

"I wait no more. Mine. I take. Then take more. Fool to try stop me." The Bocan straightened and grew tall enough to scrape the high ceiling of the chamber with his head. "I eat, I grow. A good thing, no?" The echoes of his laugher settled heavily in the room.

Korin shuddered. Would his contribution to the demise of the Bocan be enough? Would the remaining fairy folk fight together against the evil? Would the breach between fairy and gentry be sealed, allowing the gentry warriors to fight as well? There were too many questions, and no answers. "Come then, creature. You'll not find me an easy meal."

"Brave words, little one. I eat you quick."

The darkness advanced until the tip of the stave pressed against the Bocan's body. With another laugh, the Bocan moved forward, its ever-changing form flowed around the stave without harm. "Little sticks no hurt Bocan."

The light touch of the Bocan's long, icy claws made Korin gasp, and he loosed his grip on the staff. Instead of clattering to the floor, it sank deeper into the darkness and the Bocan laughed again. The fingers closed around Korin's shoulder.

The cold seeped into his muscles, inched down his arm and inward toward his heart. Numbing cold paralyzed him. He couldn't draw breath. He lost the will to breathe. Why fight the cold? There was little reason, nothing more he could do. Unable to form coherent thoughts, Korin let the darkness advance, let the cold take his will, his hopes, his life. As his vision faded, a bright light flashed. The whistle of a bladed weapon sounded over his head and the cold, fierce grip on his shoulder disappeared.

S crubbing at her face did little to hide her red nose and watery eyes, so Nanceen decided it didn't matter. Every member of her family fought the sadness, dried their tears, and contained the anger brought on by Belle's disappearance. When she returned to the cabin, she sat in the same place on the steps, took the same comfort from the presence of her brother beside her, looked at the same distraught faces surrounding her. What would they do if Korin wasn't successful?

After the sudden pain and doubt while she was within the woods, there had been nothing. No feelings, no concerns, nothing. It was as if Korin had shut a door and locked her from his thoughts. Had it been a conscious action? Or was he... dead?

Nanceen wrapped her arms about her waist and bent her forehead to her knees. When would this be over?

The warmth of Jaye's hand on her back centered Nanceen's wildly spinning thoughts. "Thanks," she whispered. "I'll be okay."

"I know. We always are, aren't we, sis?"

Nanceen lifted her head and glanced to the side. A tiny brown and very dirty face peered up at her from under the cover of a small bushy flower. The figure moved a leaf to one side and stepped cautiously into the open, swinging his gaze between Nanceen and the large black dog that focused intently on him.

Lifting her brows in question, Nanceen sat straight. This little being must belong to Korin's fairy world. Maybe he knew something... anything about Korin. She took a breath, but the little man spoke first.

"This be where the child belongs?"

All eyes turned toward her at the sound of the high, squeaking voice. Iain and Lara moved closer. Fear filled the little face and the creature seemed ready to skitter away, so Nanceen spoke quickly. "Belle? Yes, this is her home."

"I be a boggart. Once I served the king, the Fir Dhaerrig. He tooked the girl child to make a changeling. I din't think it a good thing. So, when he be gone, I tooked her back."

"Where? Where is she?" Several frantic voices asked the forceful questions, and the little man cowered under a leaf.

Nanceen held her hand out to him. "Don't be afraid. We're just concerned about Belle. Is she okay?"

Showing dirty teeth, the boggart grinned. "She's comin'."

With a shake of dark fur Noid leapt toward the forest, the happy barks accented by his wiggling greeting for the small girl who walked carefully from under the trees. Iain and Lara rushed to their daughter, while the rest of the family held back. The soft sounds of sighs and relieved tears filled the clearing. Nanceen gave the tiny man a smile.

"Thank you for bringing her home, my friend."

The boggart bowed low. "'Tis me duty, miss. We bringed him, too."

"Him?"

Nodding toward Belle, the boggart bowed again. "The new king, miss."

"King? I don't care about a king. Where's Korin?" Nanceen peered past Belle and into the forest. "When is he...?"

"Be careful, Da. I carried him like this." The soft lisp of Belle's words carried through the clearing as she handed something to Iain. He straightened and turned a mournful expression to Nanceen. With his hands before him as if in supplication, he herded Belle and Lara before him toward the cabin.

"Nance, I dinna..."

Nanceen knew what he carried, who he carried. She dashed the tears from her eyes, rose and waited until Iain reached the steps. Only then did she take a deep, but ineffective, breath and looked at his outstretched hands.

Barely filling Iain's large palms, Korin's bruised and broken body lay still. Too still. One leg bent at an awkward angle, dark splotches and scrapes covered any of the normally fair skin she could see. She couldn't breathe, and her heart stopped beating. There was a hollow emptiness in her chest that would never be filled again. "Is he..." she managed to gasp, "... is he dead?"

The boggart jumped to the porch railing and tugged on her sleeve. "He be alive, but our healers din't know what to do. Nothin' helped."

Riding on Lara's hip, Belle pointed to Korin. "See. My Bu'fly man. Uh, I mean Korin. Granda? Can you fix him?" She turned her dark gaze to Jaye. "Please?"

"I don't know, darlin'. Maybe we should just let him rest."

"No. Fix him. Granda, he needs fixed." Belle looked at Nanceen from under dark, spiky lashes. "Auntie 'Ceen wants you to."

Jaye chuckled. "How could I deny either of you? I will try, pumpkin, but I don't know if I can."

"You will." Belle nodded emphatically. "An' I'll give you a big kiss to help." She reached her chubby arms out to him. Jaye leaned into her hug and accepted a noisy, sloppy kiss. "How's dat?"

"That will help, Belle. Now, you go show your brother you're okay. Your da and I will take care of Korin."

"Auntie 'Ceen, too?"

After his affirmative answer, Belle wiggled to be released from her mother's tight hold and slid to the ground. She skipped toward Antin, where he stood with one arm hugging Derrik's leg. Belle stopped before her brother, tilted her head to one side, and patted his cheek. His serious expression didn't change, so she took her finger and stretched one side of his mouth into a smile. After doing the same with the other side, she wrapped her arms about his neck and kissed him. Antin gave her a look of such disgust as he wiped his lips with the back of his hand, making the adults chuckle. The tension surrounding the small cabin lifted.

Except for the tight knots winding their way across Nanceen's shoulders and down her spine. Korin looked so... so...

Where was the spark, the joy of life that drew her to him? Where was the way his eyes darkened to liquid silver when he looked at her? Would he ever look at her again?

"Come on, sis. Let's see what we can do for Korin. Although the last time I healed him went fine, I can't promise anything. I just don't know about his size." Jaye took her arm and herded her toward the cabin door.

The boggart, momentarily forgotten, clutched at her arm as she turned. "There's more I needs tell you. More about the king. 'Bout wha' happened. 'Bout the book."

Curiosity warred with concern in Kaelea's face and she moved closer to bend and peer closely at the boggart. He withstood the intensity of her gaze for a few moments before bowing. "How do, miss."

Without losing eye contact with the boggart, Kae spoke to Nanceen. "You go take care of Korin. I'll talk to this little man."

"I be a boggart, miss."

Kae grinned. "This boggart, then. If I find out anything important, I'll let you know right away." She straightened and gathered Nanceen into a tight embrace. "He'll be okay, Nance," she whispered. "I know he will."

Silent, Nanceen, Jaye, and Iain entered the cabin. The rest of the family gathered about Belle and continued to fuss over her until she crossed her arms over her small chest and stomped her foot. One hand on her hip, she glared up at her family then grinned, giggled, and let them continue to hug and kiss her.

Kae motioned to the boggart and led him to the end of the porch. The boggart stared at the parchments and books spread over a length of cloth. He let a grin pull his lips. He'd done the right thing in bringing the Goodfellow here.

Derrik left the family group and silently joined them. "I need to hear this as well."

The boggart glanced up at the tall gentry warrior. After a brief pause, he nodded, pulled a crooked stick from the air, and waved it four times. Two thick, leather clad volumes appeared and grew until they were of a size the gentry could easily read. Kae reached greedily toward the books, but the boggart tapped her hands none too gently with his wand.

"No. These be for the king. You give them ta him when he is well enough."

Kae rubbed her hands. "You keep mentioning a king. Who?"

"The Goodfellow, of course." The boggart cocked his head toward the cabin door.

Derrik snorted. "Yer sayin' Korin is yer king?"

"Aye." The boggart looked Derrik up and down before he explained. "Rightful, as we now unnerstand. The books will tell all."

"Can't you tell us anything?" Kae eyed the books and her fingers twitched.

The boggart chuckled. "That be why I be here. Tell yous wha' happen' an' why the Goodfellow be our new king." He settled cross-legged on the books, closed his eyes, and began his tale.

CHAPTER TWENTY-FIVE

Tain lay Korin carefully on a low, padded stool and stepped back. Jaye bent over the tiny form and gently moved his wings and his limbs to normal positions.

"Looks like there's only a little more damage to his wings, sis." Jaye glanced up at Nanceen. She lowered herself onto the couch and leaned forward, hands tightly clasped. What else was wrong? What other injuries--what if Jaye couldn't heal him?

Jaye continued. "Lots of bruises and scrapes. But, the worse looks like his knee. I would say by the looks of it, the kneecap is probably shattered."

"Can you..." The words caught in Nanceen's throat.

"I'll do what I can. For one our size, it would be no problem. But, in his natural size, I'm not sure how much power to use. And I don't know if he can handle a full healing so soon after the last one." At Nanceen's nod, Jaye closed his eyes to gather his healing power.

Nanceen looked away and stared down at her hands. The knuckles were white from her tight grip. She tried to relax, but her fingers only cramped tighter. Having the confidence her brother would do what he could to help Korin, she let those worries fade. It was her fault Korin was hurt. But would he blame her for his injuries? She lifted her eyes to his tiny form. Would he ever be able to become large again--would he even want to?

The blue glow emanating from Jaye's extended hands encompassed Korin. His head rolled from side to side and he cried out a denial. The tiny sound shot daggers of pain and anguish through Nanceen's heart. He'd given so much to her. How could she hope to return even half so much to him?

"Please, Korin," she whispered. "Let Jaye heal you again." At the sound of her voice, Korin's thrashing ceased and his face turned toward her. The tense lines marring his forehead eased and the turned down corners of his lips straightened.

Jaye took a deep breath. "That's all I dare do right now. It looks like he's going to sleep for a while." He rose from his crouch and backed from the stool. "Iain, let's go join the reunion." Casting Nanceen an enigmatic look, he slapped his son-in-law on the shoulder and turned away. Iain followed him from the cabin, leaving Nanceen alone in the silence.

She watched Korin. Counted the rise and fall of his breaths. Winced at each restless movement of his body. How long would he sleep this time? What would happen when he woke? He shivered, and Nanceen looked around for a covering appropriate for his tiny body. She rose, found a clean towel in the kitchen and covered him carefully. It was like tucking a doll into bed. How did he grow to the size of the gentry?

Curling into a ball of misery on the end of the couch, Nanceen rested her head on the overstuffed armrest. She laid her hand beside Korin, but jerked away when she mentally compared his size to her hand. How would this end? She knew what she wanted, but was it possible? Or would Korin become nothing but a tiny memory she'd try to stretch to fill the rest of her life?

His lips moved in silent speech and he smiled. Even fairy sized, he stirred her, brought warmth and wild tingles to her body. Nanceen rolled to her back and stared hopelessly at the ceiling.

. . .

"Let me get this straight." Kae stared at the boggart, who returned her gaze with a mischievous grin. "What I discovered in this scroll is true, and there really was an Oberon and Titania. Then, in the text that's missing, it says that when they left the fairy realm, they named Puck king of the fairies."

The boggart nodded happily.

"But, a Fir... Fir..."

"Yes, yes. A Fir Dhaerrig."

"A Fir Dhaerrig made some sort of a bet and Puck was tricked out of his kingship."

"Yes, yes. All in this book, words of all Fir Dhaerrig kings." The boggart patted one of the books.

"And then, after all this time, Korin, Puck's descendent, made a bargain with the current king. And was tricked as well?" At the boggart's nod, Kae sighed. This was a dream, the dream of any scholar. Actual volumes that showed what was once thought myth and fantasy to be true. To be able to touch the pages, read the words... she sighed again.

"There be many who disagreed with this Fir Dhaerrig king. But when he tooked the girlchild, we knowed he were no king. I be there when he told the Goodfellow how his many great grand-sire stoled the rule from Robin. I be there when Korin challenged him for the child. And, I be there when the Bocan comed."

Derrik leaned forward eagerly. "What is a Bocan, my friend? Is this the creature within the portals?"

The boggart eyed Derrick sideways before he nodded. "Aye, gentry warrior."

"How can I find it? Destroy it?"

"No need, warrior. Done been destroyed."

"Did Korin..."

Shaking his head sadly, the boggart gave a negative answer. "The Bocan meaned to kill, to eat..." He shuddered. "After it maked the king disappear into some world beyond the veil, it holded Korin. But before it could do more, somethin' else comed from that world. It be a creature of shadow, too. But, it fighted the Bocan. Cut the hand holdin' the Goodfellow clear from its body.

"This new one standed in front of the Goodfellow, protected him. The battle be fierce, the new creature fought silent-like, but Bocan screamed and cursed each time the new one's sword bit deep into it's filthy hide. Finally, the new one sliced through the Bocan and it falled apart."

The boggart laughed. The rich, earthy sound brought a smile to Kae's lips as well. Derrik glared at the boggart as if willing it to continue. When it stopped laughing, the boggart returned Derrik's intense gaze. "Ya know, warrior, the fighter that comed to defeat the Bocan looked kinda like you. Only a woman."

Derrik leaned back in surprise then a look of consternation took over his features. "A woman?"

"What does he mean, Derrik?" Kae rested one hand on his arm.

"I'm not sure, Kaelea. But the rare times when a Faerie..." He glanced at the boggart. "When a member of the gentry must be punished by the Alastriona, they are banished to a place between the Otherworld an' the world of the humans. The last... the last to be so punished was my cousin, Searlait."

"Hee hee." The boggart giggled behind his hand. "Din't matter much. The shadow warrior be a hero now to the fairy folk. Saved the king. Now, the king gots to return."

A fission of misgiving skittered up Kaelea's spine. What if he didn't recover? And if he did, what if he refused to return?

And, more importantly, how would her sister deal with these questions?

Korin woke and stretched his cramped muscles before remembering how he should feel after his fights with the Fir Dhaerrig and the Bocan. Tentatively, he stretched again. There was no pain, and only a slight pull around one knee. When he opened his eyes, bright sunlight blinded him and he covered his eyes with one hand. Where was he?

He rested on something soft, so he was no longer within the throne chamber. A puff of air blew over him and he inhaled deeply. It was not the air of the fairy realm. His eyes popped open behind his hand. He was in the gentry Otherworld. How had he been returned? Jerking as he sat, he slowly lowered his hand and tried to focus in the brightness. Belle. Where was the child?

A chatter of voices, not quite close enough for him to understand, sounded in the distance. And in the midst of the voices was the high, soft lisp of the girl. His shoulders slumped in relief. Mayhaps he had not been a total failure after all.

With his vision cleared enough to look around, he discovered he was within the cabin where he first met Nanceen. And, he was fairy sized. Worry centered just above his belly. He'd not wanted them to see him like this. He'd only wanted the gentry to know him in a size to which they could relate. What would Nanceen think of him now?

He turned toward a soft sound. Nanceen curled on the couch, eyes closed in sleep. Korin took a step toward her, stopped and turned away. He couldn't face her like this. Could he find the strength for a transformation to gentry size? Sinking onto the cushion, he rested his elbows on his knees and his chin in his hands. He watched Nanceen's sleep until the desire to touch her grew too great and the need to feel her lips against his burned through him. And he realized, although he had risked much that day, he would always risk more to be with her.

Glancing toward the door, he hoped no one would enter during the magical transformation. He watched Nanceen as he softly spoke the words and the magic grew within him. When he expected the agony of the growth process, he received only a gentle stretching. When he tensed, waiting for the cramping of his muscles, there was only a tingle passing over his skin. Nanceen seemed to grow smaller, and he stepped from the stool and stood next to the couch until the magic dissipated. He stood gentry tall.

He could wait no longer, so knelt beside the couch. He pressed his lips against the warmth of Nanceen's forehead and inhaled the flowery scent of her hair. She mumbled sleepily and her hand lifted lethargically to his shoulder.

"Endearment. My sweet Nanceen. Wake to me." Korin kissed her lips.

The soft, full cushion of her lips welcomed him, parting slightly with a soft exhale of breath. He kissed her again and leaned back in time to see her eyes open slowly. A sensuous smile filled her face and the hand on his shoulder tugged him closer for a kiss that scorched him to the marrow of his bones.

But Nanceen jerked away and scooted into the corner of the couch. Her hands lifted to her mouth. "Is it really you? I'm not dreaming?"

"No, endearment, no dreams. It appears I am real. I don't understand, but I'm here. If you will but have me at your side, I shall never leave you again."

Her entire body shook. She reached to touch him. Korin leaned closer and her fingers landed upon his face. Nanceen traced the firm line of his jaw, the sharper angle of his nose. She ran her fingers lightly over his eyebrows and across his forehead. When her fingertips skimmed his lower lip, Korin groaned, wrapped his arms about her and drew her into his embrace. He kissed the top of her head. "Say you will stand at my side, endearment, say you will join with me, forever."

Korin leaned back just enough to look into her eyes. Shining with tears, the dark brown depths were luminous and filled with a swirl of emotions. Had he mistaken her desires, and her declarations?

"Korin. I thought you..." Nanceen shook her head fiercely and gazed up at him with such tenderness, stinging moisture filled his eyes. "How do you need even to ask, my love? I will... forever. In any world."

CHAPTER TWENTY-SIX

W atching from a picnic bench in the park across the street, Titus frowned at the noise of a celebration rising from the rear of his competition's house. He hadn't expected his underhanded rumor mongering would do much to damage Zeroun's, but he had hoped for more.

And now, even using *her* was beyond his ability. He leaned back on his elbows and drummed his fingers against the edge of the table. What to do next? What would his next move be?

A fluttering of insects swirled around his head. A lightning fast swipe of his hand caught one of the creatures and he squeezed until the fluttering stopped. When he opened his hand, he stared down at the tiny winged creature and his eyebrows lifted. Tossing the tiny, winged woman to the ground, he stood and kicked dead leaves over the figure.

"Fucking fairies."

He strode toward his car, but stopped after five long strides and turned back to stare at the pile of leaves. A slow smile graced his face. Ah, that was it. Not a direct attack, but effective. Zeroun was doomed.

· · ·

K orin reclined on a lawn chair in Jaye's human world backyard, watching the celebration. A party in honor of his marriage to Nanceen, a fairy celebration of his acceptance of kingship, and the renewed contact between fairy and gentry, he was sure the dancing and toasts would go on long into the night. The tiny, brown form of a boggart perched on the back of his chair. Korin spoke to the fairy. "I don't know if I have the knowledge or the ability to lead our peoples."

"Ach, yous gonna do fine, sire. Cain't do no worse than the last king."

"No, that's true. But will they accept me when I stay gentry size?"

"Oh, aye, sire. Since yer queen's sister gave back the books and all heard the rest of the great Oberon's words, they's be glad to have a gentry king. They's tired of fairies that don' know what they's doin'. Wants somethin' different. Wants Korin."

Korin chuckled as the boggart jumped from the chair and skittered away. "And, I have the support of the gentry clans."

Convincing the widespread clans, first of the existence of legendary fairies, then that he was the rightful leader had been easier than he had expected. Autonomous in most of their decisions and actions, once Kaelea showed them the newly discovered genealogies linking each clan to Oberon and Titania, they came together easily. As long as he didn't threaten the rule of those clans.

Since he didn't really want one rule, why would he wish for more? All Korin wanted was the joy of loving Nanceen, a joy without conflict, a love without bargains.

A tall, willowy brunette sauntered up to his chair. "Hi there. Bet you don't remember me."

"I take no bets."

"But, do you remember me?" The voice was low and vibrated with something Korin couldn't identify. He peered up into the artfully made up face and frowned. There was a hint, but when the woman tossed her hair, it was gone.

"I fear I do not."

The woman clapped. "Ah ha. It worked." She half turned her body, skimmed her hands down her tight skirt, and called across the yard. "Bryce. Honey, you were wrong. He doesn't know me." She turned back to Korin. "But, I know you, sweetie. I met you the night you stripped down at N B Tween."

"I'm afraid..."

Bryce jogged to the woman's side. "Okay, you look good enough to pass. So what's your next dance gonna be?"

She poked Bryce playfully in the chest. "You'll have to wait and see. Reintroduce me to your new family member."

"Korin, this is Nightshade. Remember? You met him--"

"At the N B Tween." Korin chuckled. "Yes, I do remember now. But, I don't understand."

Nanceen joined them and sat in Korin's lap. After kissing him soundly, she turned her gaze to the others and grinned. "Hi, Nightshade."

Rolling his eyes, Bryce led Nightshade away. "Let her explain to you--if she can."

Nanceen curled against the warmth of Korin's body. How long did they have to stay at the party? She stroked his chest. "I wish you could have kept your wings."

A deep sigh lifted the chest beneath her fingers. "I do as well, endearment. But, the last battle left them too damaged."

"The amputation didn't hurt, did it?" Concern filled Nanceen's eyes and Korin hurried to reassure her. "It was magical, there was no pain." He rolled his shoulders. "Although, sometimes it feels as though my wings... foolish, I know, but it feels like I still have them. At times, I still feel the pain of the injuries."

"You have pain? Have you spoken to the healers?"

"It's nothing to be concerned about, endearment."

"I know. It's just..."

The tip of his tongue ticked her earlobe. "We can still fly, can't we?"

"Even if we never left the ground, my love." Nanceen lifted her lips for a kiss, but before she met the firm mouth she so desired, a clanging rang through the backyard.

"Come and get it." Jayse shouted. "Barbeque's up and hot." Korin's brows lowered and he reached for the small leather bag he still wore at his waist. "Tell me about this Nightshade."

"Nightshade? Oh, he's just trying to develop a new drag show."

"A drag show?"

Nanceen nodded. "Um hmm. That's where men dress up and pretend to be women. They do songs and dances. I think Nightshade wants to try out a strip routine, too."

"Men as women?" Korin began to chuckle. He laughed until his eyes filled with merry tears.

"What is it, Korin?" Nanceen patted his chest to gain his attention, but Korin continued to laugh. She shook his shoulders and his laughter continued. But, when she tried to scramble from his lap, Korin stopped laughing and held her tighter.

"Wait, endearment. I need to show you something." He placed his small leather bag on her thighs and opened the drawstring. A many times folded parchment crinkled when he pulled it from the bag. "You have always wondered what I carry."

"Oh, no. I'm not curious at all."

Korin pressed a kiss to her lips. "Liar. You know I made a bargain with the Fir Dhaerrig in order to be able to be with you."

Shuddering, Nanceen crossed her arms under her breasts. "I don't want to talk about him."

"Nor do I, endearment. But, look. This is the bargain." He unfolded the parchment and spread it on her lap.

"I can't read fairy, Korin. What does it say?"

"In this are listed the conditions I was to meet in order to court you." He pointed to what looked like a list. "Here is the list of conditions I completed." He moved his finger to an empty space. "And here is the list of those the Fir Dhaerrig won."

"There's nothing there."

"Yes. I know. When each condition was met, the sound of a bell signified the completion."

"Bells? Like in the movie where every time a bell rings an angel gets its wings?"

Korin shrugged. "I don't know anything about angels, Nanceen. However, when you accepted me as I am, as a fairy, Belle laughed. At the N B Tween, when I danced, I mesmerized without magic."

"Oh, you were magical, my love." Nanceen kissed his cheek. "Are there more?"

"At that time," Korin continued as if he hadn't been interrupted. "Belle called on the phone and laughed again. At the faire, thanks to Jayse, I passed fully winged through humans without them knowing what I am. Remember the dancers at the gate? They carried bells. And when we joined the first time, we flew without wings. The claxon calling us to Belle's abduction sounded."

"So, why are you laughing now?"

"There was one condition yet to be met. I was to find a man who was woman and yet man. Look, there is nothing left under the conditions. This line denotes where the condition has moved and been tallied in my column. The dinner bell has sealed our fate, endearment. All the conditions have been successfully met. Now..." His kiss was deep, satisfying and left them both breathless. "Now, I must love you forever."

DEAR READER

Thank you for reading this tale. Bringing stories to life is one of my greatest delights and I hope you enjoyed your time in one of my worlds. Readers like you spark the energy needed to tell these tales. Again, thank you.

With today's world of vast reading choices, word of mouth is the best advertising. So please let others know about this book. Tell your friends, relatives, acquaintances, the dog next door (hey, you never know...). And please consider leaving a review at your favorite retailer or review site.

To keep up with new releases, sign up for *Starr Words*. Yes, it's a newsletter, but will appear in your email only occasionally. Your email is safe with me, will never be shared, and you can, of course, unsubscribe at any time. You can find the link on my website www.lizziestarr.com

Next, there's a bit about each of my books. Enjoy the love and discovery! Happy reading!

Lizzie Starr

NEXT IN THE SERIES

Enjoy the next book in the series

Falling in love was easy. Telling Carrie about the Otherworld risks that love. But demons resurfacing from both their pasts and evildoers intent of destroying the present are intent on tearing them from their newfound love. Will their love survive a world of deception, lies and revenge?

KELTIC MULTIVERSE: THE DOUBLE KELTIC TRIAD

By Keltic Design: *Double Keltic Triad 1*

It ain't easy to be fey when you don't believe in fairy tales.

In the fey Otherworld, a half-faerie child is born. To protect him from evil's crusade to ensure the purity of the faerie race, he is abandoned in the human world, never to know of his magical heritage.

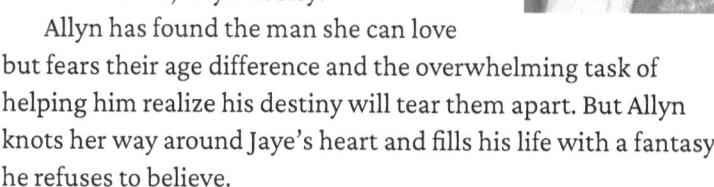

Now Jaye Zeroun is a successful businessman, rooted in reality. Fantasy is only something from an undisciplined imagination. Until he meets Celtic artist and friend of Faerie, Allyn Keeley.

Allyn has found the man she can love but fears their age difference and the overwhelming task of helping him realize his destiny will tear them apart. But Allyn knots her way around Jaye's heart and fills his life with a fantasy he refuses to believe.

Until danger threatens their love, forcing him to either accept a deadly battle or lose the very things he never planned for in his life' a family and a love beyond his wildest imaginings.

Fires of a Keltic Moon: Double Keltic Triad 2

Can love find a way through time?

Lara Zeroun needs an adventure, so she opens a portal in time and travels to the ancient Scottish Highlands. She meets two mysterious men but dares not trust her heart with either.

Under a matriarchal line of succession, Iain is unable to claim his father's holdings--his home. With no lands or possessions, he fights the temptation of a golden-haired woman who came to the manor on the arm of a wandering storyteller.

The storyteller's deceptions bring danger in Iain's time and threaten the destruction of Lara's present. Will Lara and Iain defeat the power of this growing evil and find their ways through time to the love they both desire?

Keltic Flight: *Double Keltic Triad 3*

What does she need to believe in love?

Even as a mythical faerie, Nanceen doesn't believe in the legends of tiny winged fey. Until a soft voice compels her to search... for love. She doesn't know what she believes but what she discovers changes everything.

Korin Goodfellow has loved the gentry maid from afar. But showing himself to her is forbidden by the fairy king, until using deceptions hidden by dark plans, the king forces Korin into an agreement with seemingly impossible conditions. Fueled by his pure emotions, Korin appears to Nanceen as a wingless man. One she can see. Touch. Believe in.

The evil fairy king keeps Korin's heritage hidden, warping the conditions to force Korin into battle after battle until he discovers his true place in the fairy world. Will Nanceen stand at his side as he risks everything for love?

Wild Keltic Carouselle: *Double Keltic Triad 4*

Falling in love is easy, the possibilities endless.

After months of searching, Bryce accepts he'll never find the masked dancer who captured his heart. Time to get on with life. But when his darlin' daughter climbs onto the lap of a captivating woman in a coffee shop and calls her Mommy, he certainly wouldn't mind exploring the possibility.

After a lengthy vacation, Carrie dreads returning to the job she once loved. Especially when a blond-haired cherub insists on calling her Mommy. The tiny girl's father is intriguing, and Carrie believes she's ready for a real relationship. But memories of a horrific attack surface making her doubt and fear a happy future.

Although he's human, Bryce's family ties are to the Faerie Otherworld, so when one of his fathers is kidnapped, no one knows if the abduction was of human or fey origins.

Falling in love was easy. Telling Carrie about the Otherworld risks that love. But demons resurfacing from both their pasts and evil-doers intent of destroying the present are intent on tearing them from their newfound love. Will their love survive a world of deception, lies and revenge?

Keltic Dreams: *Double Keltic Triad 5*

Passion blazes hotter than the desert sun.

A spiritual quest throws Bard, naked and alone, from his world to the desert Sahara. In search of answers, each grueling step through the shifting sands only adds to his questions and

confusion. What did the seven Guardians
mean for him to learn in this strange
place?

An ever-present evil continues to stalk
her family, so Kaelea researches possible
protections at the Fey Library of Alexandria. The appearance of a stranger at the
oasis is an unwelcome interruption. Her
instant fascination with the man, and the
overly possessive actions of a fellow
researcher are even more distracting.

Time alone might bring solutions to Bard's quest. But will
unknown danger and the search for knowledge drive a wedge
between him and Kaelea? Will they survive a passion that burns
hotter than the desert sun?

(*Author's note:* The action of the book *Prince of Dark Ness* takes
place between Triad books 5 and 6. While it's not necessary to
read *Prince of Dark Ness* here, it does give background into
Lucidea's life prior to meeting Jaysson.)

A Faire Keltic Renaissance: *Double Keltic Triad 6*

It ain't easy being fey... and the subject of prophecy

Lucidea had no idea her father wasn't
human—until a chance assignment as a
forensic artist leads her to Scotland and a
family she never knew. With her uncle
imprisoned in the World Between Worlds,
she's forced to assume leadership of a
parallel, underwater world as his half
Alfar-Sindhu heir.

Then she meets Jaysson Zeroun who
has Otherworldly issues of his own. Once
again evil plagues his clan and protecting
a newborn child takes priority over personal dreams. When

Lucidea offers to hide the family at her uncle's manor, Jayse accompanies them to Scotland. He's falling for Lucidea, but he fears how she'll react to the fact he's part Faerie.

Three worlds are in peril. A pieced together ancient prophecy might defeat the separate evils, but will it also bring them love?

KELTIC MULTIVERSE: OTHER TALES

Prince of Dark Ness: Keltic Mulitverse

(Author's note: This story takes place between books 5 and 6 of the *Double Keltic Triad* and introduces the heroine of book 6.)

An ill-prepared Alfar-Sindhu prince struggles to protect two worlds from an ancient fire elemental.

Torn between duty and love, Morghan stands alone to protect both his Alfar-Sindhu underwater world and humanity from an ancient fire elemental bent on escaping the World Between Worlds. While he's loved Coralie long upon long, he never acted on his desire.

Raised in the royal household, Coralie has remained steadfast at Morghan's side through long human years. She's hidden her true feeling for him, even from herself.

A forensic artist from America, Lucidea Galvagin travels to Scotland to determine the identity of a skull found on Morghan's land. What she discovers changes her life and possibly the fate of two worlds.

Will Morghan's two worlds be lost if he chooses family and Coralie over battle? Or will his actions doom a multiverse of worlds to fiery destruction?

Blue Keltic Moon: Children of the Triad 1

Love and redemption? Only under the blue Keltic moon.

It's been twenty years since Morghan, leader of the Alfar-Sindhu, was trapped in the desolate World Between Worlds. Now blue moons are aligning in a multitude of worlds, signaling a magical opportunity.

Devoting his life to the Fey library hasn't saved Gowthaman from the agonies of his past, and the long moments he spent in the World Between Worlds. Now, the woman he loves stands ready to lead others into that cursed place. Only he holds the knowledge enabling them to enter. And with luck, safely return with the prince. The risk to his mind doesn't matter, as long as he keeps Breanna from harm.

A competent warrior, Breanna sets aside her personal desires to lead the rescue mission, facing the unknown to bring Morghan home. While she's loved Gowthaman forever, he claims their age difference is too great. But she's seen their soulfire and knows he loves her as well.

Together they must face the World Between Worlds. Can a place filled with despair and loss also be a discovery of love and redemption? Perhaps... only under the blue Keltic moon.

Candy Guy and the Chocolate Brownie: *Keltic Mulitverse*

A short story

Who better to assist a struggling chocolatier than a Brownie?

Candy Guy is in trouble. Winning a design contest will prove his abilities as a chocolatier, but creativity eludes him. An enchanting intruder invades Trace's workspace. She may be real, or she might be a dream. It doesn't matter. Desire consumes him at her lingering touch and the deep chocolate flavor of her kiss.

Deleesi hopes to end the ancient fey curse haunting her family, but the handsome wisher defies her sleep-inducing magic. Something about this human calls to her soul, and, unbelievably, to her heart. The sensual distraction proves impossible to ignore, even while granting his unspoken wish.

By the end of the rainy afternoon, Trace has his inspiration. But will he ever again see the tiny woman who captivated his heart and became his muse?

ASPEN GOLD SERIES

The Aspen Gold Series

The Aspen Gold Series is a multi-author series set in the small, but affluent tourist town of Spenser, Colorado. I'm delighted to join with these six fantastic authors to bring you these tales. Find out more about the entire series at www.aspengoldseries.com.

These are my contributions to the series... so far.

Ryder's Heart: *Aspen Gold Series Book 3*

> *Ryder discovers an intriguing woman in his bed...*

Five celibate years in Hollywood didn't ease Ryder Barlow's guilt over his father's death, and now he's coming home to Spencer with a new purpose—to create a camp specializing in equine therapy. When he discovers a beautiful woman in his bed, his plans aren't exactly derailed, but definitely knocked off kilter.

Escaping her past hasn't been easy for Vianna Harrison, but she thinks she's found a welcoming home in Spencer—as long as she can keep her ability as a psychic medium hidden. Not an easy task when spirits need to speak of forgiveness and joy to so many loved ones. Or when the owner of the exquisite cabin she's been allowed to live in comes home unexpectedly.

Neither can start a new chapter in their lives until they stop rereading the old ones. Will acceptance overcome their secrets and show them their Rocky Mountain path to love?

For Keeps: *Aspen Gold Series Book 4*
Hiding the truth is like denying the sun.

Widow Kate Michaels kept a secret from the man she loves, and from the entire community of Spencer, Colorado. She's content running her bookstore and life is good. But in order to pay for his medical care, she must sell the ranch that was her father's dream, and in doing so disappoint her 8-year-old, horse loving daughter. Madison makes an unlikely friend in someone Kate would rather forget.

Veterinarian Jackson Samuels is intrigued by the charming girl, and occasionally lets her shadow him in his nearby clinic. He's enamored with the child's mother, but her defenses are so sturdy, not even his charm or their shared past can make a dent. When Jack uncovers a family secret, the truth makes him question who he thought he was.

Will two people who once shared a heartfelt love, allow their lonely secrets to consume and define them? Or will they help each other, forgive each other, and build a future together—For Keeps?

(Author's note: Barbara Gwen was one of the original authors who created the Aspen Gold Series. When I joined the group and planned my own story, we discovered our heroes were best friends. When Barb left this world much too soon, how could I not finish the book of her heart. **For Keeps** is by her and for her.)

Speechless: *Aspen Gold Series Book 8*
How many peonies does it take to get married?

It's a beautiful day in Spencer, Colorado, and the peonies are in bloom. A perfect day to gather for a wedding, filled with love, traditions, fun, and maybe even a prank or two.

Vianna Harrison and Ryder Barlow would love the honor of your presence as they celebrate their marriage.

Fortunate Cookie: *Aspen Gold Book 11*
This woman. Wearing Frosting. And nothing else...

Cookie Lamont owns a successful cupcake shop in Spencer's trendy tourist center. Life would be perfect if not for the escalating unwanted attention from a self-important town trustee. She has everything she needs—and a man is the last thing on her mind.

Until he walks into her shop.

Treehouse builder and TV personality Anthony Burnham returns to Spencer and finds focus building cabins for a new camp. His passion for treehouses is rekindled as a sweet, sexy new love blooms.

But the past haunts his steps and threatens his growing relationship with the alluring baker.

Some Days are Diamonds, is a short story included in:
Yesterday's Promise: *Aspen Gold Series Book 16*

A high-stakes poker game, first meets, a dog rescue, loves lost and rekindled, and life-altering choices fill the history of Spencer, Colorado. Discover the challenges faced in these heartwarming stories crafted by the multi-author group who brings you romantic fiction at its finest in The Aspen Gold Series.

This collection includes:
The Card Game~~ M.A.Jewell
Some Days Are Diamonds~~ *lizzie starr
Ah, Venice ~~ Debra Hines
First Chance ~~ Donna Kaye
Racing Hearts~~ Bernadette Jones
Rescue Me ~~ Cheryl St.John

FANTASY ROMANCE

Double Moon Destiny

On the night of the Double Moon a
child is born, and the destinies of an
acolyte and a rebel are changed forever.

Jermanah, acolyte of the religious
Compound, has never been given the
opportunity to make her own choices.
Although she accepts her way of life and
yearns to rise higher in the order, she
learns ancient, forbidden healing from the
Seer. On the night of the Double Moons, a
child is born and given into Jermanah's
care until the boy is taken to the king.

Kierigh was born moments before the rising of the Double
Moons, but his twin brother wasn't so lucky. Rumors flow from
the Stronghold—following an ancient prophecy, the king sacri-
fices the baby boys to increase his power. But Kierigh senses that
even after five cycles, his brother still lives.

When Kierigh's rebels attack the procession, he takes the
babe, and Jermanah, to his hidden camp. The captivating acolyte
disrupts Kierigh's ordered and simple life. He opposes her religion

and all the Compound claims to stand for. She's everything he doesn't need in his life. Yet she is everything he desires.

No longer considering herself one of the Compound, Jermanah discovers freedom, and truths she finds difficult to believe. But when the babe is taken from the forest, she will do anything to save the child, including face the leader of the Compound—and the king.

Can a rebel and an acolyte set aside pride and differences to find a lost brother, defeat evil, and discover their prophecy fulfilling destinies?

CONTEMPORARY ROMANCE

Birds Do It!

A search for truth, switched babies, and a threat from the past...

Macaws as lovebirds?

An avian expert, Birdie Simons is called to help control a cantankerous hyacinth macaw during a young girl's birthday party. Inexorably drawn to each other, she and single father Garr Logan share an afternoon of joy and bittersweet memories, for Garr's wife died the same day as Birdie's newborn child.

Something about Rachelle makes Birdie wonder if the golden-haired girl is her daughter, switched at birth. Then her child's father returns, dogging her search for understanding and throwing her deeper into fear and confusion.

Ready to move on after his wife's death, Garr wants the intriguing woman, but Birdie keeps the search, threats, and hidden relationships to herself, driving a wedge between them.

Will discovering the truth from nine years ago bring them closer, or forever tear them apart?

SHORT STORIES

Written in Stone: *'Structs in the City 1*

Fantasy Romance

Undercover agent Stone Mason must find a data-link before a demonstration for underground bidders leads to mass destruction. His search of a posh hotel is risky, but time is up.

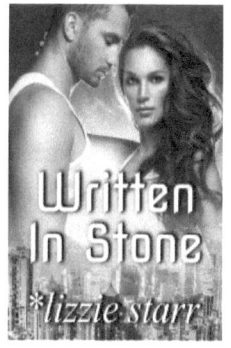

Monika Linberg returns to her hotel room after her boss dumps her and assumes the striking, robotic sex-struct is her consolation prize.

Stone is no construct, but a living, breathing man whose touch and need for information and assistance turn her world upside down. Will working with the sexy agent to keep the city safe be too dangerous for her heart?

Dead Lily Blooms: *At Death's Gates 1*

Fantasy Romance

For ages uncounted, Master Death has assisted souls in transition. But what happens when love gets in the way?

Someone wants vampyre Lily dead, and a bargain with Death has been struck. Death sends servant Agaar to bring Lily to him, but the task becomes more complicated than either Death or Agaar anticipated.

This short story originally appeared in the anthology **Tales From The Mist***. This re-release has had minor corrections from the original edition.*

Death and the Dryad: *At Death's Gates 2*

Fantasy Romance

For ages uncounted, Master Death has assisted souls in transition. But what happens when love gets in the way?

What's Death to do when a dryad appears at his gate without her soul? She can't move on, nor go back. Will Death find a place for her--at his side?

This tale appeared originally in the **Martini Madness** *anthology and this re-release has had minor corrections and additions from the original.*

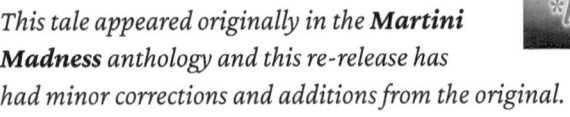

FUN STUFF

*lizzie also enjoys creating journals and guided workbooks for authors and other creatives. Look for them on her <u>website</u>.

ABOUT THE AUTHOR

*lizzie always made up games and stories to keep her company. So, a cunning witch lived in Grampa's weather research station and was only held at bay by waving a certain weed. An ancient road grader morphed into a boat carrying wild adventurers to islands filled with fierce lions and dangerous cannibals, which really looked a lot like sheep.

Now filled with fantasy, love, and romance with a sparkling twist, the stories of her imagination swirl their way into the mundane world.

*lizzie recently retired from her more routine life of being *the

Lunch Lady* at a private school. According to the kids, she was 'the best cooker!' Yes, she misses the students and teachers, but is delighted now to start her days by telling stories rather than opening cases of chicken nuggets and counting milk cartons.

Her tag line of *Author and lunch lady~~what a combination!* no longer holds true (which makes her sad because she really liked that one).

Now you'll know *lizzie by her tales of...

~~Romance with a sparkling twist~~

Want to keep up to date with all of *lizzie's worlds? Sign up for her newsletter on her website: www.lizziestarr.com

facebook.com/authorlizziestarr

twitter.com/lizziestarr

instagram.com/lizistarr

amazon.com/*lizzie-starr/e/B003F33Y0W

bookbub.com/profile/lizzie-starr

goodreads.com/lizziestarr

pinterest.com/lizziestarr

tiktok.com/@authorlizziestarr